SCOTT ARBUCKLE

Scavenged

Never let them break you —

Scott A[...]

First edition

Editing by Michelle Hope
Cover art by Anthony J Foti

This book was professionally typeset on Reedsy.
Find out more at reedsy.com

For Matt and Joe,
with whom I've shared countless adventures.

Contents

Chapter One   1
Chapter Two   15
Chapter Three   29
Chapter Four   43
Chapter Five   55
Chapter Six   68
Chapter Seven   80
Chapter Eight   95
Chapter Nine   106
Chapter Ten   119
Chapter Eleven   131
Chapter Twelve   140
Chapter Thirteen   153
Chapter Fourteen   168
Chapter Fifteen   180
Chapter Sixteen   192
Chapter Seventeen   202
Chapter Eighteen   213
Chapter Nineteen   228
Chapter Twenty   243
Chapter Twenty-One   256
Epilogue   266
Afterword   268
About the Author   270

Chapter One

Almost there, the scavenger thought. *Just a little farther.* He slid the damping piston the rest of the way down into the shock and reached for the motor oil with his right hand, pouring it into the open assembly with a soft little *glug-glug.* He used the sound to gauge when the oil level was near the top, because the dusky light in the garage was dim, and he couldn't risk seeing if the fluorescent lamps overhead still worked. They probably didn't. He had to get this right, or he'd die alone in a filthy garage a few minutes from now.

Orion Danes liked the sounds of his work—the soft whirring and grinding of something being fixed up, something old and broken being made new again. He concentrated on these sounds, shutting out the screams and gunfire in the streets outside. He replaced the rubber seal and tightened the nut back down on the top of the repaired shock, then removed the shock from the vise on the workbench and carried it to the dirt bike in the corner. He'd ducked into this abandoned garage just as the raiders had come charging into the little town. Orion had originally intended to stay the night here, moving on in the morning; now, rest was the last thing on his mind.

Finding the old bike in the corner had been a godsend, even in its present condition. Somebody had landed hard on the back wheel, cracking the rear rim and busting the shocks. Not such

1

a tough job for Orion, who had spent most of his fifteen years hanging around the trade caravans that scavenged junk in the wastelands. Most things could be fixed, if you knew how to do it. Somebody needed to fix the entire world: clean it up, replace what was old and broken, and make it all new again. It just seemed like nobody knew how.

The United Corporations Order couldn't fix what had happened—they might have their shiny towers in the Great Cities with their legions of Protectorate officers and herds of obedient vassals, but it was just a veneer, a fresh coat of paint on something that was headed to the scrap heap. And the UCO was in better shape than anyone; the outlanders who lived outside the cities talked a lot about fixing things, too, when in actuality, their Resistance fighters were getting slaughtered every day out here in the wastelands. An outlander's existence was short and brutal; it was better to be behind the UCO's huge city walls, if you could manage to get there. New Zaragosa wasn't much farther, and this bike just might save his life.

With the shock assembly back on the bike, Orion turned it upside down, then pumped the kick-start valve to clear the fuel line. He flipped the dirt bike right side up, pumped the valve some more, and then froze.

A chilling screech cut through the sounds of the fighting outside.

Lacerta warriors were here—drawn by the chaos of the attack. Now the slaughter was a three-sided free-for-all: Lacertas versus the banditos versus the Resistance townsfolk. He had to get out of here now.

He crouched to inspect the cracked rear wheel. Making the repair using a conventional torch would mean removing the tire altogether before welding, then replacing it on the wheel when the hot work was done. Otherwise, the heat would rapidly expand the air in the tire and cause it to blow up in his face—ruining the wheel and injuring him as well. Normally this job might take forty-five minutes, but that was time he didn't have.

He rolled up the sleeve of his jacket, exposing the bionic interface grafted into the flesh of his left forearm. He no longer got chills when looking at it—but the cold prickles still came every time he remembered the Greys bending over him on the table, staring with inky bug eyes and blank, lipless faces. He'd been awake through part of it, feeling the sickening tugging on his arm from their bizarre tools and cold, clammy flesh. He'd had the crazy thought that he was lying on a workbench and they were fixing him like a machine, taking an old, useless part and throwing it away, replacing the scrap with a new piece that worked better.

Pushing these memories away, he danced his fingers across a few keys on the interface. The computer's scanner bathed the wheel in pale-yellow light. He held his left arm steady with his other hand as a piercing red laser shot out from the interface, stitching the crack in the wheel rim into a shiny line of solder. The job was done in seconds. He pumped the kick-start valve a few more times, threw his leg over the frame, and then started the bike, unable to suppress his grin when the engine roared to life on the second try—

"Nice work, son," said a gravelly voice from behind him. Orion looked back to see an unkempt man standing near the door of the garage. A wide-brimmed hat and duster hid most of his face except for a ragged beard, which parted to reveal a yellow-toothed sneer. The man held a thermal pulse rifle in both hands. "Sorry to do this to you, kid, but you get off that bike nice and slow." Orion tried not to look at his own 9 mm ballistic pistol lying on the ground with his tools nearby. He had no choice; the outlaw wouldn't hesitate to fry him. Orion dismounted, relinquishing his prize. Without another word, the criminal seized the bike and was out the door.

Orion scooped up his tools, glimpsing the carnage outside through the open door. At this point, the aliens were massacring the entire town. He crept out into the street, which was littered with empty weapons and mangled corpses. He could smell smoke and fresh blood. There were no Lacertas in sight at the moment, however, and his eyes darted to a panicked, riderless horse flying down the street toward him. With an outstretched hand, he made a leap for the reins as the beast approached. His fingers closed around the rough leather straps, and he took a moment to calm the animal before swinging up and into the saddle. As he did so, a bolt from a thermal pulse streaked by so fast it singed the peach fuzz off his face.

Head down, crouched low over the horse, Orion charged through the street. Burned and ruined buildings went by at a breakneck pace. He passed the town's outskirts and escaped into the desert at a full gallop. The destroyed landscape rushed by in a dusty blur. After three minutes, he still couldn't ease back in the saddle, still wouldn't think of how close a call it had been—and then something smashed into him with crushing force, tearing his left side open, bowling the wild-eyed horse over and trapping him on the ground underneath it. Warm, sticky blood, both his and the animal's, washed over him as he kicked his legs, trying to free himself.

The Lacerta had lain in wait behind a boulder, striking with precision as Orion flew past. Now, the giant crocodilian loomed over him, standing on two legs. A scaly green-black hide covered

4

the alien, but its reptilian face lacked the cold impassiveness of an earthly lizard. Instead, its features boiled with fiery hatred and rage, leaning its body forward to hiss through a triangular toothy maw. Orion's pain and fear blended into a rising tide of panic as the monster prepared for the merciless second, and final, blow.

The burning wound in Orion's side raked his concentration, and he fought to control himself. The monster appeared to be at the end of a dark tunnel... There were only seconds left in the scavenger's life, seconds with which to act. Orion's fingers, slippery with blood, closed around the pistol in his holster, and he jerked it out, aiming it at the face of the alien as it bent toward him. He pumped the trigger over and over like the kick-start valve on a dirt bike. Hot bullets tore into the open mouth of the thing, and it gargled black blood amid its unworldly shrieks. Orion emptied the clip of the gun before the reptile fell backward at last, collapsing into a twisted heap.

Without pausing, which would only weaken his resolve, Orion jammed the pistol's hot muzzle against his side. He stifled a yelp in his dry throat as the gun sizzled and cauterized the bloody flesh. Coughing and choking, he slid out from under the dead horse. In agony, he struggled to stay on his feet, weaving and stumbling through the desert. He needed someone to fix him, to make him all better again. He limped through the wasteland, a graveyard of useless things. If he stopped moving, if he let himself fall, he would become just another discarded piece of junk. Ahead, the wind eddied and curled over an object on the ground. He almost fell over it. It was the bandito from before, now clawed to gory ribbons next to the stolen dirt bike. Orion hefted the bike upright and winced as he kick-started it. Then he was racing along toward the glittering spires on the horizon.

5

Still so far, he thought with the hot desert wind drying his tears into clean streaks on his dusty face. *Still so much farther to go.*

***

New Zaragosa was like being in the palm of God's hand, the towering skyscrapers surrounding Orion reaching up to the sky like the beautiful fingers of some divine being. In a way, he was cradled within that hand, as if it were lifting him above the world to a safer place.

He was still woozy from the laceration in his left side, and couldn't help but take it slow while creeping down the street, hugging the shade of buildings and from time to time resting against their walls. It was just as well, since the battery on his active camo didn't have much left; fast movements in full daylight would only cause it to work that much harder to keep him hidden. He'd been lucky to find the photostatic disruptor out in the wastelands; just a couple of minor adjustments had made it easy to sneak into the Great City without incident. He'd anticipated trouble when trying to enter New Zaragosa; he wasn't sure of the best way to answer the inevitable questions at the South Point Salute entry gate, but it turned out all he had needed to do was wait for a returning patrol and invisibly slide right on through with them. The passive scanners at the gate had gone off, of course, indicating a discrepancy, but he had been running down the Protectorate Thoroughfare by then. The enforcers would be more likely to treat the alarm as a misfire since there was no weapons alert—Orion's empty pistol was half buried in the dirt next to a dead Lacerta 120 kilometers south of here.

It was downright odd that, despite having bled half to death, he could call this day "lucky" at all—he'd found a veritable fortune in scavenged goods. The dirt bike still had an eighth of a tank, and he'd stashed it in a crumpled, wrecked van on the highway outside the city's barrier. The photostatic disruptor had spared him an uncomfortable confrontation already, and would surely save his life in the future. And he'd even managed to kill the Lacerta, which was no small feat. After the day he'd had, it was a miracle he was still standing.

Next, he had to find medical care immediately. Here in the Grey-operated human stockyards that were commonly called "cities," treatments of all types were free...for citizens in good standing. The technology at even the humblest street clinics would ensure that Orion's life-threatening wound was just an unpleasant memory by this time tomorrow, but he wasn't optimistic about his social status. He'd likely have to either bribe a doctor or purchase the use of a medibot, and nobody within these walls would be interested in bartering. The bike and disruptor might be worth their weight in whiskey out in the Badlands, but on the Thoroughfare, one's worth always came down to political clout, or hard capitals. Orion had neither.

He wasn't sure what a "bank" looked like from the outside, and most of the holostacks of businesses he passed weren't showcasing goods but rather holographic idiots offering a three-dimensional "thumbs-up" to passersby on the streets, along with some nonsense slogan. He couldn't afford to use trial and error; if he turned off the active camouflage and walked in asking questions, the shopkeepers would take one look at the dirty vagabond, obviously an outlander, and call the Protectorate. This was life in a city, after all: you needed capitals for information, but you needed information to get capitals.

He sneaked off of the street and into a steamy alley. A square titanium housing about six inches off the ground betrayed the location of this building's supernet hardpoints. Looking around to make sure he was alone, he crouched close to the wall with his back to the street, and rolled up his left sleeve. Slicing the lock with his own cybercomputer took less than two seconds, and he folded the hinged housing up to expose the hardpoint jack. This was a gamble; he'd never hacked an active city terminal before, and if it had Grey technology, then he was about to make the worst mistake of his life. He doubted the Greys had enough of an active interest in whatever these people were selling to supply their own firewalls, though, and if it was a normal private system, his own cybercomputer, itself Grey technology, would make short work of it. In any case, the risk had to be taken; without any caps, he'd be dead by morning.

The only sound was a soft whirring as a jack extended from his metal forearm and plugged into the wall. Then he watched the soft-yellow display on his computer shoot through encryption codes at the speed of light—twelve digits, he noted. Military tech. This would scare off a lot of hackers, but Orion actually had to suppress a chuckle as he remembered the time last year he'd hijacked a parked Demistrider that he'd found outside a desert cantina while the pilot was having a drink. He had taken the walking tank for a short, wild ride. Based on his experience, military firewalls took just a little longer than usual, but they couldn't keep him out.

As he'd anticipated, a root access menu appeared. A flurry of keystrokes with his right hand brought up a number of bank accounts. Then came a moment of internal debate—how much were capitals actually worth? Orion needed to take plenty to get around, but not so much that he would spark some "crime of the century" manhunt. He settled on 125,000 caps—about 5

8

percent of what was in the particular account he was looking at—hoping that was enough for his purposes.

He erased his digital tracks, unrolled his sleeve back down to hide his cybernetic arm, and stood up. The process had taken less than a minute. The photostatic disruptor was out of juice now, and he was glad the sun was beginning to set. Orion stumbled, then steadied himself against the alley's brick wall. Help was close now. He headed back to the street.

Stepping out into the open, however, he saw a crowd of citizens coming down the Thoroughfare. Their angry voices reached Orion before he could read the homemade signs they waved in the dimming light—and the chant *"Death to freaks!"* swelled into a chorus. *Oh, no. The Anti-Augmented Foundation...* He might have preferred if the Protectorate was coming instead.

The AAF viewed themselves as the redeemers of a purist vision of mankind; they hated anyone who was "augmented" or "evolved," whether through psionic ability or cybernetic enhancements. Although augmentation clinics littered the city, many of their patrons tried to keep up the ruse of being normal until they were trampled down in the streets. AAF members almost never demonstrated in numbers of under a hundred—and no individual, no matter how gifted, could stand against that. Orion had no reason to suppose they were after him specifically—most of the time the AAF just came out to raise hell and show a strong presence for their cause—but things could turn ugly fast if just one keen-eyed zealot spotted something unusual. People with cybernetic implants could be torn to pieces in the streets, sometimes even with armored soldiers standing a block away pretending not to see anything. Orion supposed the civil unrest likely to result from a mechanized Stomper opening fire on "peaceful demonstrators" would be a hundred times worse than the unsolved murder of some tough-guy mercenary with a flamethrower for an arm. Another one of city life's little pleasantries. He'd be better off staying out of the street.

He ducked back into the alley, hoping the movement didn't make him look too suspicious, and broke out into as much of a run as he could manage. He settled for a wincing jog through the shadowed alleys. There might be psychos and murderers here as well, but he'd manage if they were in smaller numbers than at the demonstration. After a couple of minutes, he slowed to an agonized walk. He spotted a junkie curled up next to the warmth of a steam grate. Orion looked the other way as a scowling tattooed man crouched and rifled through the unconscious vagrant's pockets. He wished for at least the tenth time that evening that he still had his gun—the empty space on his right hip was a worrisome nuisance in contradistinction to the burning, bloody torment on his left side.

He came to a wooden gate in the alley. It was latch operated but not locked, and his sense of direction told him that another major street would not be much farther. Nudging aside bags of trash with his foot, he gripped the rusted latch and thrust it upward, shouldering the wooden door inward.

Then, directly on the other side, he came face-to-face with a lean, solemn Grey. Stick-figure thin, it was leaning forward with its skinny shoulders hunched under the large, bulbous head. The alien was physically diminutive, but its predatory stance heightened the terrifying visual sense that it was towering over Orion. He screamed out of blind panic, staring into giant eyes that were colder and blacker than the deepest, farthest reaches of obsidian space.

The alien reached out for him with one spindly hand. All the nightmarish insanity in Orion's memories of his previous encounters with the Greys struck him like a wrecking ball, and he tumbled backward, scraping his palms on the filthy ground, kicking and scrabbling to gain purchase, trying to run before he could even stand. The thing took a step forward, and Orion saw a foot that was just a weird knob at the end of a stalklike leg. With smooth gray limbs like straw, it probably weighed no more than eighteen kilograms. Orion's mind shattered, trying in vain to either cope with the sight of this horribly attenuated being or reject it altogether.

Orion fled through the alley, which was a dark maze around him. There was no direction, no logic or reason, except to get away from this thing that came walking after him as if on tiptoes with its arms swinging in gentle arcs at its sides. Terror replaced Orion's pain, overriding it. His legs pumping faster than ever before, he ran and ran, only to feel as if the alien were always walking calmly right behind him.

Orion burst out onto the street in a surge of speed. Panicking, he didn't register the impossible situation on the Thoroughfare for several moments: all around the street, the AAF demonstrators were frozen stiff, many in midstride or with mouths open in a hateful grimace. They were unaware and unreactive; time for them seemed to be standing still as Orion ran through the crowded street with motionless human statues on all sides of him. No one was witness to the horror unfolding in the middle of the busy street.

But then one person was indeed awake and moving, a dark silhouette in the garish neon-lit wax museum at the end of the street. Orion saw sinister eyes framed by a hood pulled low over a lean, aristocratic face. The man was clearly a psionic—an augmented ally of the Greys. Any hopes of help or rescue from his pursuer died in his stomach.

Still running at full speed, Orion slammed into a solid, invisible wall—if he had run face-first into the side of a building, it wouldn't have arrested his flight any more. Bouncing off of the unseen barrier knocked all the breath out of him; he was flying backward through the air, limbs flailing from the force of the impact. He landed on his back a few meters away, a crumpled rag doll, supine and helpless. Gasping, Orion stared up at the sky, seeing the towering skyscrapers all around reaching up to the sky like fingers, framing his field of vision. Once more, he was in the palm of some omnipotent hand, this time with the fingers closing in on him to squeeze the life out of his frail body.

He was aware of the skeletal Grey and the psionic approaching him, although he couldn't turn his head. He couldn't look away from the sky as an enormous Grey spaceship, an unmistakable flying saucer the size of several city blocks, crawled into view far above. It was massive, hovering over New Zaragosa with a heavy and foreboding presence. As Orion watched, it seemed to fill up the very edges of his vision. There was nothing but the gigantic black shadow floating there, perfectly silent and ominous.

***

Orion awoke to a metal table beneath him and the cold, slender hands prodding and touching his side. The pain was still present, but weaker. His most prominent sensation was the unnatural tugging at his left side. He couldn't look around, as his head wouldn't move, but the slippery squishing he heard sent his drowsy brain teetering on the edge of mindless horror all over again.

"Relax, young man," came a glassy voice near his right ear.

"You won't be needing those worthless organs much longer." The psionic man's hood had been pulled back, and part of the handsome face now came into view. "Don't be concerned at all—they know exactly what they're doing."

Orion mumbled something unintelligible in reply. The aliens were shoving metal parts into the hollowed-out place where his entrails had been. It was so cold, like ice being packed inside him.

"I realize this is quite uncomfortable for you in the moment, but I can assure you that you'll find it all worthwhile." The psionic's voice had an edge of excitement just under the placid demeanor. "You really should think of this as an honor, you know. They don't just choose people at random anymore. The Greys have gotten increasingly selective about with whom they share their gifts. You've proven to have a pleasing aptitude for the previous technology they bestowed upon you. This time they'll be giving you quite an upgrade."

Shallow, quick breaths to deal with the shock to his body and mind—Orion was hyperventilating. Then a bone-jarring spasm convulsed his entire body, and his breathing was cut off completely. The cold, clammy hands kept working. He anticipated drawing a frigid, ragged breath and then another, but the relief of fresh oxygen never came. At the edge of his vision, he saw one of the creatures holding a freakish instrument the size of a flashlight, one end of it dripping with blood. It placed one hand on Orion's neck at the collarbone and the other hand, with the tool, was angling toward his chest.

The psionic man rested his own hand on Orion's forehead. "No, this is not the end for you. You were almost killed by the Lacertas today, but you used all of your assets to survive. Some of these you were born with and had to learn to utilize; some you were given by the Greys. After today, you will see how those assets might overlap with each other."

Now a smooth whine as the aliens bored into the side of his head. The action of the drill moved his head automatically in a sick parody of nodding in affirmation. As the alien surgeons stuck a long metal tube into his skull for a moment, then withdrew it, the only pain he was left with was a mild headache.

"That headache will pass on its own," the man whispered, his voice now emanating from inside Orion's head. *"You've been doing very, very well. We're nearly finished now..."*

Orion closed his eyes...and began to see.

Chapter Two

Orion's eyes snapped open again. He'd been squeezing them shut against the onslaught of freakish words and images bounding through his wearied mind. When he cried out in shock, the sound now had a raspy edge: an artificial note that bastardized the cadence of his voice. His vision cleared, and a group of aliens came into focus. They were clustered around him, staring down, bordering his view of the smooth ceiling above.

The Greys. What mind could fathom the unearthly secrets within their oversized heads? What bizarre perplexities had those passionless, inky eyes pondered? Even now, his second time in their clutches, they seemed somehow less than truly alive. Aloof and disinterested, they regarded him in silence as he wondered at what they had done to him, wondered if he was now less than truly alive as well.

Orion's final breath had been drawn some time ago. His torso no longer rose and fell with suspiration, and many of the organs within had been replaced with their alien contrivances. Of this he was certain. He touched the dried blood matted near his left temple, but the hole in his skull was restored somehow from where they'd drilled into it. He struggled to sit upright, feeling the tautness of the restraints loosen and then release.

The aliens retreated by one or two paces, giving him room to swing his aching legs over the edge of the table and hop down to the lustrous metal deck. He still had to lean against the operating slab, but Orion was surprised at how vigorous he felt. After only a few moments, he was able to take a couple of unsteady paces. Again, the aliens moved back to allow him a wide berth.

Silence reigned in the spacious cabin. Stillness echoed after his tentative steps. Regaining his surefootedness, Orion found his way to an open door and passed into the corridor beyond unmolested.

The hallway was dim and pulsed with low, ambient light. The path curved gently to the left as he walked, suggesting the contour of the alien craft he was on board. There were viewing bays to the left and right as he walked, massive windows looking into operating rooms like the one he had just left. The first two were empty and dark. The third was a scene of horrendous revulsion.

A human man was restrained on the slab, fully conscious as the cosmic outsiders administered freakish violations to his writhing body. Gore-drenched utensils were employed with callous objectivity, and blood pooled and oozed into troughs along the sides of the table and drained into canisters on the floor. Orion's eyes flicked over the modifications to the tortured man's form: twisted metal tentacles sprouted at sickening angles from the victim's chest and sides. These mindless appendages squirmed around him, flailing and grasping at nothing, indifferent to the panicked shrieks that reached Orion only as muffled crescendos. The man's shrieks were a grisly soundtrack to his body's twitching dance.

Orion turned away, shuddering, and cringed again as a new, sickening tableau greeted him: the next viewing bay showcased a pair of Greys bending over a restrained female. Her head was shaved smooth and bald, lending her a faint air of similarity to the hairless alien captors. One of the aliens placed both hands on the sides of her face, holding her still, while the other drew a spinning rotary saw in a straight line around the top of her cranium. Deft and careful movements removed the dripping dome, exposing the brain. The alien that held the girl's head immobile stared knowingly into Orion's eyes, its mouth a thin line upon an emotionless face.

Orion stumbled backward, away from the viewing bay, and rested one hand on the sleek bulkhead. Meager, throbbing luminescence revealed that he was not alone in the corridor: several Greys were shuffling toward him from the direction he had come. Repulsed, he continued along the hallway. Up ahead, there were more sticklike silhouettes, eerily backlit, shambling forward. A side door was open, and he ducked through it, wondering how long he could wander this peregrine craft, avoiding the schemes of his captors. This room was shadowed and bare; as he turned back, the door slid shut with a menacing hiss, trapping him inside.

Pale, teardrop-shaped faces with glistening black eyes regarded Orion through the viewing bay. The panic began to well up in him again, manifesting as a jittery tingling that prickled the patches of skin between his cybernetic grafts. The whispering in his head returned from the edge of consciousness, from where it had left him in a fitful slumber on the operating table.

"You may not be familiar with the concept of action potentials," the psionic man uttered, *"so allow me to explain your latest gift."*

"Who are you?" Orion asked aloud.

"A humble servant of the Greys. I am what is called an Illuminatus—a human with the ability to communicate with these higher beings. You see, although they comprehend the vulgar system of

spoken words that we use, the human mind is not capable of receiving thoughts from their heightened faculties. Not without aid, anyway."

This time Orion projected the words with a concise thought. *"The chip they implanted in my brain."*

"Excellent. You're learning quickly." The serene voice was pleased.

"So what is an action potential?"

"When a neuron 'fires,' sending a signal through a nerve, the membrane of the cell begins by rising sharply in voltage. It does this by opening gated channels in the cell wall to allow an influx of positive ions. As more channels open, the voltage spikes and transmits an electrical signal to the axon terminal, where it, in turn, signals other neurons. The channels close when the influx is completed, preventing the signal from traveling back the way it came. This is the process that results in the majority of neurological functions, such as moving the muscles of your arm or interpreting your sense of touch. These short-lived electrical events are known as 'action potentials.'

"You're probably aware that all living things survive due to bioelectrical impulses," the psionic man continued. *"The electric current innate to your body makes your heart beat, for example, and allows your brain to send commands throughout the body. But suppose that your body's circulatory and neural systems were modified by the use of nanoconductors, amplifying your bioelectrical impulses by thousands of times what they were before."*

"The machines they put in place of my internal organs—they create and dispatch trillions of microscopic robots, conducting the electricity of each action potential as if it were an electric synapse, and making it faster and stronger." Orion was in disbelief. Was he alive? Was he man, or machine?

"There you are. Your mind is working faster already. And that's just the beginning."

A hiss cut through the dark chamber. Orion's adrenaline surged—he wheeled around, facing the far wall opposite the viewing bay, where a previously unseen doorway bled feeble illumination into the shrouded room. The unmistakable silhouette of a bipedal reptilian beast staggered through, and the portal hissed shut again.

Half crouching in a combat stance, Orion groaned, fighting despair. His empty fingers seemed to twitch of their own accord. No weapons, no aid, no escape. He was locked in this room, unarmed, with a murderous Lacerta, while those manipulative freaks watched from outside. Was this their version of sport? Were the Greys, with their astounding technological advancement, yet rooted in the barbarism of gladiatorial combat for their amusement? Was he a slave to this bunch of space-age savages?

Hooked claws chattered with staccato clicks on the metal floor. The lizard-like tail whipped back and forth. Then the beast charged, crossing the chamber in three giant bounds. As teeth and claws flew at him like a storm of glittering daggers, Orion sprang aside, dodging the Lacerta just before it collided against the bulkhead. The impact didn't faze it, though, and it whirled around, pushing off the wall to pounce again. This time Orion couldn't get out of the way fast enough, and the jaws locked on to his left forearm—the one that was mostly metal, housing the cybercomputer that was built into his flesh. The Lacerta's teeth squealed against the alloy; Orion felt pressure but no pain. With his right fist, he hooked flurries of hard punches against the tough hide of its neck and head, doing minimal damage but succeeding in making the Lacerta flinch away. Its mouth opened to release his metal arm.

Orion leapt backward, avoiding a further melee, but there

19

were no environmental advantages offered in this empty room. The reptilian beast seemed to be sizing him up as well, taken aback by this unchewable foe. Its maw hung open as it panted, and Orion saw jagged, broken teeth. His frame tingled with the hormones released by battle and fear; the fuzzy ionization of static electricity surged all around him.

The beast didn't charge again; instead, it maintained a distance of about two meters. Its mouth began to gurgle, the reptilian head dipped, it took a lightning step, and then the broad, muscular tail crashed against Orion, knocking him off-balance. Another second, and the beast was upon him. Orion fell, lying with his back on the floor and one foot planted on the scaly chest, pushing as hard as he could to keep it off of him. He writhed from side to side, avoiding slashes—it was true, his movements were quicker and he could anticipate his opponent's moves, but it was a losing battle if he stayed in this defensive posture. Then the crackle of energy and adrenaline in his body climbed to a crescendo, begging for release. His own feral monster within was crying out for a victim.

Orion kicked hard and then, shrieking, rolled out from under the monster. The Lacerta readjusted with animal flexibility, poised to strike, to flatten him to the deck and eviscerate him, but sparks flew as Orion's fingertips contacted its scaly skin. The Lacerta's form seized and went rigid. The scavenger's hands found purchase on its shoulders and chest, buzzing hot current into the reptilian body. Electric convulsions jerked and twitched through it, but Orion's grip tightened with fury. The alien's jaw locked down, grinding its broken teeth together, splintering them into ruined shards. Its flesh cooked with an eye-watering stench. Its yellow eyes rolled back in their sockets and then burst into thick pus that dribbled down the sides of its paralyzed visage. By the time the charred carcass fell away from Orion's arcing fingertips, smoke was curling through the air in a lazy dance.

Orion rolled over onto his hands and knees, but did not pant for breath. In truth, he felt invigorated. As he rose to his feet, the serene whisper hailed him for a second time.

"They've made you a superior combatant. The bioelectric impulses of living organisms are mandatory for reflexive processes, and yours are now off the charts. You'll find that you react more quickly and can survive harsher environments—in addition to the more dramatic potency that you've just displayed."

As he surveyed the blackened corpse, a vista of realization spawned in Orion's heightened thoughts. *"The Greys want me to kill Lacertas."*

"You're certainly equipped to do so," the Illuminatus answered. *"Use your aptitudes and your gifts."*

Short-lived electrical events...

"That's what my life is to you, now: an action potential. Something that can be fired off, activated, to fulfill a command. Are you...giving me instructions?" Orion's heart hammered. Had they truly killed the last vestiges of what was human in him—his free will—and left him as a shambling robotic shell, a deadly plaything to be wound up and unleashed? *"Am I under your control?"* He choked the question out, dreading the answer.

A glassy chuckle. *"Of course not. While gifted savants can achieve some mild neurological manipulation in their subjects—lowering heart rate or spiking adrenaline, for example—'mind control' is far beyond the scope of actual science. You maintain your free will...although I'd say that ignoring the purpose for which you are so well adapted would be a crime against nature."*

Orion regarded the computer interface grafted into his left

forearm. *"Nature? That's a sick joke."*

Inscrutable faces still lined the window, examining him. *"I assure you that no one here is joking,"* the Illuminatus replied.

"Let me get my hands around one of their scrawny necks." The fuzzy, static feeling continued to dance over his arms.

"You won't get the chance," came the reply. *"They're returning you to the surface, in the street where they found you. The people there will experience what's known as 'lost time,' but only you will remember the Grey spaceship overhead."* Light pulsed over a sleek amber lens that had heretofore lain dormant in the floor. *"Step onto the biotransporter, please."*

"So that's it? You expect me to go back down and just kill Lacertas until one day they finally tear me apart?" Orion paced the empty room, his mind pounding for an alternative. *"What if I say no?"* As soon as he formed the words, a sadistic cinema in his mind looped through revolting alien experiments, and he regretted having asked the question.

No other answer: the simplest of choices lay before him. He could either remain trapped in this bare room on the alien ship or accommodate his captors by returning to Earth. He tarried a moment longer but acknowledged that it availed him nothing. Orion stepped squarely onto the burnished platform.

His sight was honed into crisp contrast. The room's interior became sharp and distinct, and the air warmed around him. Then a few terrifying seconds of blackness, and Orion was in the city Thoroughfare once more. As he'd feared, he was standing on the outer fringes of the AAF demonstrators who had been present before. Orion was on the outside of the group, near the shade of a building; no one had witnessed his instantaneous return firsthand, but heads turned at the movement. The zealots focused on the strange newcomer, giving him no chance to conceal himself.

Shouts and insults filled the air. Orion looked down at himself, knowing what they saw: a tattered jacket and tank top that failed to cover the mechanical supplementations to his wiry frame. The Anti-Augmented Foundation was often hungry for just such a scapegoat during one of their demonstrations. Did he have a chance to convince an angry mob that he wasn't, in fact, some sort of agenda-driven spy, following orders from the Greys? Could he, in truth, even make such an argument to himself?

"Look at him! See his arm?"

"He's modded, you can see it plain as day!"

Orion backpedaled and turned to run, but coarse hands seized him from the sides. Squirming, he was dragged farther into the street, his protests drowned out in a bedlam of accusations. He'd been careful not to run afoul of these zealots all day, and the injustice of being made a sudden target for their unthinking hatred was maddening. He'd be denounced and shot in a matter of minutes, and the Protectorate would do what they did best—pretend it had never happened. How could it be that the Greys, with their gruesome vivisections and their callous designs, had more respect for life than the human race of which he was now only marginally a part?

Tanned faces regarded him with hate-filled eyes. An unwashed brute curled up a meaty fist and drove it into Orion's stomach, where some hard metal apparatus now lay within. The thug drew back howling, cradling his broken hand. Someone behind Orion smashed a splintering piece of wood over his shoulders. Orion staggered as a burst of white pain exploded through his bones and muscles. His pulse intensified, growing sonorous and more rhythmic. Hormones flooded into his system, prickling the patches of skin between his cybernetic grafts. *Oh, no. No...*

He tried to steady his nerves, failing, unable to utilize the old standby of taking deep breaths because his mechanized body would no longer do such a thing.

He wrenched free of his captors just as a massive torrent of voltage unleashed. A crackling flash ignited the air in a shock wave that tossed members of the crowd in all directions. His metallic voice croaked; it was an awful sound that cut the pained, echoing cries of men colliding with walls, with cobblestones, with each other. For several slow, amaranthine seconds, he was at the epicenter of a deadly flower of destruction. Forks of current branched from him, vellicating nearby fallen bodies. Flesh sizzled and scorched. He was the king of a world of pain, standing supreme above his writhing, groveling victims.

Then it ended. His eyes were seared with visions of horrid electric death. When at last the color returned to his reality, things that he had broken and ruined lay scattered all about.

***

Short-lived electrical events...

Orion turned the faucet off, and settled back in the tub. Could there be a way to somehow mitigate the damage he'd done? Could a mangled human life be repaired? For the entire fifteen years he'd spent in the Badlands, his skills had been so well attuned to taking something old, broken, and cast aside and restoring it...perhaps even improving upon the original.

And then the Greys had come, ostensibly to improve upon his own original form. To cast his prior existence aside and replace it with a new purpose.

He was a destroyer now—a walking catastrophe, strewing carnage in his wake. Could he regain control of his humanity?

An action potential could not go back the way it came...

After narrowly avoiding the Protectorate, Orion had traversed the deepest reaches of the unknown alleys in the metropolis. A rank, rotten honeycomb at the core of New Zaragosa, these twisting urban mazes were rife with criminals and thugs—but the hard men left him alone, turning their weathered faces down to scowl at filthy, beaten shoes and steaming sewer grates. Holostacks like those advertising businesses on the Thoroughfare were absent here, and he'd searched for asylum using the faded signs above rusty, ramshackle doors.

His luck had seemed to hold. He'd booked a room in an unassuming hostel using the caps he'd stolen from the supernet terminal earlier in the day, which required only a feeble mimicry of registration. He'd discarded his tattered rags in favor of a black long-sleeved sweater and loose-fitting cargo pants. These garments were now slung over a scarred wooden chair nearby while he soaked in a four-legged brass bathtub in the washroom down the hall from his room.

A single naked, fly-specked bulb hung from the ceiling like a noose. The water had been comfortable but was now growing cool. In contrast to the technological marvels abundant in the more upscale regions of the city, here in the brick-and-mortar core of the metropolis, working amenities were uncommon.

"Hot water?" It was a gentle female voice, spoken aloud, that seemed to read his thoughts—not the persuasive, clouded speech of the Illuminatus that Orion kept expecting to hear again. He twisted to look at the doorway, which was cracked open a few inches. A raven-haired teenage girl wearing a yellow flowered kimono held a dented metal bucket with a small towel wrapped around the handle. Steam wafted from the liquid within, curling into light, misty curtains in the air.

25

Orion smiled, nodding but not wanting to speak, not wanting this lovely creature to hear his freakish voice. She nudged the door open further and cascaded the water into the tub, raising the temperature back to pleasant warmth. He expected her to retreat with the empty pail, but instead she lingered nearby.

"It's you that they're looking for, isn't it?" she said. "The Protectorate."

Orion's lips parted, but he couldn't exhale. He felt that he had better not speak, but his thoughts could not be silenced. *Yes, they're all after me. Everyone: the Greys, the Lacertas, and the Protectorate.*

"It's okay," the girl continued. "I won't tell anyone you're here. You're safe."

Orion's body was immovable, but his brain was electrified. *No, I'm not safe. I never will be again. It's just a question of which of them will get me first.*

The girl's kimono had slipped down to reveal one slender white shoulder.

"I can help you relax," she said, taking a step closer.

His voice still wouldn't come; he couldn't think of anything to say—but instead of interpreting his silence as refusal, the girl tossed the yellow kimono over the wooden chair and climbed into the tub with him. She cradled herself under his left arm, not flinching at his bionic grafts. Water sloshed. The perfumed steam was dizzying.

"You have money, right? It's five thousand," came the gentle purr.

Conflicted, he nodded, trying to stay motionless. Something stirred in his blood, a hesitant arousal, a contradictory excitement. She rested against his shoulder, tracing designs on his chest, trailing narrow fingers across the pale, raised

26

disfigurements latticing his body. The palm of her hand found his thumping heart. He was sweating from the hot bath and from the anxious sensation that wrapped around him, ghostly and light, like a kimono.

"No," he croaked.

She was taken aback by the sudden, raspy flexure of his voice, but quickly regrouped. "Shhh, it's okay. Don't talk."

"No. No." His pulse was rising, as were the hairs on his arms. "No, don't," he murmured.

The girl's body snapped rigid, her eyes locked, her teeth clinched. Shuddering, grimacing, she was imprisoned in an immobile dance of death. Orion couldn't extricate himself, couldn't disengage their tangled limbs, couldn't scrabble out of the smoothly burnished brass tub. Steam wafted from the liquid within, curling into heavy, funereal shrouds in the air.

When it was over, he stood in splotchy puddles upon the aged linoleum, studying the blue forks in her sizzled skin. The black hair was arrayed out in the water, floating in gauzy clouds. He draped the silken robe over the slender body before recovering the baggy sweater and cargo pants. He pulled the clothes on hastily, and fled down the hallway to the gloomy, claustrophobic staircase.

Orion exited to the street once more and chose a random direction in which to walk. What did it matter where he went? There was no rest, and no escape from the walking death that he carried with him. The girl had died for the simple crime of being close to him. She had offered kind words, a comforting touch—no matter the reason—and met the same fate as those hateful radicals who would have murdered him in the street.

How had it happened? The water in the bath? No—the augmentations would have to be waterproof to work within his body. The voltage was contained until...until something happened to make him lose control of it.

The dying rays of the sunset yawned behind him. The alleys and gutters were piled with trash, discarded remnants of people's lives. Husks of things that were contrived, made to be useful for a time, and then consumed. He had to scavenge his own life back from the Greys, salvage some kind of existence out of the path they had made for him. He teetered on the brink of humanity, separate and alone, on the verge of a plunge into some monstrous unknown.

As Orion shuffled through the landfill of human lives, one face fired a spark in his mind as it passed.

No...it can't be.

He pushed against the throng as he turned, breaking into a run. Coming up behind the retreating figure, he reached with one outstretched hand, rested it on the shoulder, and pulled to turn the stranger around.

The familiar face was that of a young woman, blinking at him in surprise and then in dawning recognition. A coral-colored scarf was tied about her forehead; he snatched it off, making her flinch. Circumnavigating her newly shaved head, in a perfect revolution, was a puffy pink scar.

Chapter Three

The firelight was dim and dusty after the harsh neon cavalcade of the Thoroughfare, and Orion welcomed the change. The Badlands were now more inviting than the city, despite the fact that the shanty they were huddled in barely had four walls keeping it together. The sheet-metal roof above them wobbled intermittently as the sandy winds raked across it outside, thumping out a reassuring heartbeat and allowing the smoke from their meager camp to float out through the gaps.

He reclined on his side on a thin mattress, propping his head against his right hand, scrutinizing the girl while trying not to be obvious about it. Her name was Lyra Vaughn. She was just a touch older than he—sixteen, he supposed, and tall for her age. She was thin and pretty, with an oval-shaped face and gray eyes. In the flickering dimness, he couldn't gauge the color of her furrowed eyebrows, and he guessed that when she'd had hair, it had been straight and blonde. Instead, she was crowned with a gauzy pinkish-orange scarf tied around her bald head like a bandana. A sleeveless tan button-up blouse and faded, ripped blue jeans hugged her frame, and she sat upright on her own mattress with her ankles crossed and her elbows resting on her knees, studying him in return.

"How did they get you?" he asked.

"I'm a courier. I run valuable items from place to place, usually on foot. I'd just escaped from a bunch of banditos in Midland. There was no one around, and I had this weird feeling, like..." She stopped, groping for words.

"Like your skin is too tight for your body," he supplied.

"Exactly. I don't remember what happened next, but I remember the operating table." One slender hand strayed to the pinkish-orange scarf, rubbing the skin beneath.

"What did they do to you? Did they tell you?"

"The Illuminatus said they were giving me a gift, that I had a good brain already and they were going to make it better."

"They made you a psionic? I didn't know that could be done."

"He said I was the first one they tried the surgery with, and they would watch me to see how I did."

Orion nodded in grim acknowledgment. "Yeah, they're watching. No doubt about that."

He rummaged beneath a pile of flat rocks near the shanty wall where he had cached some supplies weeks ago. This wasn't his house, just a shack where he squatted from time to time—in the Badlands, nothing belonged to anybody—and he was elated to see that the hidden burlap sack was still there.

Orion withdrew two cans of vegetables, sliced the tops off of them with a deft motion from his short-range cybernetic laser, and folded the lids into scoops for the food.

"That's a neat little trick." She smirked, eyeing his cybercomputer with approval.

"I'm part man, part Swiss Army knife," he joked, uncomfortable for doing so, hating the attempt at humor through the clumsy filter of a voice that sounded metallic and inharmonious.

A few seconds of silence followed, underscoring how his attempt at levity had fallen flat. Lyra's voice was delicate when she asked, "Why does your voice sound like that?"

"It's because I don't breathe anymore. They've installed an apparatus to manipulate my vocal chords so I can still speak. They're right about one thing, though: it's an inferior form of communication."

"How does oxygen get into your blood, then?"

"My bionic interfaces synthesize oxygen and circulate it more efficiently. I could stay underwater all day, or walk through a room filled with poison gas."

"It sounds like you're growing to appreciate what they've done."

Orion had no answer for this.

"I don't think we can hide from the Greys," Lyra said. "Maybe we shouldn't have left the city. The Greys can find us anywhere, but the Lacertas are more numerous out here."

"We're not hiding," Orion said. "We're arming ourselves."

Lyra raised her eyebrows. "You're really taking this seriously, then. Killing all of the Lacertas you can, I mean?"

"Everything is serious now. Whether we go up against the lizards or the Greys, we're going to need real firepower. I know where there's a thermal pulse rifle lying in the desert not far from here."

She listened as he told her about the bandito who had robbed him the day before, and the grisly end the man had met. Orion had been in no condition to recover the heavy weapon at the time, but it had remained on his mind all the same. Lyra, however, needed more convincing.

"I still think it's dangerous for us to be out here. With the caps you have, we could buy weapons in the city. They don't sell them in stores, but I've done plenty of gunrunning, and I know some people."

Orion shook his head. "It would be too easy to run into

the Protectorate, and I've already had a couple of close calls. A cybernetic and a psionic? They'd lock us up forever, and probably torture us to get us to tell them what we know about the Greys."

"So, you're scared of being tortured by someone other than the Greys for a change."

He gestured with an empty palm. "Okay, Lyra, I don't know what to do, all right? I feel better out here, that's all. I can take the rifle that could have killed me, and repurpose it, make it my own. I'm just a scavenger. How about using your gifted brain to figure a way out of all this?"

He wasn't angry, wasn't exploding at her. To the contrary, speaking about a shared problem with another human being cemented a new and unfamiliar camaraderie. In spite of having always been a loner, Orion was immeasurably glad to have an ally, even one as lost and helpless as himself.

"I am too," she said.

He blinked. "You are what?"

"Glad to talk about this with someone. Glad to have an ally."

"Oh my God. The surgery really worked, didn't it? You heard what I just thought about you." Or was it such a surprise? The Greys' track record for transformations was remarkable.

"Yes, I heard that. I think we have some kind of connection," she said. "It's not hard to guess why."

On impulse, Orion reached for her hand. He brushed her fingers, fearing the deadly reprisal that came from touching another human being—but as her hand squeezed his own, his anxiety melted into just the opposite: a feeling of more control.

"I know you don't like to be around people," Lyra continued. "It makes sense that you prefer working with inanimate objects—they perform as they're supposed to. And if they don't, you fix them. It's not that simple with people." Her insight was astounding. "But you need help. You need to realize you can't fix everything. You need to realize that you need people with you."

"When people are broken, they can't be fixed." He was staring into the fire, seeing ghosts.

"That's not true. Look what you've lived through," she pressed.

He met her gaze, despite the blurriness welling in his eyes. "I'm not talking about surgery. I'm not talking about one alien cutting you open and another one sewing you up again."

"Neither am I."

He looked back to the fire. "You're right, though. People are so unpredictable I can't stand it. Now I'm less human than I ever was, and I don't know if I should care. People cause all the problems in the world, all of this misery."

"It's not humanity's fault we were invaded by the Lacertas, or that they're fighting a war with the Greys on our planet."

"Like this place was such a paradise before that happened. Humans have fought each other as much as we've ever fought the lizards. I really think if the Greys hadn't shown up to help…" He stopped, suddenly realizing what he was saying—and, bless her, Lyra let it remain unsaid.

Outside, the wind shifted, whispering through the cracks in the shanty walls. The smoke from the meager fire twisted in Lyra's direction, and she pulled the scarf down from her forehead to cover her nose and mouth. In the crimson glow, the scar was a shiny ring around her head, a biological contrivance of a saintly halo. Avoiding the smoke, she crept to his side of the fire and stretched out on the mattress beside him. She lay on her side, nestled against his body. He was aware of her even breathing in the absence of his own. His pulse remained calm, and his skin

33

did not prickle, even when he cradled his left arm around her and closed his eyes.

***

His dreams were surreal and hallucinatory. Fleeting snatches from buried memories rose into his wearied consciousness. Once again, he roamed that peregrine craft, stumbling through yawning halls of shrouded oddity. The featureless walls reflected no visions of his own form; he traveled immaterial down narrow corridors among attenuated figures who were smoky with the fog of dreams. The viewing bays at his left and right beckoned with secret promises, luring him with intoxicating vistas of untold worlds. When he lingered at one, however, the glimpses afforded him were not the celestial bodies of unconquerable space but rather a window into the most profane depths of hell.

Aliens ripped and gutted the restrained forms of a man and woman as they writhed on metal tables. Through their contorted expressions, frantic with pain and terror, Orion discerned an air of distant cognizance. Despairing wails tickled the strings of recognition deep within his disoriented mind. Before the shadows of his fugue parted, however, he was floating on again, and the next *tableau vivant* came into view.

This room was sterile, and thankfully free of gore. A young male child was seated at a sleek, low table. A shiny metal band hugged his forehead, encircling his feathery hair like a mechanically contrived imitation of a saintly halo. Metal anodes clung to his temples and scalp. The boy was manipulating small widgets that were placed on the table one at a time by a lean, impassive Grey. Each mechanical gadget was examined, sometimes adjusted by the opening or closing of switches, and then fitted into a sequence with the other pieces by the child's busy fingers. Sockets and plugs joined tightly, forming a train of circuitry that snaked across the tabletop. Some pieces were rejected by the child after inspection, forming a discard pile at the prodigy's right elbow. All the while, the slender alien observed, and tendered new pieces as necessary. Before long, the gadgets were linked together in an impressive array; the final piece appeared to be a sort of battery, and the child beamed with satisfaction as the components all lit with dancing colors. Yellow and orange lights traveled in a blinking zigzag through the circuitry. Emotionless and wreathed in hypnagogic smoke, the Grey stared and stared.

***

Orion woke before dawn. Lying on his side, he stared ahead into the embers of the fire. Softly glowing yellow and orange lights illumined the air, wispy with dreamlike smoke. Lyra stirred as well, burrowing into his embrace against the morning's chill. His head cleared, and he felt refreshed in a way that was rare before the recent operation. He evidently needed less sleep now—but his mind was still not at peace after the night's disquieting voyage.

Breakfast was oatmeal, dried fruit, and nuts, again taken from the supply cache and supplemented with clean water from the covered well outside. The remaining goods would accompany them in a burlap sack. The dirt bike, however, was out of fuel, and there was no gasoline to be had. As the sun peeked over the horizon to frown upon the ruined landscape, Orion led Lyra west, farther into the desert, explaining that their destination could be reached on foot. After that, finding transportation would be a matter of opportunity.

"You mean we're going to steal someone's vehicle after we get the rifle," Lyra accused.

"I don't need to steal to stay alive," he said. "What do you think I am?"

Lyra nodded, her mouth turning up at one corner. "Sorry. I guess that's just how it always was with the dealers and the banditos."

Guilt and flickering remembrance prodded Orion. "Don't apologize. I stole some capitals yesterday for medical treatment. But that was in the city. Everything's screwed up there. It's all a false promise of security."

"I'll say." Lyra looked at him slyly, her mouth still twisted with a half-serious expression. "You didn't even get the medical help you wanted."

Orion shook his head, laughing despite himself. "Those ugly doctors even forgot to charge me. Wait 'til I get the bill—boy, am I going to complain."

This time, the humor felt easier, more natural. Lyra took his hand, swinging it between them as they walked.

"Okay, so forget the city," she said. "We're never going back. Out here, we're self-sufficient. What do we do for transportation?"

"We can find horses. There's lots of them out here."

"Horses," she repeated. "I've never been too good in the saddle."

"You'd better practice." He smiled. "It's how everyone in the world used to get around, for thousands of years."

"And now the world is moving backward...back to that time. What did they do before horses?"

"They walked," Orion said, gesturing with open hands. Lyra chuckled.

A journey of two hours through the flat, thirsty land, punctuated by the skeleton towers of defunct oil wells, was dusty but not unbearable. A canteen was sparingly swapped back and forth as they kept sharp eyes attuned for any salient features among the dry expanse. They spoke more of their recent experiences, with both travelers halting just before the more terrible revelations. The conversation tempted Orion to put into words what he had experienced during the night, but he was held back each time by confusion and uncertainty. The desert, so lifeless and still, nonetheless sparked some kind of vibrancy within him. Among these cracked and withered surroundings, determination flourished all the same: rugged and unkempt ocotillos and Spanish daggers reached skyward, bristling and tough. Finally, he found himself blurting out the awful words:

"I lived in the desert during my childhood. My parents were horribly disfigured by the Greys' experiments. They couldn't live among other people."

Lyra stopped walking.

"One of my earliest memories is some kind of aptitude test that they administered on their ship," he continued. "They evaluated me but didn't operate yet."

"They waited for your teenage growth spurt, so your body would be more accommodating to the implants, and then they picked you up again," Lyra supplied.

"Right. But my parents they operated on right away. It was awful—they were prototypes of something monstrous. The surgery didn't even go well, they were so mangled..." Orion closed his eyes and shuddered despite the desert heat.

"And then they dumped you out here, to scavenge for survival."

"My parents stayed hidden as much as possible. We found whatever we could at night, and fixed it up and traded it to the caravans for food when they came."

"Are they still alive?"

Orion's mouth tightened. "We'd better get moving. This isn't the place to stand around and talk."

"I see something," she declared.

Both travelers increased their pace, roving over the terrain. Up ahead, a dark, blurry shape danced in the feverish waves that rose off of the landscape. A malformed blot, incongruous against the expanse, beckoned them. Slowly it took shape: the prostrate form of a black horse, now claimed as part of the enduring wastelands, stretched on its side, heaped with dust and dried blood. Nearby, the bandito with the ragged beard, grimacing in necrosis, rotted as well.

At twelve meters away, Lyra retched from the stench. Orion's eyes swept over the gashed carcasses roasting in the sun, and he wondered that there were no vultures. Lyra gasped in shock and warning, realizing the same thing—but then a new silhouette rose, standing to its full height next to the Lacerta's corpse. A second Lacerta, obscured by the profile and angle of the fallen mustang, separated from its slaughtered comrade. Yellow-gray eyes, bearing vertical slashes like the clawed furrows on the surrounding carcasses, drove into his own. Panic clawed at him as well but fizzled under the prickling electric fuzziness as his hormones surged. Orion crouched forward.

"Wait," Lyra whispered.

The machine, the destroyer within him, was prepared to attack—but Orion hesitated. Scrutinizing the reptilian face, even at a distance, he saw what she was no doubt experiencing in greater volume. Lyra was approaching, picking her steps through the wilderness. He moved to match her strides, drawing nearer to the hulking, olive-shaded creature. They were ten meters away, then eight. There was no mistaking what he saw, although it riddled his senses with wonder: shifting emotions clung to the inhuman visage. Was it sadness mingled with fear that he detected on those bestial features, or was he overlaying his own perspective upon a distorted, alien canvas? The reptilian beast had been examining the body of its companion. Could this monster possibly be mourning the loss of its fellow? Orion glanced at its feet, noting with stupefaction the arrangement of colored rocks and boughs laid down as an altar. Disbelief and awe pummeled him.

Then the Lacerta wheeled and fled, bounding with giant strides over the rocks, leaving swirls of dust drifting in the windless air. A thin trail of cinders crawled behind it, wispy with the smoke of dreams, and settled back to a landscape that belied any signs of life.

Lyra's hand found Orion's, and their fingers entwined. At his touch, the hair on her arms prickled as well, awash with static. The latent energy seemed to bind their hands together as they gazed, transfixed, to the west.

A metallic growl broke them from reverie. The gargling sound of the hardy four-wheel-drive machines favored by the desert-dwelling Resistance could be heard approaching from the south, and the pair turned in expectation. In moments, the tawny, begrimed Jeep roared up to them and then skidded to a stop with a rumbling grunt.

Four roughnecks arrayed in mismatched tactical gear, each bearing an assortment of heavy weapons, studied them. On the passenger side, a deeply tanned man with a battered Stetson and three-day stubble hauled himself up to sit on the back of his seat.

"You kids seen a Lizzie come through here just now?" He rested a belt-fed light machine gun against the roll cage.

Orion gestured north, toward New Zaragosa. "Yeah, that way."

The militia men swapped concerned looks. On the surface, nothing about Orion or Lyra would draw a second glance from the nomadic outlanders. However, the grating sound of the scavenger's voice distracted them for a moment.

The leader's own voice, with its strong Mexican accent, was gruff but not unkind. "What are you all doing out here? It's dangerous, and we don't have room to give you a lift."

Lyra crossed to where something glinted in the gritty dirt. She stooped to fetch it and then straightened, shaking the earth out of Orion's empty pistol. She cleared the breach and returned the slide to its closed position, then tucked it at her svelte waist. "We just came to get this back. Don't worry about us, we live near here."

The engine's roaring growl surged twice before the driver shouted, "Auriga, we'd better get that Lizzie before it hits UCO territory."

The Mexican returned to his seat. The pair was scrutinized for a few seconds more before the Resistance men offered a collective shrug and thundered off to the north.

This time, Lyra did not let the troublesome statement remain unsaid. "Why did you mislead them?" she asked in a cautious tone.

"You saw its left arm, right?"

"I did. That Lacerta had a cybercomputer too."

"Yes. Older, more obsolete…but the same design as mine."

"The Greys!" she exclaimed.

A stinging wind rushed through the desert, whipping their clothes as Orion walked to the body of the dead outlaw. The filthy duster was flapping over a hidden prize, concealing it from view. He bent to retrieve the lethal treasure, half buried and forgotten.

Orion nodded. "It means the Lacertas were their previous experimental subjects."

Lyra's eyes widened. "So there's more to their relationship than we thought."

Questions spun through his mind. *How much do they know about each other? How long have they been fighting?*

Why are they now experimenting on humans like us? When will it end?

"Monsters," she spat the word bitterly, having perceived his thoughts again.

Orion's reply was to switch the pulse rifle on. A soft whine pierced the lashing of the wind for a few seconds; he was pleased to read the battery display at 91 percent, and gratified by an unexpected occurrence: his cybernetic systems were wirelessly syncing with the weapon. A yellow targeting reticle appeared in his vision, projected from his optic nerve onto his retinas. As he swept the gun to and fro, the reticle followed the barrel's trajectory, feeding him graphical information regarding distance and biological statistics.

"I always thought this was a human weapon, but it's melding with my Grey technology," he said.

"The surprises just keep coming."

He powered the weapon down and slung the strap across his torso. "I want to know more about the Lacertas," he resolved. "If there's a way to communicate with them, maybe they can tell us more about the Greys. What they've done to them, what they're doing to us."

Lyra returned his speculation with a solemn, knowing gaze. "I think I might be able to communicate with them. I could feel the thoughts of the one that was just here."

Together, they turned back to the west, to the prosaic emptiness of the desert. Buffeting gusts tore through the wilderness, but against the vast environment, Orion felt close to her—as if the two of them shared the world together.

Still staring into the distance, Lyra whispered, "I know where the Lacerta is going."

Chapter Four

The roan gelding slurped from the placid grayish-brown water, and blew through its nostrils. Orion stood nearby, the reins slack in his hand, while Lyra removed a tennis shoe and shook it until three chalky pebbles tumbled out to join their fellows on the ground.

"Is that water safe for people?" she asked with a doubtful look.

"There's no telling," Orion said. "There used to be small towns on the Pecos, but they're all wiped out now. I don't know what's upstream, so we'd better not risk it."

The girl agreed with this, albeit reluctantly, since their shared canteen was now dry. It had been a broiling one-hour walk to the trader's stable where they'd bartered for the horse and saddle, followed by a broiling three-hour ride through the Badlands, which were punctuated by the diminutive little branch before them at last. Lyra's throat was scratchy and her back ached, unaccustomed to equestrian travel. She stretched, and said nothing.

Now it was Orion's turn to ask a question. "You're sure we have to cross the river?"

"Why, is that a problem? It looks like we can just walk across."

"Yeah, it's not that. I mean that I've never crossed it. Nobody ever goes west of the Pecos."

Lyra paused, taken aback, then chuckled in disbelief. "What

do you mean? Can it be any more dangerous than what we've already been through?"

Orion's eyebrows tented. "Point taken. I just don't know what to expect."

Weird images flicked through his imagination: Bizarre, maddening alien cities. Lawless camps of savage wilderness men. Vicious, bipedal reptilian beasts.

"We have to do it," she coaxed. "If we don't try to find out more about the Lacertas, we'll never know what the Greys are doing here on Earth. We'll just end up hiding in the desert until they come for us again."

Orion shielded his eyes from the sun. She was right, of course. He gazed out at the unknown horizon as would a pioneer exploring some awful new planet. Somewhere in that arid waste, monsters thrived where no humans dared to tread. He moved to help Lyra climb back into the saddle, but she swung up and onto the horse unaided, causing him to smile. Grasping the reins, he walked into the rolling water, forging ahead into new frontiers.

***

The building would have been imposing and dark even without the dusky purple twilight. Dwarfed by its gargantuan shadow, Orion and Lyra studied the dusty, wind-worn streaks and barren windows in the pockmarked stone walls. There was no signage on the exterior, although the flattened metal fence they had ridden over had borne its share of warning notices.

After tying the gelding to a defunct light post and slipping its feed bag on to keep it quiet, the pair crept to the entrance. Spiderweb cracks in the glass double doors split their reflections into distorted effigies. Orion read the words outlined in sterile white block letters: "RETICULUM: CHARTER MEMBER, UNITED CORPORATIONS ORDER"

The door opened outward in response to fierce tugging. Inside, a cramped foyer beckoned, mottled with darkness and grime. Orion tapped his fingers twice on his left forearm, and a soft white glow illumined the chamber. This was a security station. A dented steel shutter hung across the receptionist's window on the wall to their right, and the ruined gateways of a metal detector lay collapsed in the middle of the room.

Skirting the debris, Orion examined the prominent lock on the doors on the far side of the checkpoint. It appeared to be electromagnetic, but the two round bulbs, one red and one green, were listless, dead eyes. He wouldn't even have to slice the lock.

Lyra was behind him, scanning their surroundings. He cracked the door open, and gentle light bled into the corridor. Silence reigned. He led the way into the hall, noticing the framed photographs of solemn-faced men and women who were their only companions in this facility. Lyra tugged at his right arm, leading him into an adjacent room: the one connected to the foyer via the half-shuttered window. Equipment lockers stood at attention in the corner to their left; rummaging through them, she produced a few red-and-white cardboard boxes, and he nodded in approval. Nine-millimeter ballistic ammunition.

The girl drew the pistol from her waistband, ejected the magazine with a soft click, and began to feed the rounds into the well, pushing them down one at a time with a practiced movement of her thumb. Orion followed her sure, concise operations, and reminded himself to ask later where she'd become so comfortable with firearms. The boxes of ammo joined their other supplies in a black backpack that she'd retrieved from a metal chair. Then, muffling the sound as best she could, she ratcheted a bullet into the chamber and held it against her right thigh, nodding at him to continue.

Orion forewent the readying of his pulse rifle and kept it slung at his own side instead. They'd agreed that the Lacertas would be jumpy enough at having unexpected visitors, and it might be better to retain the opportunity for diplomacy for as long as possible. He also considered intentionally making a little noise. Then his eyes caught a black-and-yellow-striped whiptail lizard darting down the hallway before them, followed by another and then one more, and he understood that the Lacertas would know they were here regardless of what they did.

They progressed to the end of the hall, passing disheveled offices and storerooms of little import. A set of swinging double doors served as the entry to a separate part of the facility. The whiptails scurried underneath the doors a few moments before Orion reached out to push them open. In the great room beyond, weak illumination fell from the heights where ruined windows combined with the ruined outside. The dusk played upon rows of massive machines, all disused, forming corridors that stretched back through time to when mankind was relevant and sure.

They picked their way forward, staying close to each other. Shadows lengthened as they walked, and they heard raspy breathing. A mutual violation of privacy, of sanity, as each side tacitly acknowledged that the other was there while hesitating to reveal themselves. What were the chances that the Lacertas would receive them peacefully, after the blood Orion had shed? How did they even expect to communicate with these strange beasts?

Silhouettes arrayed before them in the corridor. Orion flashed back to pained, phantom memories of wandering the alien ship, deceitfully tracked by slim, shadowy beings...but this was different. The hulking figures now approached them head-on, and with purpose.

Four Lacertas engaged the pair, their claws clicking with staccato rhythms as the whiptails scurried underfoot. Red-rimmed eyes studied Orion and Lyra; forked tongues danced to taste the air around them. The Lacertas carried weapons, as well: their own thermal pulse rifles were built on a larger scale, and ergonomically different from the human variety, but the similarities were unmistakable. The pair of humans was not threatened, however, and Lyra snapped the thumb safety on the pistol, stowing it in a side pocket of her backpack. Then, in a calm voice, she spoke.

"We're not here to fight. We want to talk, if you can. We need to understand about the Greys and what they've done to you."

A long silence. Licking tongues, darting eyes. Orion's gaze did not stray from their weapons, designed to blast their way through a worthless race. Their clawed digits ticked like metronomes. Tension weighed down upon them—and then one of the soldiers, its hide streaked with black bands, gestured with its chin, turning toward the far end of the factory floor.

Down dark alleys they trod, their shadows chasing each other through narrow corridors. The striped Lacerta led the way deeper into the factory, turning this way and that, winding through the monumental maze. They were lost within its dark embrace.

Seconds ticked, with Orion staring at the switching of their escort's tail. Flanked by the other three Lacertas, he and Lyra struggled to match the long, clockwork strides of their hosts. Orion studied them as best he could in the shifting shadows, and picked out occasional glints of metal in their pebbled skin: some of these beasts were cybernetically enhanced as well. He glanced at Lyra, who was studying the signs they passed in the corridors; when he began to do the same, a knot formed in his stomach.

Their destination was a humble office in a more executive branch of the facility. The lights were still off, and an electric lantern burned in one corner, casting long shadows over the shoddy carpet. The meager illumination revealed a large wooden desk with a desktop computer; a glass case with photographs and sleek, modern trophies; and dingy cloth and leather furnishings. Adjacent to the desk stood an olive-mottled reptilian; the cybercomputer on its left arm confirmed its identity as the one they had encountered in the desert only hours ago.

The stillness was yet unbroken as they were ushered in, save for the clicks and rustles of the hulking aliens' movements. Some communications were exchanged between the Lacertas, a matter of soft cues and subtle gestures too quick and strange for Orion to follow—but then their escorts withdrew, leaving him and Lyra alone with the leader. Their retreating clicks echoed back through the open door as the guard lizards vanished down the hallway.

The Lacerta fiddled with the computer on its arm. After a few seconds, an artificial voice spoke from it with soothing female cadences. "Good that you have come here."

Orion's eyes were wide, but he held his tongue, preferring that Lyra do the talking. "You can communicate with us through your computer?" she asked.

More selective typing. Then: "Yes. Tongue is thin and forked, larynx is not developed. Do not have lips, cannot use human speech. We communicate with visual and olfactory means." The Lacerta appeared to be inputting its thoughts in a shorthand manner, and the computer extrapolated them into coherent phrases before speaking them aloud. It was impressive, if slightly clumsy.

"How many of you are here?"

"You do not need to know that." The synthesized voice was pleasant but firm.

"Oh…sorry. So you're a female?"

"I am queen."

Now Orion spoke up, his own artificial voice laced with gravel in contrast to the computer's gentle tones. "What? Lacertas have royalty?"

"Many queens in a kingdom, and one king."

"I see." In truth, there were some questions about that, but Orion did not pursue the topic.

Lyra intervened, getting them back on track. "We came here to talk because we know the Greys have experimented upon your race, like they have done with ours."

"This is true. The ones you call Grey came to our home system long ago to stagnate development."

Orion scowled. Lyra, of course, broached the subject on his mind. "They stagnated your species by performing *enhancements?*"

"Yes. Natural evolution is confounded. Species becomes dependent upon artifice. Progresses backward. Senses weaken, muscles atrophy."

"Like the physical differences between a twenty-first century computer nerd and a hunter-gatherer from caveman times."

Hesitation before pecking at the computer. "I do not understand that, but my race did not display great aptitude for computers. This made us less valuable to the Grey, who intend to relegate others to subjective status."

Orion spoke up again. "By screwing with their evolutionary

process? Isn't that awfully imprecise, even if it wouldn't take millions of years to achieve their results?"

"They are simply conducting an experiment. Time is irrelevant. The Grey could perform pervasive alterations to four or five successive generations, and return in distant future to observe results. May not take millions of years. Many species exhibit dramatic changes within comparatively brief time frame. Thousands of years, perhaps."

Lyra leaned against the edge of the mahogany desk. "This is a lot to handle. You're saying that the Greys visited the Lacertas on your home planet thousands of years ago and introduced you to superior technology as a way of directing the future course of the species?"

"Should not be difficult to believe. Happened to humans too."

Chills enveloped Orion's frame. He'd been feeling odd since they'd arrived at the factory. He shook off the apprehension, trying to concentrate: there was something snagging his notice on a nearby wall. As Lyra continued speaking to the beast, he crossed to the wall where a framed photograph hung. He studied its depiction of handsome, well-dressed men and women standing around a polished oval table, with a familiar face just to the right of center. The Illuminatus peered back at him from the frame, those dark, sinister eyes and aquiline nose unmistakable.

"Lyra," he croaked.

An immediate gasp as she joined him. "The psionic man on the ship. What is this?"

Orion touched the print at the bottom of the photograph. "He was on the board of directors here at Reticulum. It says here his name is Josiah Corvus."

"These other people are board members and high-ranking executives with the UCO."

Orion turned back to the Lacerta. "The signs in the hallways on the way here seemed to indicate that this was some kind of manufacturing facility."

"Weapons factory," came the answer. "You are holding a Reticulum weapon at this moment."

Slowly, Orion unslung the rifle from his shoulder. A moment's examination revealed the truth: engraved into the polymer frame on the left side above the trigger housing were the words: "RETICULUM THERMAL PULSE PLATFORM ORLA TX."

He powered the rifle on, this time observing the "RETICULUM INDUSTRIES MBR UCO" heading that flashed on the display at startup before switching to the field targeting system. "Was this made by humans or Greys?"

"Grey technology shared with humans, as we discussed."

"And it's way out here in the desert, where no one knew about it." Lyra was connecting the dots. "The Greys helped the United Corporations Order develop more powerful weapons in secret, until a certain time came when the secrecy was no longer necessary. The Greys are out in the open now, and the UCO is uncontested."

"Likely happened as you say."

"Don't the Greys know you're here now? It seems like they would blow up the factory or something."

"Grey are not intrinsically warlike, as other races. Do not use weapons in the same manner. Instead, use others for their purposes, as we discussed. Preserve appearance of benefactors to mankind—a false appearance. Humans are not aware of the scope of these plans. Not aware of the extent to which they are manipulated by the Grey."

Orion's skin was sweaty and prickling. "Don't try to wriggle out from under this. None of this changes the fact that we're still enemies. The Lacertas killed half the people on Earth and practically destroyed the entire planet. Then the Greys came to intervene—"

"Fool," said the reptile's artificial voice. "The Grey used my race as a weapon against you, and then offered their help in order to gain your trust. Kept Lacerta and human against each other to cull their numbers and position themselves above both races." The cold yellow eyes were positively glowing in the feeble incandescence of the lantern—but sharper still was the light that shone against the monster's dagger-filled jaws. "You are correct, however, that we are still enemies."

"As if I could have forgotten." Lyra's alarmed face broke into Orion's fugue, and he realized that he had been pointing the weapon right at the Lacerta.

"Orion, easy. Get a hold of yourself," she soothed, edging toward him. Addressing the scowling alien, she added, "All we're doing is talking to you. This doesn't have to escalate. Let's just talk about this."

"They've destroyed entire cities, Lyra. The Lacertas aren't innocent victims in all this. One of them almost killed me just *yesterday*." His head pounded, causing him to wince. He didn't feel well at all. "And here they are, hiding out with all these weapons, building an army... Even if what they're saying is true, it doesn't change anything. We'll have to fight them sooner or later."

The reptile hissed, foregoing the use of its computer in an unequivocal statement. It crouched, talons splayed.

"Don't do this," the girl begged. The staccato clicks returned: Lacerta guards coming down the corridor outside.

In a flash, the creature leapt. Lyra screamed as Orion's weapon coughed twice. Fiery bolts of superheated gas tore through the

Lacerta's chest, leaving a pair of ragged holes. Black ichor sizzled and cauterized at the edges of the wounds. Flailing through the air, snarling and squealing, the reptile skidded facedown onto the carpet.

"*No!* Why did you do it?" Lyra shrieked, searching the twisting expressions on his face. She stormed up to him, reaching to snatch the weapon, but he grabbed her wrist and flung her down behind the desk. As he dove for cover after her, thermal bolts erupted through the door and its adjacent windows. They stayed seated on the ground, their backs against the hard wood while glittering glass rained around them.

Orion presented the rifle above his head, aimed backward, and blind-fired over the top of the desk. Beside him, Lyra dug into the side pocket of the knapsack, retrieved the ballistic pistol, and snapped the safety off.

"What's your problem, are you trying to get us killed?" She ducked again as the trophy case exploded, showering them with more glass. Spinning around in a forward-facing crouch, she peeked out around one side of the desk to gauge the number and position of figures outside. Long slats of blinds obscured her view, however.

"I didn't mean for that to happen, but I had to defend myself!" Orion repositioned to fire again. When he stuck his head out, and then flinched from a blistering round that missed by a hair, his vision was augmented by the assisted targeting. The reticle made it easy for him to focus on the colored silhouette drawn in on his HUD. Orion moved the gun's barrel until the green reticle on the display turned red inside the beast's outline, and pumped the trigger. His weapon kicked, and an orange jet tore through the blinds and the window to explode against the Lacerta on the other side. The silhouette jerked against the wall of the corridor and then slumped to the ground.

Return fire now angled into the room from invisible figures behind the wall against the exit door, chewing the desk into smoking splinters. "We gotta move!" he shouted.

Lyra blasted away at the entrenched Lacertas, her bullets driving them deeper into cover for an instant. The respite of a few seconds was enough for Orion to get moving again, and he launched himself into a roll that tucked him behind a padded sofa. The protection wasn't good, but the position earned him a new firing angle, and a second Lacerta was neutralized. He gestured for her to come to his position and then advanced to the doorway.

"I can't believe this. That Lizzie was singing like a canary, and you had to bring the whole factory down on top of us. What's the matter with you?" She sprinted to his side and placed her back to the wall with her elbows bent, holding her pistol at chest level, its barrel pointed at the ceiling.

"It's not my fault, okay? It would have torn us to shreds, and I had to do it. I'll make it up to you if we can get out of here." He risked a look into the hall. "Just watch my back—I don't see any right now. Let's go!"

He slipped into the corridor, hazy with the stench of sizzled flesh, and she followed, crunching glass underfoot as they ran.

Chapter Five

"Hey, *payaso*, want to do me a favor and not smoke while you're doing that?" the man called from the doorway. Martín Auriga looked back over his shoulder at the Depot Warden, and grinned with the offending cigarillo clamped between his teeth. He passed the tobacco to his companion in the back seat of the Jeep and then gestured with the nozzle of the fuel pump in a mock salute to the Warden before inserting it into the gas tank.

As the fuel counter ticked, Auriga fanned himself with his white Stetson and studied the tall chain-link fence surrounding the perimeter of the Resistance outpost. Makeshift guard towers housed slender, shabbily clad figures who perched over AK-47s, their faces obscured from the whipping dust with bandanas. How old were the faces beneath those masks? Fifteen? Eighteen? Auriga thought back to the kids he'd seen in the desert an hour ago sorting through the dead as they rotted in the sun.

Beyond the fence, a rippling haze welled up from the desert horizon. It was midafternoon, the hottest part of the day, giving the Lacertas a pronounced advantage. Although the species favored dark and humid environments, they had nonetheless adapted to Earth's desert wastelands with ease. The cold-blooded reptiles thrived in temperatures that stifled even those humans who were inured to these wilderness climes. Of course, hunting them at night presented its own difficulties: while the lizards were sluggish in the cooler hours, their keen eyesight and affinity for concealment still allowed them to get the drop on many an experienced Resistance party.

"That's enough!" the Warden marched up to the pump and reached out to slap the lever to the "Off" position. His mustachioed face twisted into a frown. "Fifty-seven liters, man. That's worth at least two hundred rounds of ammo. Or have you got any *licor*?"

"I've paid you already, amigo. I pay with dead *Lagartos*. Two this week so far," Auriga said.

"Oh, dead lizards? So you've got them on the run? Look what happened to Coyanosa, they tore that place apart."

"That's because I wasn't there, *ese*. If I were, it would have been different."

"Don't give me that King Kong garbage. You've got to pay up. What have you got?"

"You think your little fence is keeping the Lizzies out? This place looks like a kids' playground. *I'm* keeping them out. You can give me some gas to go on patrol once in a while, man."

"I'm not going to ask again."

"All right, then, fine. Don't do me any favors." Auriga produced a pea-size lump from a pocket of his vest. "Twenty-four karat, man. Almost a full gram." He plucked the cigarillo back from his comrade's lips and blew a long trail of white smoke out the corner of his mouth.

The Warden scowled, his fist closing over the nugget. "That looks like half a gram of eighteen K. You're as bad as the banditos, Auriga."

Auriga chuckled, climbing back into the front passenger seat. "No, amigo. I'm much worse."

The off-road vehicle rumbled through the Badlands, jostling up and down. The driver's face was protected by wide driving goggles and a black bandana, but to Auriga, the breeze generated by the movement, although dusty and warm, was still welcome. He kept one fist clamped to the roll cage overhead as the driver periodically swerved to avoid an outlying boulder or Spanish dagger.

"Hey, Auriga." A soldier in the back seat leaned forward with a gold-toothed smirk. "Tell us again how you think it's a good thing that the Lizzies invaded."

"He thinks it's making us stronger," the other soldier supplied, scratching the bat tattoo on his collar. "They kill off the weak and the slow, they only leave the tough guys with the big cojones like Auriga. It's good for the gene pool, man." The two men snickered.

Auriga swiveled partway in his seat to glare at them. "It's not that at all, you *idiotas*." His sharp gaze remained after their sniggering had tapered off into an uneasy rest. Then he indicated his stormy eyes with two fingers. "It's about *los ojos.*

"You can tell a predator from a prey by looking at the eyes. Look at a rabbit, or a deer: a prey animal. It's got eyes on the sides of its head." He tapped his temples. "Gives it a wider field of view, lets it see all the way around for when something is sneaking up on it. An animal like that, its defense is in running away, escaping. It has to watch out for predators.

"Now look at a lion or a wolf. The eyes are in front." His fingers switched back to where they had started, forming a V that lined up with his own eyes. "So it can focus straight ahead and give chase. So it can pursue a prey animal that is running without losing sight of it. That's a predator animal." His white teeth flashed. "Like man."

"So the *Lagartos* got eyes on the sides of the *cabeza*. They don't act like prey animals, dude."

The white smile widened. "That's because they haven't had a predator until now. They been on top in their own world. As predators, they been impressive, and now we got to hone our own predatory skills to outmatch them. That's why it's good for us. We been eating TV dinners and playing video games. We forgot we were predators until the Lizzies came along and reminded us."

"You're crazy, hombre," the gold-toothed man said. "The Lizzies are two and a half meters tall, and some of 'em are way bigger than that—big as mountains. The Titans came right out of the ground and swallowed half the cities in the world in one day, remember?"

Auriga's sharklike grin vanished behind a straight, set line. "Of course I remember the Great Harvest."

A mournful silence descended from the massacre's invocation. The engine still growled, and Auriga's voice was harsh and grating when he spoke again.

"The *Lagartos* start out as larvae—just big worms with teeth. If they can get ahold of something big enough with a central nervous system, then they take it over and mutate it into the reptilian form we're all familiar with. And if not, then they just feed on vermin and offal, and get bigger and bigger until finally they've grown into one of those enormous city-wrecking monstrosities." He spat out of the car in disgust. "That ain't a predator, *ese*. Not even close. That's just a parasite. *I'm* the predator. I hunt *them* and kill *them*. Don't get it twisted."

"How come you ain't caught this one yet, predator?" The

snickering was on the verge of returning.

Auriga turned back to face the windshield. In truth, he couldn't imagine how the Lacerta had slipped past them. While it was hard work on the eyes to spot a desert-dwelling species in the rippling sun-soaked air, Lacertas *did* behave much more like predators than prey. They often fled in straight lines, left distinctive tracks, and were still inexperienced at covering them up, if they tried at all. It was obvious that the lizards were not accustomed to matching wits with a pursuer, and so relied on their superior brawn as much as possible. Today, however, it seemed he had been outsmarted. What simultaneously bothered and consoled him was that he didn't think it was the Lacerta that had done it.

Auriga motioned for the driver to stop. Pinching the stub of the cigarillo before returning it to his hat band, he declared, "There's been some wind, but not enough to wipe out all the *Lagarto's* tracks. We're going the wrong direction."

"We should head back anyway," the wheelman agreed. "If we go much farther north, we risk running into the law."

"Take us back to where we saw those kids. That's where we lost the trail."

***

The stable was streaked with wind-worn damage to the dull gray paint, but was otherwise in good repair. A dog barked; inquisitive horses cantered to the yard as the Resistance vehicle pulled up in front of the more humble structure nearby. The Jeep hadn't come to a stop before Auriga hoisted himself over the car door and planted his boots in the dust.

Eschewing the Shrike light machine gun, which he left in the passenger seat, he drew the tactical pistol from his thigh. "You *vatos* stay here and keep an eye out," he directed.

Auriga covered the scant few strides to the entrance, and leaned against the wall while he peered in through the wooden screen door. The change in light from inside to outside betrayed almost nothing of the interior, however, and the advantage of sight lay with the building's occupants. With a snap, he tossed the door open, wide enough not to knock his wide-brimmed hat off and obscure his vision as he rushed through.

The counter of the little store was in plain view, and a snow-topped man in a faded plaid shirt smiled, wrinkles cracking his leathery face. The barking stopped, and as Auriga holstered his pistol, a steel-colored mutt trotted out to thrust its nose into the recently vacated palm.

"How are you, my friend?" the shopkeeper hailed, tucking his shotgun back under the counter.

"Very well, *señor*." Auriga strode up to the wooden slab to grasp the offered hand, which was rough from work and time. "Staying safe, I see."

"Yes, with help from the Almighty and from you."

Auriga leaned against the counter with his elbow, scratching the dog behind the ears. "Did you have a couple of kids come through here today?"

"Sure did. About three hours ago. They'd been walking and needed a horse. I might have let it go for less than I should have, but"—the leathery crinkles appeared again—"I couldn't charge them too much."

Auriga nodded. "Hope they're doing all right."

"Yes, me too," the shopkeeper said. "Especially since Comet there signaled on a Lacerta not too long before then. We never saw it, though. I half expected you'd be stopping by. How's the hunting going?"

A grin played on the stubbled jaw. "Good, good. Got any five-five-six?"

"Yes, indeed." The older man bent to fetch a large rectangular metal box, and set it on the counter with a grunt. When the storekeeper snapped the lid open, dully glinting rounds of ammunition were strewn all the way to the top. "How much are you wanting?"

Auriga's hand left the dog's head and dug into a pocket of his vest. He hefted a velvet pouch in one palm; when he loosed the drawstrings, sharply glinting nuggets of gold were strewn all the way to the top. "I think I'd better take quite a bit of it, *señor*."

***

Night had fallen as the vehicle's tires rumbled over the flattened metal fence. The shining headlights and growling engine startled the gelding out of its doze, but its feed bag muffled the protesting snort.

The driver cut the lamps and ignition. Desert stillness descended again. At the foot of the stone structure, whispers seemed appropriate. "This is definitely it," the driver breathed.

"Right," Auriga confirmed, this time not neglecting to haul the Shrike assault weapon out of the Jeep with him. The others readied their own equipment without a sound.

"Here's how it works," Auriga continued. "A place like this has got to have a jenny." He indicated the driver and the man with the gold tooth: "You and you. Go around back and find it. Turn the power on, and get inside to cut them from behind while we take them on from the front." He signified himself and the man with the bat tattoo. "Don't let them run out the back. I want clean kills. Watch your fire around the kids, but be careful—we don't know anything about them. They could be hostile too."

Whispered affirmations and the businesslike clicks of weapons answered him. Then his comments were met by an unexpected report: flashes of orange light and quiet *whishes* that leaked from the missing windows along the top of the building.

"Go, go!" The Resistance men split, and one pair scurried along the flank of the structure. Auriga and his teammate covered ground in a crouching run, heading farther down the front of the building, where a set of exterior doors led into the largest factory room. As they approached, he noted that the hinges were on their side of the door, opening to the outdoors. He prayed that the doors were unlocked; breaking off the hinges would take time and announce their presence. His comrade reached the handle first and tugged the portal open. *Bueno.* Auriga flew inside, glad that the scant illumination of the desert night would reveal almost nothing in a room with an active firefight taking place.

As the door clicked closed, the man with the bat tattoo was back at his side, sweeping the space in front of them with a black submachine gun. Auriga took two steps forward and headed left, planting his right shoulder against a massive piece of machinery while he let his eyes adjust to the dimness. The other man understood the unspoken instructions and headed right, pausing at the other end of the equipment.

While his sight sharpened, Auriga relied on his ears: the acoustics of the room betrayed concrete floors and high ceilings. The echoes of chittering claws were dampened by obstacles, so there was sufficient cover, as on a factory floor. He allowed himself a faint smile: solid obstructions to visibility would work against the Lacertas' superior eyesight where simple darkness would not.

Auriga turned back to the other soldier and hefted the Shrike with his left hand while making signals with his right. *Other side of room. Advance parallel. Fire and maneuver.*

They took the next aisle at the same time, seven meters apart as they webbed through opposite sides of the machinery. The gaps between the equipment were staggered in relation to each other, not placed in neat rows, which meant that they could continue to advance while staying in cover.

When they reached the third row, the orange blazes returned from deeper in the room, and the whispers now sounded like the rushing of powerful winds. Plasma fire. The sounds were answered by hurried footsteps—*human* footsteps—and the clang of metal as someone crashed into cover behind a machine. Auriga wasn't the one being shot at, so he was free to hustle forward again.

The fourth aisle was the last for several more meters; now the clicks of lizards' feet were sharper. Auriga looked to the left, hoping for a way to circumvent the open space, but it required too much distance. The only structure was a metal staircase spiraling up to a catwalk, and it was too widely slatted to afford any protection. He took a deep breath, preparing to launch to the other side, but then he heard the human footsteps again. Auriga ducked back into cover, his finger tightening on the trigger as he listened for where the human was headed.

For all his care, though, he was caught off guard when a bipedal shape rounded the corner three meters away, entering his own aisle. As he brought the weapon to bear, he picked out a slender outline. This was neither a Lacerta nor the human who he had heard moving through the factory: it was the girl with the coral-colored scarf, and she backpedaled in surprise while bringing up her own weapon. Auriga steeled himself to return fire.

The threat was performed by reflex on her part, however, and the pistol lowered again while she raised her left hand, palm out. "Don't shoot!" she whispered.

Auriga shook his head, shushing her. He peeked around the corner to the open floor. Silence covered the room again. Had his position been given away? He was tempted to move but couldn't gauge a safe direction in which to head. It wouldn't do to question the girl until he had a better handle on the situation. Then the hammering of gunfire interrupted his thoughts: to his right, the other soldier was opening up with the submachine gun. Lead bullets sang against the steel furnishings, chewing into them with loud pops. Auriga spun against the exposed side of his cover and zeroed in on a hulking black shape pinned against the equipment to his right. His own firing angle was unobstructed, and the Shrike clattered with deafening noise. A full-auto burst stitched its way up the silhouette, which went staggering backward into a wall of apparatus.

Auriga was out of cover, however, and orange streaks splashed the metal nearby with calefaction that seared his right arm. He ducked back into the aisle, blinking to remedy his vision while the submachine gun rattled again in answer. When he could see clearly again, he noticed that the girl was gone.

Auriga snatched the white Stetson off his head and flung it like a saucer into the corridor far ahead of him. Thermal pulse fire obliterated it from a lateral position, and he advanced into the open space, pinpointing where the attack had come from. Now the Shrike roared loud and long, grinding up the equipment with suppressing fire. He saw his partner ducking forward, threading between the machines farther to his right, and then heard the burst of automatic fire and an inhuman squeal as the bullets found their mark.

He almost didn't hear the clicking on the concrete floor amid the chaos, but four sets of long, hooked claws were now closing in fast. Two of the Lacertas had wisely abandoned their weapons in favor of close-range fighting. The Shrike was a large, heavy gun to bring around so quickly, and Auriga pummeled the alien on the left with rounds, flattening himself against the nearest obstacle. Inky ichor splattered, and as the Lacerta went down, it flailed into its uninjured comrade, slowing it up. Long claws reached out, and Auriga lurched away just as furrows raked into the metal where he had stood. He was off-balance, but so was the other Lacerta: as he planted one foot behind him, the beast pulled itself up and over its dying comrade. Slashing again, its claws came just shy of his smoking weapon, which then flashed with a merciless strobe of flame. Both aliens twitched in a tangled tarantella on the blood-slicked floor, perforated by the harsh reports of a fully spent belt.

When the din died away, shouting rose on the other side of the room. One voice he recognized as the man with the bat tattoo; the other was even more distinctive to his ears, despite his having heard it only once before. He snaked another ammo belt out of his pack and ran, struggling to perform the steps required to reload the weapon and maneuver in the inadequate light. He compensated by switching on the underslung flashlight, reasoning that the time for stealth had long since passed.

The disturbance was coming from the end of the room leading to the corridors that reached out of the factory floor and deeper into the facility. He could discern the separate shouts now:

"We won't hurt you, just drop the weapon!" This from the Resistance man.

"Not a chance, there's still more of them," replied the mechanically laced voice.

"Four of them down," Auriga said, stepping into the passage.

In the cone-shaped light, he took in the scene: the teenage boy held a pulse rifle at low-ready position, but his finger was off the trigger and the other soldier covered him, so Auriga didn't press the issue. Instead, he swept the vicinity again, and came up empty. "Where's your girlfriend?"

"She's not my girlfriend."

Auriga rolled his eyes in response—and caught movement above them. Remembering the metal staircase, he cursed himself for having ignored the catwalk. A Lacerta stalked them from above; its claws betrayed no sounds by slipping through the rectangular holes in the metal walkway, and no shadows were perceptible as it skulked underneath the pale-lit windows high overhead. He registered its shape for an instant before it pounced, but he was unable to haul his weapon up at such an angle and connect a shot before it reached him.

The enemy dropped through the air, jaws wide with rows of triangular teeth—and then its seamless flight was arrested with a jolt, leaving it stranded, dangling in empty space like a marionette. It languished, straining against unseen forces before a searing blast of superheated orange heat tore most of its face off. The monster jettisoned to the far side of the room as though propelled from a cannon. Bricks cracked as the lifeless body smashed into a wall.

Awestruck, Auriga turned his eyes to the young man, whose rifle barrel betrayed wisps of smoke and whose lips betrayed a faint, telling smile. The girl crept into the aisle from one of the farther rows, coming to join the group.

The two Resistance men exchanged looks before lowering their weapons to a resting position. A psionic and a cybernetic, working as a pair—it was devastating. The youthful age of the boy and girl made the violence they could dish out all the more disquieting, but Auriga, ever the opportunist, saw it as an advantage. Lighting a fresh cigarillo, he fixed a stern expression upon them both.

"I'm going to need some answers," he said.

Chapter Six

Orion reached for the canteen again as Lyra wiped her mouth with the back of her hand, smearing a thin trickle off of her cheek. The water made her lips glisten where they had been dry and pale throughout most of the day. Then Orion brought the container to his own lips, savoring the simple joy of a fresh drink of water.

"Thanks, I needed that," he said, tossing the bottle back to the outlanders with nothing left. The four soldiers stood leaning against walls and machinery, while Orion and Lyra sat cross-legged against the wall. It had been a casual interrogation, despite their nonchalant poses and respectable affinities for manipulation. The burly, stubbled Mexican paced and postured, asking questions, making concessions, and delivering accusations with impressive acumen. It was the oldest trick in the book, passing a canteen around among themselves in full view of their parched guests, but although Orion knew when he was being manipulated, he saw no reason not to cooperate.

And so he'd told them the truth: about the Greys, about the Lacertas, about Lyra and himself, and how and why they'd come to be at the Reticulum factory. There was nothing to lose by coming clean: the Resistance men had been enemies of the alien races since the day the Lacertas had first emerged from the earth to begin a devastating rampage through the civilizations of man. The massacre that had halved the world's population and obliterated most of its cities had come to be called the "Great Harvest." When the Greys had arrived soon afterward to aid humanity, however, the loosely structured Resistance militia had stood in opposition to the UCO-brokered "Interstellar Alliance." Ten years later, the city-dwelling vassals were now subject to the strict obligations born in those desperate and uncertain times. The majority of outlanders felt that the Resistance's xenophobia was justified, and Orion hoped that by vindicating their beliefs, he could win some much-needed allies.

And although Auriga was playing his cards close to the vest, Orion was optimistic. His bioanalyzation systems, evidently sensing that they were still needed, had remained active after the firefight and throughout the questioning, and Orion had been able to study the larger man's responses. Auriga's bio-electric signature had remained stable, surging only in reaction to the more lurid details of what Orion and Lyra had been through—and most notably when Orion relayed the Lacerta's statement that the Great Harvest had been a matter of timing and convenience for the Greys. Occasional glances to Lyra earned her confirmation: Orion knew that she was reading Auriga's reactions with more accuracy than he could ever hope to. Lyra signaled that, as of now, the Resistance men had no violent designs. It pleased Orion that he was learning to communicate with her through nonverbal cues. Was this a function of her psionic abilities, or some other connection between them? Then, not wanting her to know he was thinking of her, Orion turned his thoughts back to the matter at hand.

"So," he announced, rising to stretch his sore muscles, "instead of sitting around here in the dark, how about we get the lights on in this place? Then maybe we can see what the UCO has been up to."

The man with the gold tooth sneered. "The generator don't work, dude. You think you can get it going again, I'll show you where it is."

"You should let the kid try," Auriga said. "And don't give him a hard time—he was in here blasting *Lagartos* while you were playing with the stupid jenny, missing all the action."

"You *told* me to turn the jenny on," the soldier shot back.

"*Sí*, exactly. And you didn't do it." Auriga chuckled.

Muttering to himself, the gold-toothed man escorted Orion and Lyra through the factory floor. When Orion stole a look at Lyra, he saw her brow crinkle in worry, then clear again. She shook her head in Orion's direction once, then tucked her chin down with her eyes up as they walked.

An exit door at the rear of the building opened adjacent to a caged area with massive power equipment. Orion located the smaller backup generator at one end—there wouldn't be enough fuel to turn on the plant's main turbines, which would be a large job anyway. All they needed was to get some electricity for the lights and computers, not start up the entire facility.

As Lyra and their escort looked on, Orion plunged the primer button. The generator produced a sharp snap before the button sprang up again. He did this twice more, then found himself at a disadvantage. Touching buttons on his cybernetic interface, he asked, "I can't smell anything since I'm not breathing. Do you guys smell propane?"

"Maybe a little, yeah," the Resistance man replied.

Orion studied the readout from the passive air analysis on his computer. There was indeed a trace amount of the gas around the generator, which was normal. "It's just been sitting for a long time; the gas is still good, but the air-to-fuel ratio is off." He fired the primer twice more and then held it down; the generator hummed into life but shut off again when he released the button. "Easy fix. I just need to adjust the air flow..."

He turned and walked around the side of the machinery, locking eyes with Lyra for an instant. The man with the gold tooth took a step back to allow him to pass, gesturing for Orion to move in front of him. The scavenger began to comply—but then rushed forward two paces to place his left palm on the soldier's chest. A blue arc popped; the air crackled with static, and the man seized and stiffened, falling onto his side in the sand. Trying to shake off the effects of the stun, he rolled, his right hand slapping at his pistol until Orion's boot stomped onto his wrist. Lyra, kneeling, plucked it from its holster and held it to the man's head.

"You were out here for several minutes and the lights never even flashed once. Did you even *try* to start the thing up?" Orion's rifle whined as the power switched on.

The Resistance man grimaced, his mouth twitching twice before he regained the ability to speak. "You're crazy. What are you doing? The jenny wouldn't work."

"It would have if you'd held the primer down. That didn't occur to you in all the time you were out here?"

"I don't know nothing about generators. Let me up, you maniac." Rage and guilt boiled in the man's eyes. Orion ground his boot harder into his captive's wrist.

"You can't live in the desert for one week without knowing about generators. You're not a Resistance fighter, are you?" Orion accused. "Either you've lived in the city your whole life, or you didn't try to start the power at all. Which one is it?"

"I don't know what you're talking about."

"Lyra, which one is it?"

The girl had been studying the protesting man, and now she rose from her kneeling position. "He didn't try to start it," she reported.

"Last chance," Orion threatened. "Why didn't you turn the generator on?" His finger curled around the trigger.

The militia man gasped, squinting, turning his face against the sand. "It was the other guy! He paid me, but I didn't have a choice. He held me at gunpoint and said that everybody in there was going to kill each other in the dark—"

Orion reached down, zapping the man into unconsciousness with another tap from his fingers. With the resulting convulsion, capchits spilled out from the man's trouser pocket and embedded their square edges partway into the soft dust. Orion stepped on them while hurrying to the regulator on the hose leading from the generator to the propane storage tank. After some fast adjustments, he hit the primer again; on the second try, the spark caught and the machinery hummed into operation.

"We'd better get in there." Lyra frowned.

"Yeah, right after we take care of one more thing," Orion said, sprinting out of the utility cage and around the side of the building.

***

The facility was now awake with ample illumination, but the noiselessness from the banished shadows remained. Orion and Lyra kept a brisk pace, returning to the mouth of the hallway that led back to the offices. The scavenger swept the corridor in front with the readied pulse rifle, while behind him Lyra covered room entrances and side corridors with twin pistols equipped.

"Auriga!" Orion shouted to an empty hallway. "Don't trust

him! The guy with the driving goggles!"

An answering shout tumbled down the corridor far ahead. The pair hastened, monitoring the side doors for a possible ambush. Far ahead, a baleful shape rested near an open doorway, one of the few doors with light spilling out from the frame. A man lay facedown in a dark, asymmetrical pool. Orion quickened his pace, and as his targeting reticle passed over the prone figure, the tactical display confirmed that there was no helping this man.

"Auriga!" he called again.

"In here," came the answer. It was another office, not far from the one in which they had met the Lacerta. This room, too, was ruined with gunfire. To Orion's relief, however, there were no more corpses, and the Mexican peeked at them from behind an overturned table before rising to his full height.

"Where is he?" Auriga asked.

"We haven't seen him," Lyra said. "The other guy was paid off and we left him sleeping out back."

Back in the doorway, Orion turned the fallen man over to confirm the black wings and pointed ears that crested at the dead man's throat. "Shot in the back of the head."

"He tried to get me right after that, but I was already moving," Auriga said. "We each traded a full clip, and then he was gone. I don't think he was hit."

The three exited the office, and Lyra crossed the hall to the windows in the next room that looked out from the front of the building. Auriga peeked through the blinds with the barrel of his weapon, which left a seared black stripe on the plastic.

"The Jeep's still there, but the horse is gone. He had the keys, why—"

"Here's why," Orion said, displaying the vehicle's distributor cap.

Auriga nodded in approval. "Smart thinking. You know, you could have shot the horse too, though."

Lyra fixed him with a concerned glare. "You could have shot the bad guy."

The militia man shrugged. "Point taken. Let him go, I hope the Lizzies eat him for breakfast."

Orion unshouldered his gear, laid his rifle on a cheap pressboard table, and seated himself on a plum-colored couch. "Meanwhile, what have *we* got for breakfast? I can't remember the last time I ate."

Lyra was pensive for a moment before she approached the couch. "We'll get something together. Right now, while it's safe, you should rest for a while."

"No, I'm okay. We should—"

"Shhh," she soothed. "Look at me." She gazed into his eyes.

Orion began to ask a question but forgot what it was. Maybe resting wasn't a bad idea—all at once, he realized that he was exhausted. He stared back at Lyra, captivated by her face. She was so pretty.

"I know you know that I just thought that," he said. The sentence sounded like drunken rambling to his own ears. "But I don't care."

"Relax, you need to rest."

Orion's mind swam as lethargy took hold. Something about the feeling wasn't natural, and he found himself floating in the two large gray pools of her eyes.

"Sleep. Don't worry, everything's fine," Lyra whispered. "Lie down and close your eyes…"

Exhaustion pressed down upon him like a physical weight, and despite himself, he reclined upon the sofa. As his head came to rest, his vision grew dim and fuzzy, and then the sounds and the light were gone.

**

He was alone in the desert, insignificant and weak against the vast horizon. The ground unfurled like the conveyer belt in a factory, moving him forward to some unperceived destination. All around him, a desolate world decayed, cracking and flaking into pale shards that curled between his listless feet as they dragged on. The monotonous wasteland crawled past, out of sync with his abated steps. He turned his eyes upward to an anemic sky, which fled from his sight, forsaking this etiolated realm.

The conveyor belt plodded along. The horizon fractured, with the earth no longer meeting the sky but riven by something in between. Angular beings rose in demented, blasphemous majesty above the world.

His wearied feet lifted from the ground, and he floated upward. He saw Lyra hovering nearby, her hair spread around her like a golden cloud. Above them, a gargantuan flying saucer pulled them up and up. Light bathed them in wondrous colors. He reached for Lyra and gathered her in a tight embrace. She clung to him; suspended in space, entwined together, they rose toward the inexorable alien ship.

He buried his face in her long yellow hair, breathing in its clean honeysuckle scent, reveling in the sureness of her arms around him. Then her grip loosened, and the divine scent faded. She pulled away from him, drawn upward by the enormous craft. He stretched out an arm, trying to hold on, but she slipped away.

Colossal and supreme, the Greys leaned forward, their inky eyes filling the void where the heavens had once been. They reached for him. Sluggish and dumb, he gaped in fascination as they plucked pieces of him away. Parts of his body vanished from any semblance of material being. He felt nothing. As the yawning mouth of the saucer prepared to swallow him, other ashen, nimble hands spanned forth their long fingers to apply bizarre permutations to his form. He was no longer what he remembered, if he remembered anything. He was merely a construct, a plastic man, a secret weapon built in a secret factory.

***

Orion awoke with a jump; the desert rushed by in the newly formed daybreak. He was in the back seat of the Jeep. He bolted to a sitting position: Auriga glanced back at him in the rearview mirror, and Lyra twisted from the passenger seat to offer him a smile, the wind whipping the ends of her scarf like flags.

"Hey there. Hope you slept well."

"What did you do?" he asked, more confused than angry.

"Don't be mad, okay? I'm sorry, but it was honestly the best way. We needed to plan our next move," Lyra said.

"And I don't get to be a part of that?" He shifted in his seat, restless. The back of the Jeep was filled with supplies: weapons and ammunition, assorted equipment, food and water. Much of the ordnance bore the newly recognizable Reticulum sigil; Auriga and Lyra must have found some useful items at the facility.

"Better eat something to keep your strength up," Auriga called from the driver's seat. "We're gonna need you ready for action."

Sullenly, Orion complied, tearing open an MRE and eating. His appetite was powerful. "I think you have the wrong idea of me. I don't just take orders. Not from the Greys, and not from either of you."

"Listen, that's exactly what I need to talk to you about," Lyra said. "There's a good reason for why I did what I did. Ever since your last operation, Corvus—the man we've been calling the Illuminatus—has had access to your mind. I don't believe he's able to watch directly through your eyes and control you like a robot, but he's exerted some influence on your decisions."

A flicker of recognition surfaced. "Like when I killed the Lacerta in the office."

"Yes. I'd say he flooded your system with aggressive hormones, and engineered the most likely outcome," she said. "We have to take measures to stop this. It's going to be ugly, and I don't like what it entails, but there's no way we can continue to allow him to manipulate you."

"What about you? They messed around with your brain even more than mine. That doesn't give you permission to do the same thing to me." Now that he was all right and sure of his surroundings, anger eclipsed his bewilderment.

"That's true," she conceded, her eyebrows raised in concern. "But as a psionic, my mind is more guarded than yours. I've felt visitors knocking at the door a couple of times, and didn't let them in."

Orion gazed at the looming skyline ahead. Spindles climbed from the edge of the world, separating the earth and sky. He reflected on her words: slaughtering the Lacertas was one thing, but the thought of killing a human being—however vile—unsettled him, as it no doubt did her as well. In order to even reach Corvus, they would need to eradicate untold numbers of Protectorate officers first. Troubled, he thought back to the lethal scene in the streets two days before. The demonstrators had been about to take his own life; of this he could be certain.

His response, even if not under his own control, was surely justified—and yet the smoking corpses of his accusers pierced him with smoldering eyes from the depths of memories that would remain with him forever.

Was he not now under such duress? Loath as he was to elicit more bloodshed, what might happen if he did not take these steps to reclaim command of his actions? What price could he refuse, what chance could he not be willing to take, in order to have his own mind returned to him?

"There are different ways to perform a good deed," Lyra prompted. "One is to help good people. Another is to destroy evil ones. Either is a positive outcome."

He found himself nodding as he ate. For some time, no one spoke; the engine's grating charge carried them forward. The city of New Zaragosa was near again.

"You could have just asked me to wait in the other room while you planned this," he said.

"If Corvus had been listening, he would have gotten suspicious. He would have had time to prepare. I didn't want to put you to sleep, or make these decisions without you, but when I saw what was going on, I had to."

Orion broke the seal on a bottle of water, and drank. Was he not, in truth, choosing his own path? Could his thoughts and feelings be every bit as artificial as his body parts? He studied Lyra's gentle face, the large gray eyes beneath the whipping scarf. Could what he felt for her be spurious as well? If not, could he be compelled to turn against her?

"Look, you know what I'm thinking, so I shouldn't have to say it," he said.

Lyra unbuckled her seat belt and climbed into the back seat with him. "I don't always know what you're thinking," she said, holding on to him as the Jeep bounced along. "And even if I did, I would still want you to say it."

"This isn't fair."

"You mean, because you can't read my mind but I can read yours?" she asked.

He chuckled and turned away from her. "Of course."

As he watched the dusty scrubland flying past, Lyra spoke softly into his ear. "I bet you could know what I was thinking if you tried."

Orion looked back at her. Her eyes fixed on his, and he grazed his fingers along her smooth cheek. He paused for only a moment before leaning toward her.

The Jeep lurched, throwing them apart. Orion grabbed the back of the seat in front of him to steady himself; Lyra, with no seat belt, toppled backward in the seat, laughing. The rearview mirror displayed a conspiratorial smile on Auriga's face.

"What about you?" Orion addressed the outlander. "I take it you're good with all of this?"

"Taking out a UCO executive on his own ground?" Auriga replied. "One that's helping the Greys to carve people up and mess with their minds? Believe me, I'm *very* good with all of this."

An inexorable tower swallowed the rising sun. The shadow cast by the massive skyscraper engulfed them.

"We're going to need an army to pull this off," Orion muttered.

"They're going to need an army to stop us," Lyra said.

Chapter Seven

The double doors exploded inward, ripped off their hinges as though by an unseen juggernaut. With the doors tearing in midair across the expansive lobby, the safety glass did not shatter but instead crystallized into an opaque spiderweb of jagged shapes. The weighty projectiles caught two security guards in their path, flattening them as the doors crashed against the unyielding walls behind them.

A trio of assailants burst into the building's foyer: on one side, a burly man bedecked in tactical gear retreated inward while exchanging heavy weapons fire with forces out in the street. On the other, a teenage girl marched forward with the fingertips of her left hand touching the temple of her shaved head, which was wrapped in a pinkish-orange scarf. Her right hand grasped a gleaming machine pistol. Between them, a young, sandy-haired cybernetic swept the surroundings with a thermal pulse rifle, scrutinizing the room with certain, percipient vision.

The receptionist behind the expansive marble counter cowered next to an activated alarm button beneath the marble edifice. Orion crossed behind the desk and reached down to grasp her shoulder with an outstretched hand; the woman shivered with electricity and slumped to the floor. Then Orion's fingers danced over the keyboard as his eyes studied the screen and the room's various entryways.

He began by lowering a security gate at the front entrance; as it unrolled from the ceiling, he noticed the flexible barrier seemed to be made of a clear plastic sheeting. When the gate locked into place, however, it pulsed once and then took on the solid, semitranslucent aspect of a thick acrylic wall. Auriga's suppression fire ceased, and the sextet of spinning barrels on the heavy weapon crawled to a stop, reverting from cherry red to gunmetal gray.

"His office is on the seventieth floor," Orion reported. "Elevators are locked, but I can change that. It's better than fighting our way up seventy staircases' worth of soldiers."

A team of eight black-clad Protectorate men rushed into the lobby, fanning out and taking up strategic positions behind statues and low marble walls. They opened fire as one; the room filled with the crackle of submachine guns. Auriga dove behind the stone ledge of the circular fountain in the lobby's center; Lyra vaulted over the receptionist's counter and took cover with Orion. Bullets stitched a zigzag path in the wall behind her as she leapt.

Orion lay in a prone position and shimmied forward on his elbows to the end of the desk. Chips of stone and metal rained on both him and Lyra as the unceasing gunfire dug into their position. He waited for the click of a magazine change, and snapped his head and rifle around the corner while lying on one shoulder. His HUD lined up a firing angle, and he blasted one soldier into a bloody, backward dance. He ducked beneath the desk a second before hot chunks were torn out of the floor where his head had rested. Over the clattering chaotic roar, Auriga's minigun whirred like a helicopter, churning walls and obstacles into gravel. Two more agonized screams mixed with the tinkling music of shell casings pouring onto the tile.

The opposing assault renewed in force. Orion's surroundings disintegrated under a hail of bullets, keeping him pinned in place. He couldn't risk even a glance around the corner of the desk, much less over top of it. If Auriga had as much fire concentrated on his position, there would be no help coming; the Mexican had fallen silent, and was probably reloading or similarly immobilized.

Then a chilling metallic racket caught Orion's attention as a pineapple grenade bounced over the desk and landed less than a meter away from his right leg. He had nowhere to take cover, and the blast would obliterate both him and Lyra in a maelstrom of shrapnel. Lyra reacted instantly, motioning from her own position farther away. Her left hand shot out, making a flinging gesture, and the untouched grenade whipped back up and over the shelter to the other side of the room. A second later, a deep thud concussed the air and another man shrieked in pain.

A momentary decline in the attack was granted. Orion prepared to spring to his feet for a counteroffensive, but Lyra was first: as he crested the top of the marble counter, he saw her push out with both hands, toppling a steel sculpture across the room. The operative sheltering behind it was crushed before he could escape.

There were three Protectorate men left now, who elected to retreat from the lobby while spraying the intruders with covering fire as they went. Auriga's cannon whirred again, ripping a trail of devastation right on their heels. The officers vanished down a corridor just as the heavy weapon fell silent; Auriga unshouldered the empty gun and let it crash to the floor amid a mountain of spent brass.

The cybernetic resumed his outbreak of keystrokes at the terminal. "This is just a network computer. I've performed some operations here, like sealing the exits, but they'll just undo them unless we get to a security console."

"Where is the security office?" Lyra asked. Several Protectorate officers were clustering outside by the barrier at the building's entrance; two were kneeling by an access panel on the outside. Auriga paused in equipping a carbine rifle to gesture rudely to them.

"First floor," Orion responded, crossing the foyer to the front gate. "I could use their terminal to unlock the path we'll take to Corvus's office, and shut down all the others. Then we can wreck the place behind us as we go. It'll give us more time alone with Corvus." He wrenched open a small metal door beside the acrylic gate; reaching inside with his left hand, he grasped the electric motor that raised and lowered the barrier. Sparks popped and sizzled, and acrid smoke billowed out in a bitter wave. Orion then unhooked the manual release chain from its brake and held it taut. A few seconds' attention with his short-range laser snapped the chain, which rattled loosely against the inside of the compartment. He slammed the panel with such force that it dented inward, stuck. "Let's go."

The team hustled through the decimated lobby, withdrawing to the corridor through which the response team had retreated. Glossy artwork and potted plants, resting on square stone pedestals against the walls, adorned the hallway. An elevator bank dominated the left side. Gentle lighting was violated by ruby-red pulses from emergency indicators near the ceiling, casting an urgent sheen in intermittent beats. Auriga moved to take the point position, and the trio scurried along with focused resolve.

Then, rounding the corner twenty meters ahead, a larger team of paramilitary operatives poured into the hallway. Orion couldn't count them with precision, but there were more than a dozen; their opening salvo was already pounding around him as he sheltered behind one of the stone pedestals on the corridor's right side. The planter above his head burst, showering him with soil and shards of pottery. As Orion pressed against the narrow refuge, he risked a desperate glance at Auriga across the hall. The Mexican had dug into the elevator alcove, gritting his teeth as countless bullets whizzed past.

Orion blind-fired around the side of the pillar a few times, gambling that some shots would hit home if only due to the high number of targets. Then he remembered that Lyra was somewhere ahead of him and lost to sight, and decided against such recklessness. Instead, he watched Auriga to try and coordinate a plan, but the outlander was pinned down, crammed into a tiny space with his chin tucked, muttering to himself in Spanish while fishing for some object on his vest. There was so much enemy fire; Orion's own cover was degrading, withering under compressive streams of gunfire that would not relent even for a moment.

"*What do we do?*" he shouted, his voice cracking.

Her voice, calm but feverish in its intonation, was unexpectedly close—seeming to come from inside his head. "Get ready to hit them with everything you've got," Lyra said. Orion caught a glimpse of Auriga snapping to attention as well, as if he had heard the same commission.

A strange sort of vertigo took hold as the world slowed around Orion. The crack of the bullets was replaced with a distorted booming, as if by a sound traveling underwater. The pedestal no longer disintegrated next to him, and he chanced to peek out: Lyra knelt behind another pillar, facing forward with her hands pressed against the sides of her head. Farther down the hall, the strike team held to a rigid firing formation, with some operatives kneeling in front and a second row standing behind them. Their gun barrels flashed in uneven intervals. Orion distinguished individual bullets floating through the air toward him and his allies, moving so slowly as to appear harmless. His targeting reticle glowed red as he swept it over the enemies. Still crouching, he fired the pulse rifle at one of the combatants in the front row.

The hot jet tore the air in a flash of speed and heat and splashed in a shock wave against the man. The stricken operative wheeled backward with lethargic grace, his gun going wide and peppering the ceiling as he fell. Auriga opened fire now, raking through the line with leaden projectiles. Splotches of crimson blossomed over the black uniforms; men grimaced and tumbled in ponderous disarray. Orion rose out of cover, finding it easy to sidestep the bullets as they crawled past. One by one, he picked off the Protectorate soldiers in their lethal stasis. Auriga came to his side, still strafing the remaining subjugated victims. In a matter of moments, they demolished the entire line. A few last operatives writhed on the floor before joining their comrades in stillness.

The psionic girl stood and opened her eyes to view the carnage with obvious distaste. Orion's vertigo evaporated; Auriga was mute with amazement but did not neglect to replenish the carbine's magazine with a mechanical action.

Orion searched for words, but had none for what they had just witnessed. He moved down the hall, stepping with care over the corpses. Lyra followed, and then Auriga.

The security office was vacant and forsaken. As Orion swiveled behind the main terminal, jacking into it with his bionic interface, Lyra sank into an office chair with a muted groan. His eyes searched her with concern, and then flicked back to the screen. "This is good," he said. "I'm revoking clearance for everything we're not going to use on our way up. Everything's locked down except for where we're going; the other Protectorate teams are going to be moving very slowly."

Orion reflected on the irony of this choice of words for a moment, until the rattle of Auriga's rifle jolted him back to attention. The soldier had positioned himself at the door of the office, shooting at unseen foes farther down the corridor. Orion began to get to his feet, but Auriga's rifle fell silent again and he nodded back at the teenager to continue.

The task did not take long, although Orion encountered packets of Grey technology in the programs he attacked. It was not difficult, however, to subvert the system into working for his own ends; the building was well within his means to manipulate.

"This place actually has some of the aspects of a prison," he said, surprised. "Who ever heard of an office building with sally ports? Or holding cells?"

"We'd better be able to leave when the job is done," Auriga warned, peering down the hallway. Then his rifle clattered again.

"I'm more worried about something else. Is Corvus even here, or have we just walked into a trap?" Orion finished up, jacked out, and slid the keyboard away.

Lyra now stood, her expression distant yet sharp in its resolve. "Yes, he's here."

***

The elevator doors parted in a smooth crawl. Orion engaged the manual lock on the elevator and stepped into the chamber. The lighting, ambient and reserved, was complemented by the brilliant illumination of the seventieth floor's towering height. Aesthetic treasures adorned small pedestals, but unlike the decorations they had seen downstairs, these had an element of the unearthly. Smooth, twisted features beckoned the mind with hypnotic allurement. Orion shuddered, turning his thoughts from their enchantments.

Ahead, their destination endured in the silence of space. Thick glass partitions revolved to admit them into the spacious room, which was alien in its sterility. Glossy furnishings cambered with simple grace. The windows opposite them reached floor to ceiling, with two transparent doorways opening to a dizzying balcony outside. A wide ledge wrapped halfway around the skyscraper; Orion had a partial glimpse of some modern vehicle parked outside. The office afforded a magnificent view of the city's skyline—but as Josiah Corvus stood with his back to them, he was not studying the immense grandeur of man's achievements.

The Grey spaceship hovered a few kilometers away and roughly equal to their altitude of seventy stories above the city. Sunlight kissed the familiar saucer shape, the only admission to its coexistence with mundane things.

"Marvelous, isn't it?" Corvus murmured in admiration. "The flawlessness, the functionality. The supreme marriage of simplicity and complexity. The absolute pinnacle of conscious thought, made manifest in physical form." He turned to them, smiling. "Of course you can understand my appreciation."

His three visitors kept their weapons trained on him. Corvus unbuttoned his suit jacket, smoothing the slate-colored silk against his slim, athletic form. "Now, I can only assume you've come to inform me of your progress and receive new instructions."

"You know why we're here," Orion said darkly.

"In fact, I do," came the amused reply. "I know a fair amount about your motives and intentions. You may have performed this visit on short notice, but don't be a fool—you couldn't possibly kill me."

In answer, Auriga pulled the trigger of his carbine, sending a burst of rounds at the man's head. Corvus never flinched; the projectiles were deflected by an invisible force and only left smoky scuff marks on the reinforced glass behind him.

A smirk crept onto the handsome face, and Corvus's brow darkened for an instant. An invisible giant punched Auriga, sending his feet flying out from beneath him. The Resistance man flew backward, slammed against the glass partition at the office's entrance, and crumpled to the floor.

Thermal blasts streaked from Orion's gun, washing past Corvus's body and melting with warm slipperiness into nothing. Lyra's pistols hammered in rapid succession, sending white-hot chips of metal tracing their way up his torso, but these, too, fell away, harmless. The Illuminatus flicked his wrist, spurring a blossom of energy in his hand; a spade-shaped projectile of blazing phosphorescence appeared between his fingertips, and he cast it with furious speed at the cybernetic. Orion turned his rifle to the side, deflecting the dagger along the broad side of the weapon, and it sizzled into thin air with deadly beauty.

"I'd rather not kill either of you," Corvus announced, more blades appearing in his fingers. "We've invested time and effort to make you what you are, and you show promise. It's a shame that a human's potential to transcend must always be tied to stubbornness in equal measure."

"You speak as if you're not human," Lyra said. "Worshipping the Greys and doing their dirty work doesn't make you one of them."

"Physiologically, you may be right," Corvus admitted. "I may have the body of a man, but men are more than the sum of their parts. Wouldn't you agree? Is your mind not more than a simple network of neurons transmitting electrical signals?"

Short-lived electrical events, Orion recalled.

Auriga got to his feet. Past the balcony doors, the saucer was moving in their direction. The three allies spread out: Lyra remaining in the center, Orion creeping right, Auriga maneuvering to the left.

"The Greys have so much to share with us," the Illuminatus continued. "Why remain earthbound when you can soar among the stars?"

"Is that what you call hunting an entire race to extinction?" Orion said.

"Don't be a hypocrite." Corvus sniffed. "Your companion was doing his part to annihilate an entire race long before you ever met me."

"That's self-defense. You're just killing off the Greys' old slaves so that you can take their place," Orion countered.

"The Lacertas were only fit to *be* slaves. They didn't display any aptitude for the gifts they were given. Mankind is quite another story—and you are living proof of that."

"You're insane."

"No, I'm able to grasp these concepts with perfect clarity. You will too, in time...or you will die like the Lacertas."

"Let's see who is still alive five minutes from now," Auriga said.

Corvus shook his head. "Very well, we'll do this the hard way, if you prefer."

Corvus unleashed the handful of projectiles across the room. Ribbons of opalescent light followed behind the spaded knives, forming streamers that variegated the room's reflective surfaces. Orion hurdled out of the way, and Auriga threw himself against the wall; the blades flew past both of them and fragmented into the closed entryway. Lyra stood firm, and as two of the projectiles coursed toward her, they bloomed into rainbow shards against an invisible shield and faded from view.

Orion and Auriga opened fire in tandem, sending bullets and orange jets to bombard Corvus in a dual-angled crossfire. His defenses remained active, scattering the deadly waves to either side. Lyra lashed out with her mind, hurling a psionic spear of energy through the air; as the Illuminatus countered the missile, the resulting collision discharged in a shock wave that staggered everyone in the room.

Orion regained his initiative and changed tactics, blasting objects off the large metal desk between Corvus and them. Sparks and shrapnel showered the Illuminatus as ornaments and equipment swept off the desk's surface. The smithereens sizzled and died against Corvus's unseen barrier, but a slight flinch betrayed a minute break in his concentration. Lyra seized the opportunity and hammered Corvus with a mental assault that hurled him off his feet and against the window with an audible crack.

Corvus rebounded at once, pushing off of the glass while delivering a salvo of concussive force that shook the room. As the shock wave bulldozed them, all three allies tumbled backward and skidded to the far wall. In the next instant, Corvus flung more of his discarnate knives with renewed vigor. The dazzling spades rained down on the trio—Orion rolled and twisted, but one projectile stabbed into his thigh and a second one embedded in his armor. He thanked the heavens for the tactical vest he'd shrugged on underneath his sweater before they'd arrived.

Colored slashes assailed his two companions as well. Lyra flew upright again, regaining her feet. But Auriga grunted in pain, still on the floor, a spare magazine for his carbine lying out of arm's reach. Instead of retrieving it, he readied an item from his vest. Auriga heaved a black canister in a smooth arc up to the front of the room and then covered his head with his hands.

Orion followed suit, shielding his eyes. A deafening clap filled the air, and the concordant white flash pierced his vision, even with the precaution he'd taken. He resumed his assault, however, and unleashed a fresh barrage of gunfire against Corvus. The psionic man appeared disoriented, but he was still able to deflect the missiles; the viewing window behind him was now scarred and fogged in patches from the pummeling it had taken. Auriga snapped another magazine home with a loud clack and added to the fusillade.

Corvus stretched both arms out before him, trembling with exertion. The massive metal desk wrenched free of the floor and rose nearly a meter in height. The barrage of shots glanced at varied angles off of the smooth expanse, scattering hot stripes over the walls and ceiling. Lyra flung her hands forward as well, and concentration shadowed her face. The desk hung in midair, shivering with unspent force. A tug-of-war ensued as the heavy furniture was pushed with incredible force from both directions simultaneously. The gleaming contours warped with the strain.

Orion continued his battery, attempting to line up an angle that left Corvus exposed, but the enormous metal object obscured his sight. Auriga was doing the same; automatic weapons fire chewed up the floor in jagged lines leading under the obstacle, but no connection was made.

Lyra groaned, gritting her teeth. The effort was taxing her to her limit. Orion's weapon display pulsed with a dead gray: the battery was wearing down. Auriga changed magazines again but fired more sporadically, conserving his ammunition. Then Lyra gasped, faltering, and her focus broke. An instant before she collapsed, the desk rocketed through the room with all of the deferred momentum that had been withheld from it. It struck Auriga with bone-jarring violence, carrying him through the glass partitions, which exploded into glittering debris. The desk, and Auriga's pulverized body, flew several yards out into the hallway behind them, colliding with the wall before sliding to a stop.

Orion now faced the Illuminatus alone, the wasteland of the ruined office sprawled between them. Corvus was bent at the waist, regaining his composure; the scavenger lined up a shot and pulled the trigger, but the weapon was dead. Frustration and rage wracked him. Orion seized the rifle with both hands and pumped it full of current until it convulsed with bluish forks. He flung it at the psionic man, who had recovered from his momentary vulnerability. A spidery burst of lightning was unleashed in a torrent as the weapon bounced away from Corvus; it clattered end over end to a corner of the room, useless.

Without pause, Orion drew a pistol from his right side. As he brought it up, Corvus gestured and the gun jerked from Orion's hand. More movements from the psionic man brought a flurry of blows against Orion's head, chest, and stomach. He was battered with merciless strikes; there was no defense from the unseen assault.

Fighting through the pain, Orion lowered his head and charged forward, crossing the empty room in leaping strides. His fists crackled with voltage, and he drew back, preparing to swing. Corvus sidestepped, however, and the phantom force redirected Orion's flight, crashing him to the ground. Standing over him, the Illuminatus hauled him up in an incorporeal stranglehold; Orion's feet dangled above the floor, his hands joined at his throat as it squeezed shut. He strained with his right hand: Corvus was centimeters out of reach, and Orion's fingertips arced with feverish menace but did not connect. Orion glared into the dark eyes, seeing in them the void of space. He floated, languishing and helpless, as one would drift through its infinite emptiness. Darkness reached to envelop him.

Then twin shots rang out in the stillness. Blood splashed against the windows as Corvus spun and went down. Orion collapsed as well, his strength failing him. He turned his head with arduous effort: Auriga lay on his stomach at the office doorway, with Orion's own discarded pistol smoking in his hands. Auriga's head slumped, and the gun tumbled free of his grip.

Orion struggled to rise, but couldn't. He rolled to face the windows. Outside, the Grey craft hovered meters from the balcony. He shifted his view to the man lying nearby: Corvus scrabbled on the floor, palms slippery with his own blood. He'd been hit in the neck and shoulder. Orion stared, gratified yet repulsed, and moved almost to pity for this dying man who was wrestling to live just a little while longer.

They were not alone. The presence in the room was an eerie, familiar aura. Two Greys were entering Orion's field of view, coming from the balcony. They paused to survey the ruined office with attentive eyes.

"Help me," Corvus begged.

The diminutive, ashen aliens crossed the room to where Lyra's unconscious form rested.

"No." Orion dug for strength, managing only to rise to his hands and knees. "No, please God, no."

The two Greys gathered her up, one taking her by the arms and another by the ankles. They carried her toward the balcony where the ominous saucer waited.

Orion stole another look to the doorway, where Auriga began to stir. "Take me instead," Orion said to the Greys. One of the aliens aimed a blank stare at the scavenger as they withdrew.

"Take...me...instead," Corvus echoed before swooning.

The balcony door swung closed. Orion squinted to see through the scarred, bloodstained glass as the alien ship pulled away into the open sky.

He crawled to the incapacitated man. Auriga was limping forward, pistol in hand. He aimed it at Corvus, but Orion shielded the fallen Illuminatus.

"Don't do it! We need him. He's our best chance at getting Lyra back." Orion worked to stop Corvus's bleeding by removing the man's silk tie and using it to apply pressure to the wounds. Auriga seemed about to argue the point, but there was no time: a distant elevator chime preceded the sound of boots in the hallway. The scavenger fished in Corvus's suit pockets for a set of keys. "We've got to get him out of here."

Auriga holstered the weapon and heaved Corvus's limp body off the floor. Orion and Auriga gathered him up, one taking him by the arms and another by the ankles. They carried him toward the balcony where the convertible vehicle rested.

Seconds later, waves of Protectorate men stormed the room. Shattered glass mixed with pooling blood in the heavily scarred chamber; burn marks and bullet holes pockmarked every surface. Outside, an engine rumbled, and an onyx machine took flight, spiriting its three passengers away into the sunny morning.

Chapter Eight

O rion splashed water on his face and stared into the cracked mirror. Bleary, reddened eyes contemplated him in return. He wrung the washrag into the chipped sink and smoothed the bandage on his thigh before cinching up the cargo pants and pulling his shirt back on.

In the main room, Auriga tended to the unconscious man, who slumped in a battered office chair with two broken wheels. Corvus's hands were bound behind the back of the chair with a tight strip of duct tape at the wrists; his head lolled to one side, allowing Auriga room to examine the bandages at his neck and shoulder. Although rusty stains discolored most of the front of Corvus's shirt and suit jacket, the gauze was clean and white.

"The bleeding's stopped," Auriga reported, "but he's lost a lot of blood, and we'll have to watch for infection. He's not out of the woods yet."

Auriga, shirtless and wearing faded blue jeans, placed a palm at his ribs, which were taped on the right side. Orion noted a tattoo over the man's heart, written in an elegant script: "*10 de julio de 2022.*" Other dressings and discolorations adorned his chest and arms: Auriga had taken quite a bit of punishment in the battle. The Mexican appeared to be adept at medical aid, however, and had treated them all as soon as they'd arrived at his hideout.

They were in a tiny four-room house in a place Auriga had called "Loving County," prompting Orion to raise an eyebrow at the unfamiliar, antiquated term.

"How old are you?" Orion had asked.

"Old enough to remember the good old days," was all the man had said, with a grin.

Now, Orion observed Auriga's ministrations upon Corvus with growing concern. It was odd how events could turn—the worry he felt for the injured man's fate had its root in his ability to help them recover Lyra, of course, but it also bordered on an unexpected sympathy for the Illuminatus with whom he had so lately been in combat. Corvus's zeal and vision fascinated him. How could the man be so sure and unrelenting on his course, when Orion's own constant companion was uncertainty? They were both human—or slightly more, perhaps—but the difference in perspective was unreal. On the ground, Orion looked up to see the Greys reigning from their majestic ships; Corvus, from his office in the sky, viewed them on an equal plane.

What mystic mirror could Orion ever step through that would replace his loathing for the Greys with the admiration that Corvus felt for them?

These questions would drive him crazy; right now, Orion could allow only one concern to occupy his thoughts.

"Anything I can do?" he asked.

Auriga nodded, motioning to a rickety chest of drawers blocking sunlight through a grimy window. "Second drawer, there should be pills. Bring me anything that ends in '-cillin' or '-romycin.'"

The scavenger complied, rummaging through several bottles with handwritten identifications. There was a lot of pain medication here, but the antibiotics were harder to find. A torn photograph mixed in with the drawer's contents drew his attention, and he examined it, awestruck.

Auriga was recognizable in the photo, despite being younger and clean-shaven. His dark eyes were alive with joy, as were those of the midnight-haired woman beside him. His affectionate arm was pulled close about her waist; with the other, Auriga hefted a toddler boy on his hip. In the background, the tall structures of an amusement park heralded wonder and diversion. Orion had seen rusted skeletons of such things, and had only imagined what they might have looked like when lit against the night.

Orion flinched as the photograph was snatched from his fingers and tossed back into the drawer. Auriga scattered the pill bottles around, selected one, and then slammed the chest closed. On his return to the injured man, Auriga retrieved a bottle of water from a scarred wooden table. After unscrewing the caps of both containers, he laid two pills on the table's surface and crushed them with the flat side of a bowie knife, then swept the dust into the water bottle. He screwed the cap back on and shook the bottle to dissolve the medicine.

Orion approached the incapacitated figure and pulled two folding chairs to face him. The Resistance man slapped the lean face, grabbed a fistful of the thick dark hair, and held Corvus's head back until his eyes opened and came rolling into focus. Auriga brought the water bottle to the man's blanched lips and held it for a few swallows, then turned the folding chair around and straddled it with the chair's back facing their captive.

"Okay, amigo, I guess we'd better get started." Auriga's tone had a menacing edge beneath the superficial, cordial words.

Corvus tested his binds once and then appraised his surroundings in silence; Orion prepared himself for what was to come, as well.

"Very well," the Illuminatus replied. "I'm ready when you are."

Orion leaned forward, clasping his hands with elbows on his knees. "The Greys took Lyra. What are they doing to her?"

A pause while Corvus gathered his strength and his thoughts. His words came in halting groups. "She was displaying...some psionic abnormalities. They're going to rectify that."

"More surgery." Orion envisioned himself breaking all the furniture in the shanty, but he restrained his temper. He had to remain calm for this brief window of opportunity, or it would be wasted.

"Not necessarily. She may just need...additional training to use her gifts."

"How do I get on the ship?"

Corvus narrowed his eyes. "What a ridiculous question."

"Answer him, man," the Mexican warned.

"There is no answer to that question. They control who gets on and off the ship." Corvus slumped in his seat; his chin and eyes drooped. Auriga smacked him, and the prisoner's features focused again.

"What do you mean by 'abnormalities'?" Orion pressed.

"You saw it. She isn't ready for the amount of power she wields. It's...not uncommon."

"Not uncommon," Orion repeated. "I didn't realize this kind of thing happened all the time."

"It's happened...for thousands of years."

Orion thought back to what the Lacerta queen had told them in the factory. "The Greys visited Earth in the distant past and bestowed 'gifts' upon mankind. Then they've periodically visited to see how the race was progressing with those gifts."

"Yes. Not just through surgery either. As I'm sure you're aware, many cultures on Earth have benefitted from their influence. The Pyramids, for example...and many monolithic structures in South America..."

"And weapons factories in the desert west of here," Orion broke in. "They're not just building pretty stone statues, you psychopath. The UCO has 'benefitted from their influence' most of all, haven't they? You would know—you were on the board of directors at Reticulum when it was active. Then you took a nice desk job at Alien HQ and helped the Greys do whatever they wanted to the human race."

Corvus chuckled weakly. "An oversimplification, perhaps...but your premise is correct. The United Corporations Order has always been tied to the Greys' operations on Earth. There are many of its subsidiaries, past and present, which serve the purposes of the Greys: weapons factories, vehicle factories...research facilities, medical facilities...even colleges and universities are all part of the UCO's extensive influence on behalf of the Greys. Before it became what it is today...the organization was better known as 'Majestic 12.'"

This time Auriga spoke. "Care to explain that?"

Corvus grimaced, then took a deep breath. "Almost a century ago, there was an alleged...extraterrestrial incident at a ranch in Roswell, over two hundred kilometers north of here. It was believed to be a UFO crash...but although it turned out to be a failed attempt to spy on the Soviets using a mundane weather balloon...the government's response to the incident, when it was broken to the public, was quite telling."

Corvus stopped, enervated. Auriga supplied more water before the prisoner lapsed into unconsciousness again.

They waited in silence for a time. "I think he's stalling, taking us for a ride," Auriga judged. "He might tell us more about the

UCO, but he's not going to give us anything that will help get Lyra back—assuming he even knows anything."

"He probably knows more about the Greys than anyone alive. We've just gotten started."

"I know, but we really don't have a lot of time here," Auriga said.

"He seems coherent enough. If he were dying, it would have been harder to wake him up just now."

"I'm not worried about him dying, muchacho." Auriga's expression was dark. "Quite the opposite. I don't want him getting stronger."

Orion turned back to the incapacitated figure. "I know he's dangerous, okay? But right now he's too weak to pose much of a threat. If it were you on the Greys' ship, believe me, you'd want us to do everything we could to get you out of there."

"If it were me, I'd understand that there was nothing you *could* do. Assuming that she's alive, man, she's on her own. I'm sorry to say it like that, but there it is."

"No. There's got to be something we can do. He has to know something." Orion paced the shoddy floor, thinking aloud. "If we only had access to some of their equipment...we could get into his mind or force him to cooperate somehow."

Auriga's apprehension escalated. "Do you know what you sound like? Taking a captive and subjecting him to invasive procedures? You're thinking just like the Greys."

This accusation gave Orion chills, but he fired back anyway: "As opposed to you, who just wants to beat the information out of him?"

"He's too dangerous. You know what he's capable of—we should put a bullet in his brain and be done with it."

Orion sneered. "You're not exactly taking the moral high

ground here either."

The Mexican shrugged. "Don't ask the question if you don't want the answer, man. I think it would be a mistake to let him walk out of here."

"If we kill him, it's like giving up on Lyra completely."

"If we don't, it's a matter of time until he takes us out. Any information he did give you would probably just lead you into a trap."

"If you don't want to be a part of this anymore, that's fine." Orion tried to find somewhere to rest his gaze, but everywhere he looked in the cluttered room shook his senses with discomfort. "I know you didn't ask for any of this. It would be a lot simpler to shoot him, like you said, and just walk away. But I've been on the operating table. You have no idea what it's like to have parts of you snatched away, to have your body and your mind violated, your identity and your entire life hijacked..."

Orion trailed off, seeing the anguish beneath Auriga's stony visage, knowing that there was a photograph in the second drawer of the chest that would disprove what he'd just said. For several seconds there was silence; then a groan cracked the stillness, and they both turned back to Corvus.

The Illuminatus's head still hung limp, and his eyes were still closed. The relaxed posture of his form, in fact, suggested unconsciousness—and yet his lips moved, designing words that floated from them as if in a trance.

"Orion, can you hear me?"

Auriga's eyebrows rose at the question, and he cast a worried look at the teenager.

"Orion, it's Lyra."

Orion stared, aghast. The voice was Corvus's own, with the only departure being a slight drowsy cadence. He shot a glance to the Resistance man, who knelt by the captive, examining him closely.

"He's out cold."

"Yes, I can hear you," Orion said cautiously.

"I've established a link to Corvus while he's unconscious," Lyra reported. "I can hear and speak, but I can't see anything and the link will be severed when he wakes up."

"I didn't know you could do that," he said. It was difficult to conceive that he was speaking to her via a surrogate.

"It's not too difficult since we're both psionic. He's not actively using most of his brain right now, so I've moved in for the time being. My body is unconscious too."

"And you're on the ship," Orion supplied, his skin prickling.

"Yes. Listen carefully: there may be a way for you to destroy it."

"Destroy the ship?" he repeated. "I'm not doing that with you on it. I'm coming to get you."

"No, don't be foolish. I want you to destroy it. Their ship uses energy in surges, because the power source is too strong and too unstable to supply a steady stream. It's what facilitates faster-than-light travel or biotransportation: immense bursts of colossal energy, followed by a dearth while the system recovers."

Short-lived electrical events...

"Action potentials," he said in disbelief.

"Yes, but on the scale of a spaceship. The energy travels in channels, to be used for applications in the ship that are in need of it. If you could build a device to siphon that energy, like a massive power sink, the ship would be forced into a constant deficit and would lose all of its power."

"It would have to be made from Grey technology for the ship to accept it as one of its own applications. That kind of stuff isn't easy to find," Orion objected.

"I have faith in you," she said. "This is important—you have to try."

"We've got problems," Auriga cut in. He had retrieved a combat shotgun and was peering carefully through one of the dirty windows facing the front of the house.

Orion leapt to the window on the opposite side of the front door. Protectorate soldiers in black tactical gear skulked around the neighboring porches. "Oh, no, the car," he realized, thinking of the vehicle they'd hidden under a canvas tarp out back. "They must have been able to track it."

Auriga whirled through the crowded room, digging through boxes. He fetched a rectangular olive-green plastic assembly; Orion spied the words "Front Toward Enemy" on the convex side. Auriga's carbine rifle lay on top of two short filing cabinets, and Orion equipped it, racking a round into the barrel with a deliberate motion.

The outlander propped the metal legs of the land mine between two bricks that were otherwise employed as a doorstop. He angled the weapon toward the front entry. As he stretched a thin wire behind the doorway, Auriga called out, "Hey, we got Corvus in here! Anybody tries to come in, we blow his brains out, got it?"

He waved Orion toward the back door. As he crossed into the cramped kitchen, the young man spotted more officers positioning around the rear of the house. "We're surrounded," he told the Resistance man.

Auriga joined him in the kitchen, ducking beneath the window at the sink. "We're gonna clear them out at the back door, okay? Get ready to bolt as soon as you get the chance."

The cybernetic nodded, and concentrated for a moment to

upload a targeting reticule to his HUD. The crosshairs syncing to the M16 didn't offer the same tactical information as the more advanced thermal pulse rifle, but it would provide a valuable advantage nonetheless.

"Now!" Auriga popped up at the window, discharging a twelve-gauge volley through the curtains and glass. Orion swung the back door wide and crouched behind the doorframe while delivering bursts of automatic fire. Their initial assault caught two men unprepared and tore ragged holes in the black-clad figures who tumbled to the earth. Auriga remained at the window, assailing the team with shotgun blasts, shucking shells into the weapon like clockwork. Enemies receded against the assault; sporadic gunfire was returned in their direction, and Orion deftly picked out the hostiles, silencing them with carefully aimed salvos.

Commotion erupted at the front of the house. "Let's go!" Orion urged. "Get to the car; I can take the device out of it when we're gone."

"You go, muchacho. I'm staying here," Auriga replied, still stacking shells into the shotgun's chamber. "I'll cover you and slow them down so they can't chase—" He faltered for a moment, losing his grip on the weapon before catching it again. Orion's eyes widened: a stream of fresh blood welled from a bullet hole in the man's chest.

"Come with me!" Orion begged. "I can't do this alone!"

"No time to argue! Go!" Auriga said, pushing Orion backward out the door. As he lurched onto the back porch, the door slammed, and a sharp click sounded as Auriga engaged the lock. From the kitchen, Orion's comrade shouted, "Good luck, man—been nice knowing you. Do what your girl said and take that ship down, all right? Do us all a favor and make the Greys sorry they ever came."

Two paramilitary operatives rounded the side of the house, raising their weapons. Orion rattled the M16 in their direction, driving them back around the corner. He vaulted off the porch, bounding for the vehicle at the back of the little shack, tearing the tarp off of it as he skidded around to the driver's side. As he turned the key in the ignition, a thunderous boom sounded from the front door of the house: the Claymore mine tore the building to shreds. The car lifted off the ground and Orion spun the wheel desperately, facing it toward the beckoning oblivion of the desert. From within the dwelling, an eruption of gunfire swelled into a black storm that rang in his ears as he jammed the pedal to the floor.

Chapter Nine

D olorous and bare, the wastelands flashed by Orion yet again. He kept the vehicle throttled high, putting as much distance as possible between himself and the hopeless tragedy that he'd just skirted. The wind whipped his face, stinging him with the shame of his flight. The stigma of cowardice chased after him—he'd come full circle, alone in the desert once more.

When there was nothing but bleak isolation in every direction, he throttled down and shut the car off, resting it on the arid sand. When he used his cybercomputer to scan for a tracking signal, it revealed a convex disc tucked inside the engine compartment; the tracker was built into the cylinder block so that the engine wouldn't function if it was removed.

The hard aluminum case had no seams or tabs, so Orion bisected it neatly on the horizontal axis. As the top half fell away, a tiny bead with a wire-thin antenna was revealed; he crushed it between two rocks and closed the hood. With the protective case open, the heat from the vehicle's engine would fry the rest of the exposed circuitry in no time.

Orion resumed his course, speeding away from the spine-lessness reflected in his own eyes in the rearview mirror—but fearfulness always kept pace with him. He watched the skies, anticipating the great silver saucer to come for him, gleaming overhead like the sword of Damocles. The saucer would need no tracking device to find him, no matter where he fled. One day it would inescapably be there, the last day of his life.

It was innate, the path that he took. Past scarred, wind-worn edifices and time-ravaged ruins he flew, circumventing the wreckage of towns that served as portents of untimely death. Keeping a southerly course, he journeyed through places that humanity had long since abandoned or been driven from by the Lacertas—two species in retrograde, locked together in a reckless spiral toward the dust of extinction. Orion was not fooled by the grandeur of the city spires he'd spurned, or even by the mechanical wonder he piloted at this very moment: they were concessions from superior beings, consolation prizes like the gaudy baubles children clung to at a carnival after driving themselves to bankruptcy.

He was alone; of this he was certain. He was harassed neither by the Protectorate in the wastelands behind him nor by lurking lizard-beasts in the demolished structures ahead. He was indeed alone: Auriga was dead, and Lyra merely floated incorporeal and unreachable through such vulgar vessels as she might find. She was captive in that inscrutable disc that might as well have been light-years away for all the power he held over it.

And yet, despite all of this, the tiniest kernel of hope beckoned from within his thoughts. The report Lyra had shared, brief though it was, had sparked in him a deeper understanding of the physics of the craft. Could he guard his thoughts from outward molestation long enough to put that revelation to use? Corvus was either rescued or dead; the balance hung between relief and disaster.

It would require the pinnacle of Orion's skills to achieve his designs; success would likewise hinge upon his ability to recover such artifacts as he would need, and to remain hidden while the precarious task was done. In his mind, though, a blueprint was unfurling that might provide him the means with which to board that peregrine craft.

His ruminations on this subject were well advanced by the time he achieved his destination. A derelict hovel, forsaken by time and the living world, bowed squat and ugly upon the outlying reaches of a bleak and Acheronian village. He settled the vehicle in back, hiding it from view with large pieces of splintering plywood, and tested the back door.

It opened to a world of phantasmal wretchedness. Orion stood in the doorway for long moments, casting a stretching shadow forward into the impoverished chamber. As he surveyed the shack, he was struck by its shrunken look. After spending so many childhood hours here, he now returned to find its furnishings on the order of a dollhouse.

Debris and detritus littered the place. Its scant effects were ruined and strewn in ill-lit anarchy—when he entered, he knew he would have to watch his step, but for now that action was unthinkable. A battered wooden chair would be in one corner of the room, but he dared not look. Not yet. He remained where he was, standing in the narrow portal between two wastelands, one without and one within.

✳✳✳

Sitting cross-legged on the shanty's floor, Orion tinkered with the ocular device, loosening the telescopic band and removing the ruined shards of glass from the groove that housed the shattered lens. His small, agile fingers plucked out the pieces and laid them in a pile to one side; then, taking up a coarse-bristled brush, he swept away the grit and sand that coated the scope's interior. He held the device to the overhead light, angling it to examine his handiwork.

"Good, son," came a slow, thick voice. "Now we add the new lens."

Orion took the proffered item from the mottled, lumpy arm that extended from the dark obscurity of the chair in the corner of the room. The doubly convex disc of glass shone like an opal, rainbow bands weaving across its smooth surface. He studied it, mesmerized, and began to fit it into the space vacated by the missing piece.

"Use your shirt," the slurred voice spoke with tenderness. "No fingerprints on the inside of the lens, or you won't be able to get them off."

Orion nodded, wiping the lens with the soft cotton of his T-shirt. He used the cloth to drop it into place, set the hard plastic ring with its tab into the inside groove, and spun it until it locked. The telescopic band now rotated in a smooth arc, and he aimed the sight around the little room, focusing on little objects or softening large ones to make them blurry. His operations did not, however, reveal the obfuscated form in the corner.

"Very nice, Orion. You did a good job."

Orion's pleasure at the repair's success, and the praise that followed it, supplanted for a time the unease that had been growing within him of late. His father had taken increasingly to the darkness, seldom leaving his spot in the shadowed corner; when he did so, his movements were pained and sluggish. Likewise, his mother could seldom be roused from bed anymore, and her whimpers of agony were not wholly muffled by the musty pillow she cried into.

Orion carried the restored scope to the nightstand that served as one leg of the workbench, wrapped it in a cloth, and laid it amid the other treasures. The caravans would arrive soon, bringing food and water that might stave off their desperation a little longer. His parents were loath to leave the house in daylight, and Orion would cajole a single one of the traders into coming to barter with the sick tenants of this ramshackle house.

It would be a day or two, three at the outside, and Orion patrolled the nearby village the next day, waiting for the convoy of merchants to come slogging through the sand in their tracked sage-colored vehicles. Nothing broke the horizon, though, and when he returned home that evening, his mother would not accept the morsel of food that he tried to share with her, saying that she and his father had already eaten.

In despair, he returned to the small town again in the morning, scanning with the newly repaired scope for any sign of visitors. Today there was indeed a convoy crawling along, and he rushed to meet his saviors outside the village borders. In his elation, he did not stop to wonder at the unfamiliar black vehicles until the burly men exited, formidable and grim in their tactical gear.

"What's the matter, son?" one of them had asked. "If there's something wrong, you can tell us. Hey, don't be scared, it's okay. We're the Protectorate."

He'd grinned uncertainly in the back of the black SUV, directing the men to the humble shanty outside town. Refreshing cold air blasted from the vehicle's vents, and Orion marveled at the interior climate and cushioned seats. His parents would be glad; they would thank him for bringing help, and they wouldn't be sick anymore.

When the convoy arrived at the shack, the man who'd spoken to Orion asked him to stay in the car with him and show him how his scope worked while men from the other trucks went inside to talk to his parents.

He'd been so engrossed in the demonstration, and reveling in the enthusiastic delight of his audience, that he paid no attention to the subdued commotion from the shack. When the doors slammed on the other vehicles a few minutes later, he broke from his distraction with a rush of apprehension. Once again, the officer calmed him: "Your parents are going to be fine, okay? They're sick now, and they're going to go to a hospital to get better. Don't worry..."

***

In the demolished, abandoned hovel, Orion's boots crunched over the remnants of another time. The chair in the corner lay toppled on its side. With cold purpose, he crossed the room to the large workbench, uncovered it, and tossed the shroud to the floor behind him in a billow of dust. Tearing the plastic off of a twelve-volt battery, he attached two alligator clips to the leads and snapped on a caged lamp. When he hung it from a nail in the wall, the lamp's brilliance shone down upon a marvelous array of tools, parts, and equipment.

Orion bent to the aged nightstand at his left, slid the drawer open, and dug through the assortment of findings. The items he sought were easy to separate from their earthly and mundane counterparts: Orion lined up odd and alien appurtenances on the workstation. Each one could fit into the palm of a child's hand. Each one had. Strange contours crafted their bizarre outlines. Although these devices were not altogether unknown to him, having lingered in that drawer for years—neglected but unforgotten—their purposes remained a mystery. What was unmistakable was that they were of Grey origin.

***

The woman in the lab coat led the child down a narrow corridor lined with viewing bays. When he turned to peer into one, the restrained forms of his captive parents writhed upon hospital beds flanked with sterile surroundings. Facility workers, alien in their protective suits, ministered to their deformed bodies. His escort turned his head away from the sight. "They're going to be just fine, my dear. We're going to go right in here and take some tests."

In the next room, the boy was seated at a sleek metal table. His hostess, a prim black woman with carefully colored burgundy lips and a spotless white lab coat, sat across from him. She opened a manila folder and slid a few sheets of paper and a silver pen to him across the table's smooth surface. He traced his finger along the asymmetrical chevron emblem embossed near the top of the paper.

"Just answer the questions at your own pace," she coached as an assistant placed a metal band around the child's forehead. A troubled expression washed over the youth's face but dissipated at the woman's reassuring smile. She observed his progress with silent watchfulness, from time to time glancing at the associate who monitored his results with a handheld tablet. He found it difficult to concentrate at times, but eagerness to indulge his new friends won the day.

There were some questions he didn't know how to answer, and as his frustration surfaced, the lady in the white coat bolstered his spirits: "Don't be upset, my dear. If you can't answer something, just leave it blank."

Before the child had finished scrawling answers on the page, the man who'd placed the band on his head made a pronouncement. "Readings are totally normal," he said. "He doesn't display any psionic potential—his brain activity and cognitive function is that of a regular twelve-year-old child."

"I'm nine years old," he'd objected.

Just then, the hallway door swung open; a doctor removed her quarantine suit's helmet to address the woman seated across from him. "They're in late-stage chronic transplant rejection. Should we start corticosteroids?"

The woman in the lab coat shook her head, remaining seated. "It's *much too late to begin immunosuppressive therapy, and obviously a bone marrow transplant isn't an option either. Take careful note of the antibodies present near the cyberimplants and halt everything except hypertonic saline in a central line."*

The doctor hesitated, then cast a stricken glance at the boy. She seemed about to speak, but a severe glance from the seated woman sent her withdrawing from the room. The child could not understand a great deal of the words spoken, but his vexations returned anew. She turned back to him, smiling pleasantly.

"So, you're nine years old? That's wonderful!"

***

Orion assessed the contrivances laid out on the workbench. These morbid trappings had stolen two lives from him; he would now subjugate them into restoring two interrupted ones. He would channel the Greys' own technology against them by building a device to siphon their ship's power. This Vinculum, as he would call it, would bind him to the ship's analog, masquerading as one of the saucer's own applications in order to receive enough energy to transport him onto the craft.

As Orion donned an optivisor and tested the condition of the soldering iron, he mused upon the maniacal implications of this act: for the entirety of his life, he'd been thoroughly petrified at the thought of returning to that ship of demented harvest. Nothing could have swayed him to seek it out or entertain any notion of gaining entry to those horridly curving corridors—and yet now, as he labored with every resource available to revisit the very foundation of all his nightmares, it would be the aliens themselves that would resist those efforts.

***

"Can I speak to you for a moment, my dear?"

It was the following day, and the woman with the white lab coat had knocked at the entrance of his dormitory before sliding the doorway open. The child had been awake for hours, as evidenced by the wide dispersal of electronic parts and pieces he'd requested as playthings.

The woman entered the sparsely furnished chamber, smoothing the coat against her thighs as she sat down in a plastic and metal chair. Orion tendered his attention, laying aside the trinkets and climbing up to sit on the narrow cot.

"Orion, when your parents came to us, they were very sick. Do you remember what happened to them to make them that way?"

Resolute nodding. "The skinny men with the black eyes put things into them. They wanted to see what would happen."

"Yes, they did," she agreed. "I'm afraid their bodies rejected the things that were put into them. It took some time, but what the skinny men were trying to do didn't work, and it hurt your parents badly. Do you understand?"

Eyes downcast to the parts and pieces on the floor. Slower nodding. "You can't fix them either?"

Her voice was soft. "No, I'm afraid not."

He picked up a pair of snips, fiddling with them in his fingers. "Dad told me they weren't going to get better."

There was the slightest crack in her smooth façade; then the serene sympathy returned. "I'm sorry, but he was right. They didn't get better, and...they're gone now. I know this is hard, and you're very grown up for your age, but it's okay to be sad anyway. You'll be taken care of, I promise."

The boy laid the tool down with care and then wiped his eyes, still looking down at his lap. Moments passed before he whispered, "I can

114

take care of myself."

"No, son. The Protectorate will have to care for you."

His angry gaze pierced her steadfast demeanor. "I don't like it here. I don't like the Protectorate."

"It's okay," she soothed. "I understand that you're angry—"

"Shut up," he interrupted. "You don't understand anything."

The doctor paused, taken aback by his sudden harshness. However, it wasn't an affront to her feelings that engendered the response; she was instead considering how best to maneuver forward. She rose from the chair with resolution. "I'll give you some time to yourself," she announced. "And then we'll have someone for you to speak with about what's going to happen next."

The youth didn't respond, and she punched a sequence on the keypad by the door, letting herself out before the portal hissed shut.

***

Orion laid down the separating disc and scrutinized the inner workings of the alien gadgetry. The organized lines of wires and circuitry foretold a maze of branching roads, and he was lost within the multitude of options. He picked up a fine-point pair of tweezers, preparing for the first fateful probing into the technology of another world, but he hesitated for several moments, paralyzed with uncertainty. How on earth could he even hope to begin such a task? He was a teenager, working alone in a defunct shack with mediocre tools, whereas teams of scientists with access to cutting-edge resources had been stymied by the physical concept of teleportation for the entirety of human history. What hubris could possibly deceive him into believing that space and time were his to control?

In fragile futility, he nearly swept the instruments from the board—but the thought of doing so made him recalcitrant. Could it be denied that he had learned much from the Greys? Could he pretend that their attentions had not bolstered his skills beyond those of ordinary humans? Who else could attempt what he was about to perform? He alone was suited to this task, having been thrust into the Greys' unearthly designs from his earliest recollection. Indeed, he had been spinning his own machinations since a time when he could hardly be aware of their future significance.

***

The keypad next to the door could be pried open to expose organized lines of wires and circuitry. The boy selected a newly assembled device from the pile of playthings he'd spent the morning tinkering with; it was rectangular in shape, with two protrusions ending in copper leads. Using a fine-point pair of tweezers, he teased two wires out of the keypad's maze of branching roads. After connecting them to the leads in the handheld device, he spun a small black dial clockwise until it stopped. The electronic array on the lock froze in a display of nonsensical symbols, and the door disengaged from its housing.

***

The overhead lamp burned into the night. Orion's eyes were bleary and strained from fixating on the tiny objects; stretching his hands against cramps, squinting at the sharp and acrid tang of solvents, he rolled his head against the ache in his neck and shoulders. He didn't know, didn't want to know, how many hours had elapsed in the stillness of the ruined cabin. He was getting nowhere, fumbling with the alien gadgetry with no proof of concept in sight. He rubbed his eyes and dropped the optivisor back over them, leaning forward to the workbench again.

***

The child strained to reach the red plastic box affixed to the wall, turning his head back to watch for approaching figures in the hallway. His neck and shoulders ached and his hand was beginning to cramp. His fingertips brushed the handle of the fire alarm, and he leapt upward to seize it and jerk it downward. A shrieking bell clamored in the facility; red lights pulsed in their beacons high up on the wall. He hustled into a janitor's closet, wrinkling his nose at the sharp and acrid tang of solvents. Remaining motionless and silent, he bided his time until the turmoil of evacuating employees rambled past his hiding place. He waited several more seconds, then slipped out into the empty hall. Running close to the wall, he hurried to the laboratory next to the testing room where he had spent the previous day. Once again, he used his invention to slice the electronic lock, and in a flash he entered the lab. The two beds were now vacant and stripped of sheets; he glanced at them once and turned away. On the counter, he spied the items he sought: an array of bizarre and alien apparatus, six of them in total. They had been sterilized of blood after removal from their victims but seemed to be otherwise unmolested. He snatched them up and fled.

***

Dawn had come. The sun rose upon another day with Lyra at the mercy of those incalculable tyrants—another day in which Orion was powerless against them. Dirty light inspected his pathetic attempts upon the workbench; nothing had been accomplished, nothing gained from his clumsy and inferior attempts. He cast the pliers away. He had failed to save his parents, failed to save Auriga, failed to save Lyra.

By now, Lyra might have even found some way to blow up the alien ship while she was still on it. Shuddering, he imagined her being blown to bits as debris rained down over the city.

He allowed despair to cloak him, abandoning himself to the chimerical revelations that he had hitherto shut from his mind. The Greys had had Lyra for a full day now; whatever fiendish designs they had for her were likely already fulfilled. Nightmarish visions stampeded through his head, an almost tangible burden. He folded his arms upon the bench, sagged forward, and buried his face in the crook of his elbow. The optivisor slipped off and clattered to the floor.

Febrile and exhausted, he slept.

Chapter Ten

Auriga tightened his grip on the twelve-gauge, wincing against the pain. He'd taken a ricocheted round at the top of his solar plexus, and thick blood coursed from the wound. The sound of Orion speeding away in Corvus's vehicle was barely audible over the gunfire shattering the house all around him. He started for the doorway from the kitchenette to the dingy main room, but just as he reached it, a booming thunderclap tore through the house, and he ducked for cover at the open door.

An entry team had triggered the Claymore mine he'd set, touching off a vicious explosion that launched metal projectiles in a fan-shaped radius at the front door with searing velocity. He believed that he'd gotten two of the commandos with the blast, but the hazy, splintered destruction was still raining down. Just for good measure, he unleashed two more shotgun blasts at the front of the room. It gave away his position, but it didn't matter. This was the end; he'd just finish Corvus off, and that would be it.

Auriga staggered to his feet, leaving a bloody smear on the doorjamb where his hand had rested. He lugged the shotgun forward, dragging himself into the middle of the room. The weapon was too light: he'd used all the shells. The front of the house was a ragged, smoky cavity. In the yard, more Protectorate

119

men regrouped.

"You have one chance! Throw your weapon out the front door!" someone bellowed.

"Okay, I'm doing it! I give up, don't shoot!" Auriga screamed in answer. He chucked the empty Mossberg into the front yard; it bounced into the yellow dirt. He reached around to the back of his jeans and withdrew a tactical pistol; one officer rounded the edge of the splintered hole, and Auriga shot him neatly in the forehead. As the corpse tumbled off the ruined porch, the kitchen door behind him imploded under a crushing force. He pumped two more bullets into another officer at the front door. The house swarmed with Protectorate men, and Auriga swung the gun's barrel to Corvus, who still slumped in the broken chair, listless, his lean face in shadows.

Auriga's chest burned; his vision darkened, and he gasped for breath. His finger curled against the trigger, but slick with blood, it slipped off.

"*Stop.* I want him taken alive."

Corvus's frame was limp and vulnerable, but his voice carried unmistakable weight. The Protectorate men surrounding Auriga hesitated but kept their weapons trained on him. In Auriga's dizzying vertigo, black gun barrels whirled around him. He could pull his own trigger and vanish in a dark flurry of bullets and blood. The pistol was burdensome; it drooped in his hand. He struggled to heft it back on target, hearing the throaty hum of powerbinders somewhere in the room before he collapsed.

***

Auriga awoke in a brightly lit, sanitary room. He reclined upon a white bed; looking down, he discerned a clean gauze bandage on his chest. When he went to examine it, leather straps halted his wrists—he'd been restrained to the bed.

He blinked in the effulgence, taking a mental inventory of his condition. The agony from the wound in his solar plexus had dissipated to a manageable level of pain. His muscles were sore and drained from their strenuous exertion, but he was confident enough that he could stand on his own feet if he could only get the chance. Stand, and do more than that, if need be.

Then a frightful concern plowed into his stirring thoughts: for all he knew, he was on board the alien ship. He froze, searching the stillness for the hum of engines or the ethereal weightlessness of flight, but found his inquiry to be inconclusive. He twisted in the bed, craning his neck to take in as much of his surroundings as he could: White countertops with glass beakers methodically sorted; a gleaming medibot on standby against the wall. There were no windows, as in a hospital suite—he guessed that this was an interior room. An odd, asymmetrical chevron crest adorned one wall. Elsewhere on the wall hung a nickel-satin hook; it was shoulder-height above the ground. Still inconclusive. Weren't a small number of the Greys even taller than a man? Then he realized that the hook would only be there to hang a clipboard or a lab coat.

"*Bueno.*" He sighed to himself, sinking back onto the pillows. "*Estoy bueno.*"

"That's good to hear," replied a female voice from outside his field of view.

Auriga's relief vanished like a soap bubble. He contorted again, struggling in vain to see his attendant. "Who's there?"

A handsome woman with decorous features and burgundy lips seated herself at the right side of his bed. Her smile was understated and devouring, like a predator who would circle a wounded animal to prolong the satisfaction of the moment. She withdrew a handheld device from the pocket of her lab coat, speaking while she recorded his readings for temperature and blood pressure.

"I'm Dr. Noreen Vulpecula, Mr. Auriga. You're well-known to us at the United Corporations Order, but I'll forego the trite pleasantries of how nice it is to have you as a guest."

"I'm tied to the bed, lady. If that's your definition of a guest, you've got a messed-up private life. Call me old-fashioned, but I still believe in a little thing called consent."

"Very good, Mr. Auriga," she said, examining the device's findings. "I'm glad you're able to find the levity in your current situation."

Auriga attempted a grin in response and shifted uneasily in the bed, vanquished for the moment. The grin faded.

"You're recovering from your ordeal very well," the doctor observed. "How is the pain? I've kept the doses low because I felt it was important that we talk, but if you're suffering, I can give you something that will help."

"No. No painkillers." He hesitated, then shook his head, finding his voice again. "Somehow, this doesn't look like a hospital, Doc. How about you tell me where I am?"

"Certainly. You're at Fornax Enterprises, in the northeastern Chihuahuan Desert. This is a genetics laboratory owned by the UCO. It was the closest medical facility, and you and Mr. Corvus were both badly in need of care."

"*Madre de Díos*, what about Corvus? He's here too?"

"His injuries were more serious than yours. Since he didn't receive adequate medical care when he was injured, there's only so much our medibots can do for him. We've been forced to use more conventional measures: we've debrided the wound, but he's susceptible to infection due to the ballistic fragments that remain in the body. We can't risk an operation to remove them due to the vascular complexities of the neck. We'll have to keep him on antibiotics and watch him carefully, but so far he's stable. I'm confident he'll pull through."

"He's not awake yet?"

"No, he's been unconscious since they brought him in. I heard he gave the order to capture you alive." Her brown eyes were even and vulturine. "That's surprising, considering you're such a well-known enemy of the UCO."

"Oh, stop it. You're making me blush."

Vulpecula studied him, her face blank. The silence stretched for several moments before she produced a silver pen to take notes on a clipboard. "Are you allergic to any medications, Mr. Auriga?"

Auriga laughed out loud, despite the dagger it plunged into his bandaged chest. "This is just too much, Doc. Just tell me what you're going to do to me, and then do it already."

She unclicked the pen and returned it to her lapel. "Well, Mr. Auriga, that remains to be seen."

"Don't string me along. Since I'm a prisoner of the UCO, there're only two choices, right? Execution or *reeducation*." He spoke the last word with exaggerated reverence.

"Hmph," she grunted, crossing her legs and settling into the chair. "I believe there's a third option you haven't considered."

Auriga blanched despite himself. "You're going to hand me over to the Greys, aren't you? To mess around with me like they did those two kids." His bravado fell away at the thought of extraterrestrial captivity. "What could you possibly gain from that? I killed Protectorate men, but I was never cruel."

Her sporting mien was the first trace of humor betrayed during the interview. "Do you find the Greys so cruel? I believe they've demonstrated a protective benevolence toward mankind."

"You're sick," Auriga objected. "This is all so sick." He swept the room with a surreptitious look. One corner lay outside his field of vision, but as far as he could tell, they were alone. No assistants, no security.

"Why, look at the advances in medicine they've brought us," she said. "Your very own life was saved by Grey technology just today. I'm not a woman who would use the term 'miraculous' lightly, but you were shot in the chest with a rifle—to say nothing of the injuries you sustained in the fight with Corvus. A scant fifteen years ago, your wounds would have been a death sentence."

"And what am I being healed for? To be in pristine condition when they rip me open? They aren't bestowing gifts upon mankind; they're manipulating us for their own reasons. If you were intellectually honest, you'd admit that was true."

"Their manipulations have led to a new renaissance," she said, folding her slender hands upon one upraised knee. "The advances in medicine, transportation, and electronics have allowed human achievements to develop at an astounding rate."

"Those aren't human achievements, then. If you copy off of someone's paper to accomplish something, you don't deserve the grade you get."

Vulpecula was silent.

"We're only advancing as far as they intend to let us," Auriga went on. "What about teleportation, or FTL travel?"

"Humanity isn't ready for faster-than-light travel," Vulpecula said. "There are societies out there that we know nothing about. It takes time to discover our place in the universe and learn to handle that kind of responsibility. We'd touch off an intergalactic war, or cause genocide."

"And what do you suppose the Greys are doing?" Auriga countered.

"By killing off the Lacertas? You were happy to perpetrate your own little one-man genocide until you discovered it aligned with the Greys' interests. If *you* were intellectually honest, you'd admit *that* was true."

Auriga was silent.

"The Greys are using a carrot-and-stick method," she explained. "They share some beneficial advances with the population, and observe us to see if we use them responsibly. If so, they introduce more powerful technology. I understand they've begun to implement psionic augmentations in certain subjects." Her eyes twinkled with conspiracy.

"They're running an ant farm. They're not only experimenting on individual people but entire races," Auriga exploded. "The benefits they offer are only realized by a few at the expense of many. People are stranded in the wastelands and scraping by in the slums. They're exploited like cattle."

"That's perfectly justifiable," Vulpecula responded. "It's not pretty, but it's the way nature works—the strong rule over the weak. Did you ever worry about an individual steer's place in the world when you ate a steak? Or did you reason that its purpose was being fulfilled? Your analogy is more fitting than you realize: consider that a steer is much stronger than a man, and yet mankind is the master of the beasts."

"Because we're smarter." Auriga's eyebrows lowered in concession.

"Indeed. If each individual human on Earth wrestled with an individual steer to prove which was the dominant race, the struggle would quickly fall to the cattle. However, we've maneuvered ourselves into a position of authority over cattle, and any other number of creatures, by using our own advantages to stack the odds against them. How can you fault the Greys for having done the same thing?"

"We use cattle for sustenance—for survival. We don't screw around with their entire species just because we can."

"You're wrong," she pronounced. "Mankind has selectively engineered what it considers to be favorable traits in any number of creatures: dogs are bred to become hunters or trackers, for example, even if it knowingly results in health problems specific to a certain breed. And as far as the Greys' own survival—as a physically weaker species, they depend upon the subjugation of other races to meet their needs. Again, this is comparable to man's own actions with regard to the other species of Earth. You're introducing emotion into the equation because of your discomfort with its natural implications."

"I'm sure you're just thrilled with our new alien overlords."

"You can rail against the injustice of the universe all you want. I'm talking about hard facts. Suppose a race of giants were to rise up as the new dominant species on Earth, hunting human beings for food. We would be free to defend ourselves if we were able—it's the right of any living creature, after all—but if we couldn't overpower them, what recourse would we have? It would be every bit as ridiculous to indict them for their behavior as it would be to expect any *other* predator not to consume its prey."

"'Might makes right,' then, is that it?"

"I believe a more accurate lesson would be, 'Evolve or die.'"

"So you're going to stack the evolutionary playing field. I'd love to hear this."

"I'd be happy to indulge you." Vulpecula uncrossed her legs and leaned forward. "For ages, we have wondered about the next step in human evolution. Many so-called purists seek enlightenment by becoming more beastlike and primal, developing the physical body to its limits, relying on instinct and reflex to find the path forward. They relegate the brain to being more of a fuse box than a computer—all hardware and no processing. If you compare this with the path nature has chosen among the more dominant species, however, this is regressive. Predators are among the most intelligent animals; prey are not. They succeed as a result of their brains—not just the simple fact of possessing superior force, but in knowing how to use it for maximum effect.

"Others have gone to the opposite end of the spectrum: envisioning heightened cortical development, tapping into the unknown mysteries of the mind. They speculate that the human brain will become larger and more highly developed, facilitating everything from psychokinesis to extrasensory perception. Again, nature contradicts this: the human brain is already as big as it can get. It's quite common for an infant's head size to pose drastic problems in passing through the birth canal. If our brains were the size of the Greys', for example, women and their infants would both die in childbirth.

"I believe humanity is uniquely suited to ascend because we possess both brains *and* brawn, in equal measure—unlike the Greys or the Lacertas. You, Mr. Auriga, are a perfect example of this: your physical form is outstanding, as is your knowledge of medicine, tactical maneuvering, social and linguistic constructs…the list goes on. You remember I mentioned a third option—it's something that I think may appeal to you, Mr. Auriga. You are the specimen that I need for the procedure."

"I'm flattered, Doc. What procedure are we talking about, exactly?"

Vulpecula leaned forward. "The body is subjected to cryonic shock in order to administer invasive bionic surgeries that no human should be able to live through. The cold slows metabolic function and minimizes swelling, allowing the surgeon greater control over the transplant process. It would greatly improve the integration between the host's immune system and the bionic grafts—the diametric opposite of transplant rejection."

Phantom chills covered him as she spoke, and he shook his head. "Cryosurgery is only effective for destroying certain malignant tissues by selectively freezing them. You can't freeze and unfreeze a human body whenever you want; our bodies are almost two-thirds water. The cell walls would rupture with the freezing temperatures, and when you thawed them out after surgery, the person would end up as a slushy puddle on the floor."

"I've developed a drug that will allow the subject's cell walls to become flexible in order to withstand the temperature fluctuations."

"So then the proteins in the amino acids break down. The subject's muscle tissue turns into gelatin. How many mops do you go through every week in the operating room?" Auriga said.

"Muscle tissue is actually *strengthened* by the procedure," she said. "The catalyst is only active at extremely low temperatures, when the deterioration is halted by the cold. What's even better is that the baseline for conduction velocity is reset to the temperature at which the procedure is performed."

Auriga tried to sit further upright, despite his restraints. "So at normal body temperature, the subject's action potentials become hyperactive with the relative increase in temperature."

"Precisely. Your familiarity with these concepts only reinforces my decision to utilize you for the operation."

He chuckled. "You know, Doc, I'm actually curious about all

this. You might have even gotten me to go along with it—but I'm going to have to pass. If I wanted experimental surgery, I'd ask the Greys to give me a nose job."

Auriga curled his right bicep with violent force. The leather restraint on his wrist went taut, stretching to its limit, and he ripped it free from its anchor at the bed frame with a feral grunt. As he grabbed the other strap, the doctor's hand shot out, clenching his forearm and stopping him cold with a steel grip. Her dark eyes bored into his as she wrestled his arm back to its original position. He strained against the sheer force summoned by her slim muscles, and they grappled together for a few seconds. He was unable to match her strength, however, and she pinned his arm down by his right side once again.

"The surgery isn't as experimental as you might think," she disclosed, still staring into his eyes. "There has already been one subject to receive these enhancements, and she has found the operation to be an overwhelming success."

A smile inched across her burgundy lips. Auriga couldn't take his eyes from her.

"I intend to overtake the Greys using what we've learned of their technology," she went on. "We can accelerate the development of our species and overthrow the Greys by being stronger *and* smarter—the *ultimate* predator. The time is right for humanity's own leap into realms beyond."

"You're talking about beating them at their own game."

"The Greys know only the basic framework of my research. The operations are carried out entirely by my team and myself." Vulpecula's calculating smile widened. "I've been falsifying my progress reports to the UCO for months. Poor is the student who does not surpass the teacher, after all."

The disquiet was leaving Auriga now, a crystalline sheet of ice that cracked open to reveal something wondrous underneath. Auriga recalled the words he had spoken to the Resistance men in the Jeep: *I'm the predator. Don't get it twisted.* It seemed like ages ago now, part of an old life that had ended there in the demolished house where the Protectorate men had captured him. Now, perhaps, a new life lay ahead. The thrill of the hunt, the glory of vanquishing his prey, could still be waiting for him on the horizon.

Auriga's lips pursed in a devilish smile of their own. Vulpecula's hand still grasped his right forearm, and with a calm, deliberate motion, he drew his arm straight back until their palms met. As Auriga returned her glinting gaze, his fingers closed with hers in an assertive and steadfast handshake.

Chapter Eleven

Orion floated through billows of dust and smoke. The ground and sky had forsaken it all, and he traveled through an intangible void of gently rolling detritus. Gentle illumination pervaded the boundless expanse, but shadows did not grow from the undefined light. Nothing rested beneath his feet as he walked, and the sphere was similarly free of landmarks or waypoints by which to judge his progress. The solitude was complete, and his only experience was a heightened awareness of his own consciousness and thoughts.

He would acclimate himself to this solitude, he decided. His journey had included companions in bygone days, and now they were no more. He would learn to be self-sufficient, aware of the strength within his own mind, instead of acutely aware of the empty space beside him. Solitude was all that existed: there was one universe, one timeline, one life inhabited by one being. Only one thing could happen at a time: nothing was simultaneous or manifold. Actions were taken piecemeal, by an individual with purpose. The microcosm stretched and deepened; Orion existed only within the present, observing existence as it occurred instead of vainly grasping at moments that had already passed.

But no—he was not alone. He perceived other beings through the shrouded occlusion. *Perceived*, rather than *saw*. Slim, bulbous-headed creatures stalked nearby, and yet they were not to be seen. He halted in his movement, sensing that it would be best to remain hidden. The absolute stillness that he reached was maddening; not even the stirring of living breath differentiated him from oblivion. After a time, the sensation of otherness faded, and he was able to resume his wayward journey.

"*Orion.*"

Up ahead, the swirling dust half revealed a slender silhouette. This one somehow elicited a singular impression upon his confused and cautious faculties. He plodded toward the waiting figure, wondering if it was a mirage. There was a decided incongruity between his efforts to reach the being and the progress he made toward it. The visitor seemed to approach at a crawling pace. Gradually, he discerned its features: with a round, smooth head, like those of the other creatures. Heeding his instincts, though, Orion persisted in closer scrutiny. Variances came into view: tan blouse, faded jeans, and a coral-colored scarf around a bald head.

"Lyra!" he exclaimed. "You're alive? I don't know where I am. Is this place real?"

She smiled, and he continued to approach her. Puzzled, he found that, once he was about an arm's reach away, he could draw no closer. He walked, he leaned toward her, he even took a leap through the oddly permeable space—yet he always remained the same distance from the girl.

"Yes, it's very real," she said. The dissonance confounded the sounds he heard against her barely moving lips. Everything was out of sync, like an object viewed above and below water at once.

A tapered rectangular ship the size of a skyscraper tore through the void somewhere beneath them, but its low, droning hum seemed at odds with the sight of its massive engines all aglow.

Its matte-black armor was carved into varying levels and decks, and the entire cruiser bristled with antennae and guns. The sight enthralled Orion: a space transport built by unknown hands. It didn't seem to be typical of Grey design in any way, and it surely wasn't made by humans. What other strange races traversed this mystifying galaxy? He inspected the ship until it vanished into a pinpoint in the mist.

"It's so confusing," he said, finding that he had twisted around somehow and was standing—albeit standing on nothing—sideways, with the top of his head pointing at Lyra's body. "Where are we?"

"You're not used to it," she said. "It's been called the 'astral plane,' but in the truest sense of the word, it doesn't have a name. Spaceships move through this place when engaging their faster-than-light drives, because this plane facilitates movement and proximity to any point in space. Unimaginable distances can be covered in seconds—if you don't get lost, that is. This is simply the state of consciousness—the state of *being*—and nothing else: no frame of reference or surroundings. My consciousness has established a connection with yours while you sleep."

"You did the same thing with Corvus while he was passed out."

"Yes," Lyra said. "One of the earliest known things about the Greys is their ability to approach other beings through the theta waves in their brains. It's a wavelength that surfaces during meditation or sleep—or even hypnosis, such as when driving for a long time on a straight stretch of highway. These are all conditions under which people first began to report contact with other beings—beings that turned out to be the Greys."

"You can move into people's minds while they meditate or sleep?"

"I can make contact with people while their theta waves are

active, provided that my own mind is in the same state."

"I can't move right." Orion attempted again to position himself upright. He drifted, wishing she would reach out and pull him straight. "I don't like this. Can you help me?"

"You've never experienced this type of freedom from your physical body before. As you become used to it, it will get easier. Here, the agility with which you move is a function of your aptitude for psionic actions. The closer you're able to get to someone, the more firmly linked your consciousness is with theirs. That's why we're within speaking distance—we have a solid connection and can hear each other clearly, but we can't touch. A person's consciousness can't physically touch another's; we're outside of our bodies."

"People used to report out-of-body experiences where they were made aware of extraterrestrial creatures," Orion recalled, gaining some purchase on an even level with her at last. "It was before the Greys made formal contact with humanity. And after they did, I would always have nightmares about the Greys: an endless replay of the worst memories I ever had. But this is happening right now, even though I'm asleep. It's not a dream; it's real."

"You're having an out-of-body experience right now," she explained. "The Greys are quite adept at this type of encounter." She turned her head to the right. "And one of them is coming this way. Come on."

"What?" he exclaimed, looking in the direction that she had but perceiving only clouds. Lyra moved away, her strides not matching the prodigious length of distance she traversed. Orion hurried after her, running as if underwater.

She came back to him. "Don't try to move your limbs; that's not how it works here. Just concentrate on moving. It will be easier if you focus on me."

His efforts improved somewhat, and the pair drifted through the void at a measured pace. "What happens if they find us?"

"If one of them gets close enough, it can make contact with your mind just like we are doing now. It might be able to manipulate your body, like I did with Corvus... I don't know exactly what they could or would do, but it's better not to find out. By staying far away from them, we're guarding our minds from their influence. They're much more practiced in this sphere, and will appear to travel much faster than you, so focus on staying close to me."

Orion had no intentions of doing anything else. The solitude he had accepted as his lot only moments before now seemed unthinkable. Being stranded in the middle of the desert would be preferable to seeing Lyra disappear again. He found that by concentrating on staying at her side, he could move alongside her with ease.

They progressed farther away from the other beings, and their presence faded from his mind. Soon, Orion and Lyra were alone again.

"I've been waiting for you to fall asleep so we could talk," she said. "You were up for hours and hours. Don't push yourself into exhaustion; it's not good for your mind or your body. You have to stay sharp."

"You've been waiting here for that long?" His concern grew. "You can't have been meditating for several hours. You're still unconscious on the ship—oh my God, Lyra, you're in a coma."

"I'm still somewhat conscious," she said. "They've been leaving me alone since I've been on board. I'm not in danger."

"There's no way you can say that," he admonished. "You're on the Greys' ship; you know that it's not safe. Why do they want you?"

"They must have had some reason for taking me instead of Corvus. They wouldn't have given me psionic powers if there weren't some advantage in it for them. They wouldn't have kept him around for as long as they did either. I'm guessing that my psionic potential is greater than his—I'm his replacement, but they feel that they still need to keep me under observation or..."

"Or operate again," he finished, cursing the ruthlessness of the Greys. It was obscene, the very idea that this lovely and compassionate girl before him could be any sort of proxy for the sadistic villain who had betrayed his own race to kneel before those Machiavellian outsiders. Lyra and Corvus couldn't be any more different. He was arrogant, divisive, and intransigent; she was caring and considerate. From the time she'd first displayed the ability to glimpse into Orion's thoughts, she'd only used the power to find common ground with him—even going so far as to put herself at great risk to guard the sanctity of his mind. It was the opposite of everything the Greys represented. How could they dare to make her like them?

He had never communicated, however briefly, with a single member of the race—never been allowed to share in the aloof and secret thoughts of the aliens that so unforgivingly manipulated his life. Not a sound would ever escape their blank, lipless mouths to reveal a hint at their intentions; the honor of understanding even the simplest of their motives was reserved only for the elite few who could commune with their unfathomable minds.

"Orion, you can't board the ship. That's what they want you to do—you have to stay away. Don't come to get me. Just do what I told you before and build the power sink that will crash the ship."

"I could never do that."

"Don't say anything, Orion. I know this is hard for you to hear, but if I ever do wake up, I might not even be the same person. Who knows what Corvus was like before they...brainwashed him?" Her voice had a slight hitch. "This might be the last time we'll ever speak. I need to know that, whatever happens to me, things will turn out the way they're supposed to. If you don't crash the ship, you're risking yourself and anyone else who they'll take in the future. The world will never be the same if you don't take this chance while you have it."

"No. I won't crash the ship. There's another way, and I'm going to find it."

"If you don't do it, I will," she said, looking away. "I'm never getting off of the saucer. You have to accept that."

"I do *not* accept that!" he screamed, making her gasp at the outburst.

It occurred to him, there in the emptiness of a vacant world, that his attempts at communication with members of his own race had chronically been imperfect at best. He, like any other human being, could only grope for the "right words," as a lost traveler might drift through barren clouds of dust and search among similar figures for a companion—only one being correct and true, the rest hostile impostors. Was it not the purest purpose of language to simply facilitate the sharing of thoughts between minds? Wouldn't a more direct route to that objective be superior?

Perhaps here, in this place where his consciousness communicated clearly with hers, the right words could be found. His world would never be the same if he didn't take this chance while he had it.

"Lyra, listen," he ventured. "I don't know if this is the right time to say this, but it's the only time we have."

She turned to him, her face bright in the dusky gloom.

"I'm tired of feeling like I'm barely alive," he said. "The Greys might as well have killed me on the operating table, because I was dead long before then. I thought there was nothing inside me except their machines…but when you came, you looked in my mind and saw things that even I didn't know I felt."

It was then that he realized he had been speaking, not in a synthesized metallic croak but with his own voice. His *old* voice, as it had been before: gentle, steady, a voice it seemed he hadn't heard in ages.

"I have to come for you because…I want us to be together. If we get through this, if we make it…there's a life for us if we're together."

Shimmering in the omnipresent silver glow, her eyes brimmed with tears. He knew her thoughts: not in the way of a psionic, back in the world of shrouded and deceptive understanding, but in a more perfect avenue.

He reached for her, clutching at the void between them. No matter how far apart their physical bodies were, incapacitated and alone, here in this ethereal sphere he could forge a connection with her, if he could only reach her. His arms were aching and empty. She remained just outside of his grasp, eternally unattainable.

In this plane, could he not focus his mind and make it so? He tried to envision her close against him, wrapped in his embrace. He shut his eyes and built a world in his mind in which they were tightly joined, clinging to one another as they would to a lifeline in the barren depths of space; still, his efforts were unfruitful. It was horrendously unfair: he had asked for so little in life, had built himself to be independent and self-sufficient. He had been shattered over and over again, and he had scavenged the pieces together, repaired them and gone on. If his life were broken this time, it would never be fixed.

When he looked at her again, she was a couple of paces farther away. Alarm seized him; an invisible embrace of horror clutched at him instead of the cherished one that he sought. He strove harder to touch her, redoubling his conviction, raging at the futility of it—all to no avail. She drifted farther away.

"Lyra, come back. This isn't the end."

"Go," she said, floating backward into vacuity. "You have to wake up before they find you."

The figures were drawing near again, and this time he could see them plainly. The aliens ambled out of the dust, approaching him with repulsive and morbid scrutiny. He retreated toward the empty wasteland behind him, back through the obscuring clouds toward the dingy shell of a collapsing life huddled within the dingy shell of a collapsing home.

"I'm coming for you," he shouted at the Greys. "I won't let you do this. You've always been able to take whomever you wanted and do as you pleased, with no one to stop you. The Lacertas ran away, and the humans bowed down. No one has ever stood up to you and fought, but I will. I don't care if I have to do it alone—if I have to renounce my humanity, if I have to kill you all—whatever it takes, I'll do it."

His words traveled through the cosmos, a pact sworn in the face of oblivion. Although they were far away, some of the Greys were reaching out, reaching their sticklike arms forward as they shuffled after him. He withdrew from this vacuous realm of maddening isolation, back to a place where he was even more utterly, irredeemably, alone.

Chapter Twelve

Auriga thrashed with convulsions on the narrow hospital bed, groaning as paroxysms shook him. Orderlies in white coats restrained him; he wrestled against the men, keeping them all occupied at once. Past the squirming frame of white arms and hunched shoulders, he saw one orderly recording the events with a holostacker. Meanwhile, Vulpecula stood near the steel headboard, observing in silence. Auriga's spasms continued for over a minute before abating somewhat; at last he lay still, panting through a rictus of white teeth.

Labored moans still escaped him at intervals, and he had the wild thought that it would have been better to have fallen into the clutches of the despised Greys than to be here under the attentions of his fellow man. Then he considered that the staff at Fornax Enterprises had at least provided him the luxury of unconsciousness during the surgery.

Vulpecula leaned over him to speak. "I've ordered for you not to be sedated, because you've only been awake for a short time. I want to get your heart rate up, and the increased circulation will do you a lot of good while we get your body temperature back to normal. However, I need to be reassured that you don't pose a danger to yourself or my staff. If you become violent, I will have to have you sedated and restrained, which neither of us want. Do you understand?"

Auriga nodded, still squinting his eyes shut and gritting his teeth. One by one, the orderlies' hands released his stiffened appendages, and he curled into a fetal position, shuddering. An attendant placed a heavy blanket over him, but Vulpecula took care to retrieve Auriga's right arm from beneath so as not to disturb the intravenous line. She sent the attendants away with a gesture—all except for the holographer, who continued recording.

"Your vitals are strong," she observed. "It should please you to know that the operation went smoothly. We've imbued your cells with the additional stimulants and reset your action potentials to a heightened state of conductivity. What you're experiencing now is your blood working to recirculate through your body and regain its temperature after the cryosurgical process. As I mentioned, you'll have some discomfort from the cold for a while. I think you'll find the temporary unpleasantness to be well worth it."

He was shaking so hard that the bed rattled. "The cold, it burns…" he sobbed in agony. "Everything hurts so much, all over. It feels like tiny spikes in my veins. How long will it last?"

She crossed her hands in her lap. "I don't know," she said.

"Well, how long did this last for you when you had the procedure?" he pressed, still doubled over with misery.

"I didn't have the same procedure as you," she replied.

"What?" he exploded, trying to turn and face her. The motion ended up being more of a wallowing excruciation. "You said you had been enhanced with these methods. Your strength—"

"I was enhanced with cryosurgery, yes, but not nearly to the same extent," she clarified. "My augmentations were not nearly as invasive—or *per*vasive. For the time being, I'm simply a cybernetic, albeit a supremely innovative one…but you:

141

you're now something altogether different and new. I've been recording the entire procedure for posterity, so your insights are quite welcome. I'd like as complete a chronicle as possible."

Auriga's skin, blanched with frigidity, now turned rosy. "'For the time being?'" he quoted. "Meaning that you intend to undergo these procedures yourself as soon as you've perfected them on your guinea pig."

"Don't belittle yourself with that name. You're making an unparalleled contribution to human advancement."

Auriga was silent for several moments, huddled and shuddering beneath the blanket. His body struggled to recuperate from the ordeal; a tingle crept though his extremities. It was painful to speak, even to think, but he lashed out against the frozen barrier that encased him. "You're just like the Greys," he accused. "How many people have you experimented on here? How many of them died? This Fornax place is just a man-made chamber of horrors, like that airborne butcher's shop over the city."

"We've already discussed the necessity of adapting some of the aliens' techniques in order to outplace them," she said. "First, the nature of this project demands that it be done in secret, outside of the knowledge of mankind *and* the aliens. Our remote location in the desert has already saved your life: I doubt that, with your wounds, you would have made it to a clinic in the city.

"Second, the experiment requires healthy and strong human subjects. It does us no good to perform these procedures on a creature of minute proportions and limited reasoning capability, like the ubiquitous lab rat. And in case you're not aware, pigs and chimpanzees are rather hard to come by in western Texas right now."

"How many people died?" Auriga repeated the question with fervor.

"My surgical assistant expired during the procedure," she disclosed. "The second subject succumbed to hypothermia soon after being revived. On the other hand"—she inserted her handheld device into his left ear until it beeped—"thirty-six-point-five degrees Celsius. We've managed to course correct from both episodes." She sat back with a pleased smile. "I believe foregoing the sedation and engendering an impassioned reaction from you was the right call."

Auriga uncurled, rolling his head against the pillow. "You pissed me off on purpose to get my heart rate and body temperature up," he realized.

"Yes, but it should be noted that everything I told you was true. I'd say you've earned the right to know these things."

Auriga studied the doctor. Her guile was appalling but effective: Vulpecula was distinguished in her abilities to manipulate both the body and the mind. Even now, she was drawing him in with her admitted frankness. He'd have to be careful around her—but the aliens weren't the only ones who could be beaten at their own game.

"You're even colder than I am, Doc," he said, "and believe me, that's saying something."

Vulpecula surprised him by throwing back her head and laughing at the joke.

***

Auriga bounded along on the treadmill at a galloping pace, timing his breathing in rhythm to the steady beats of his shoes upon the belt. Perspiration shone lightly upon his forehead, and wires snaked from the treadmill to round white leads stuck to his bare chest. From the corner of his eye, he watched

Vulpecula as she eyed his powerful physique with appreciation. He debated whether her standoffish persona was betraying signs of softening, or if her approving gaze was due to the readings on the exercise machine. He had, after all, been jogging at thirty kilometers per hour for the past ninety minutes. When he glanced at her, she redirected her gaze to the tablet in her left hand.

"Your convalescence has been quite remarkable, Mr. Auriga," she said. "Even with the benefit of our medibots, it's hard to believe you're only twenty-four hours removed from surgery."

Auriga maintained his pace, but he wasn't out of breath when he spoke. "Has it only been one day? I'm dying of boredom, Doc. Could have sworn I'd been here all week."

"I'm sorry that we don't have any gunfights to keep you entertained. These post-op evaluations are going to have to suffice."

"Well, I have to take my fun where I can find it." The treadmill coughed gray smoke as the electric motor burned out with the sharp smell of ozone. Auriga stepped off of the conveyor and slung a white towel over one shoulder before approaching Vulpecula. "So, do you like what you see?" he asked.

Her eyes flicked briefly over his muscular form before meeting his gaze with an unassured expression. "Excuse me?"

"The test scores." He motioned to the tablet she carried.

"Oh, yes." Her concentration surged again. "I'm ecstatic about your performance. Traditionally, the problem with nanotechnology has been finding a reliable power source that will sustain millions of tiny computers inside the human body. I believe we've solved this problem by allowing them to tap into the heightened voltage now generated by your neurological system. In fact, the bionic implants we've given you now display a synergy I'd only dreamed of. You're three times faster and more than five times stronger than before—not to mention your increased stamina. The nanobots cycling through your systems are able to supply you with an almost constant stream of energy."

Auriga paced the exercise room, picking up a massive dumbbell and curling it absentmindedly. "I'm glad you're happy with the results, Doc, but I can't help but remember the old saying about something that sounds too good to be true. You're still waiting for any possible side effects to manifest before you go under the knife yourself."

"I've been forthright with you throughout this process, Mr. Auriga. In fact, I'd be happy to share with you some of the side effects we've observed in the subjects who were augmented by the Greys."

Auriga's idle demeanor ruptured as Orion and Lyra shot into his thoughts. "What side effects?"

"Well, for starters, the Greys are more concerned with short-term results than with long-term sustainability. Their bionic implants feed from the energy of the host, rather than supplying it *to* the host, as we've engineered ours to do."

"You mean they age the organs prematurely and cut the life expectancy of the subject?"

"Significantly so. The star that burns twice as bright burns half as long."

Auriga's mouth was a thin line. He turned his back to her, still repeating the weight-lifting motion.

"And along those lines," she continued, "we've noticed increasingly aggressive behavior in the Greys' subjects. I've theorized that this may not be a wholly biological function, however."

"What else would it be? Behavioral?"

"Possibly. It's hard to make these conjectures without knowing the details of the procedures that the subjects were involved with, but it appears to me that a person's behavior might become…uncharacteristic after an abduction event."

"How so?" Auriga asked.

"I'm surprised you have to ask. A fifteen-year-old boy with no history of violence helped you massacre a large number of Lacertas in a UCO facility. A sixteen-year-old girl, also with no prior offenses, helped you shoot up the UCO headquarters in broad daylight immediately after that."

"I can assure you, they had very good reasons for doing so."

"That's precisely my point. I believe we can rule out that they were acting under the express influence of the Greys—perhaps not in the first instance, but certainly in the second. The UCO has worked hand in glove with the Greys since even before First Contact was officially recognized. It makes no sense for the aliens to facilitate a slaughter at their headquarters. I believe the teenagers, like yourself, were there for their own reasons."

Auriga returned the dumbbell to the rack and pulled on a clean black T-shirt—supplied by Fornax Enterprises, as evidenced by the asymmetrical golden chevron logo on the breast. "You're saying that the augmentations they received made violence a more viable option in pursuing their objections, and so they became more aggressive."

"Yes—behaviorally so, as an incidental result of the surgery. Our knowledge of the aliens' physiology is limited, but I don't believe their bodies use hormones in the same way ours do. They've disregarded the effects of serotonin, testosterone, adrenaline, and so forth, approaching the procedures from a purely surgical perspective and neglecting internal medicine."

"You're building super-soldiers, and they're building biomechanical freaks."

"That's a bit stronger than I would have worded it, but yes. It's almost like they're perfecting a design for powerful yet expendable warriors before putting their prototype into mass production."

"Shock troops." Prickles cascaded through Auriga's body.

Vulpecula's face was grim. "I think now you understand why I'm doing what I'm doing."

A shrieking bell clamored in the facility, making them both jump. Red lights pulsed in their beacons high up on the wall. Vulpecula produced a key card and had the hallway door open in a flash. "Stay here," she directed as the portal slid shut after her. Through the reinforced windows, Auriga watched her hurry down the hall, her eyebrows furrowed in worry.

Alone, Auriga paced the room. There were no monitors or exterior windows in the gym, and he recalled the sensation of possibly being trapped on board the Grey saucer. As he fought to shut out the obstreperous alarm that dominated all other sounds, he could discern the chaotic scramble of personnel elsewhere in the halls. A nagging itch worried his constitution; he felt coiled like a spring. He leaned against an exercise machine, folded his arms, and counted to twenty. Then he marched to the hallway door that the doctor had exited through and demolished it with a single sharp kick.

He strode into the corridor, turning to his right and following the path he had seen Vulpecula take. Up ahead, attendants hurried along, their white coats tinted with angry flashes of red from the intermittent lights. It seemed he was heading to the front of the facility, passing more laboratories and consultation rooms on either side. Most were empty and betrayed signs of hastily abandoned projects.

The hallway widened into a nexus, and the wide counters of a reception bank hosted three figures who studied the screens at a security station. When Auriga advanced behind the counter and joined them, Vulpecula looked up from the monitors to glower at him—but he did not acknowledge the stare. Instead, Auriga looked past her and the station's Protectorate officer to evaluate the third man.

Corvus appeared to be somewhat the worse for wear after their last encounter: his smooth skin was clammy, and his obsidian eyes were ringed with red. His disheveled hair had lost its gloss, but he wore slacks and shirtsleeves rather than a hospital gown, and his posture retained the pomp and dignity he had carried before, even with the betrayal of injuries lurking beneath. The two men regarded each other darkly.

"You can't be here," Vulpecula said. The man in the Protectorate uniform swiveled, his hand moving to the sidearm on his belt, but with a fast motion, Auriga caught the guard's wrist.

Still locking eyes with Corvus, Auriga said to the doctor, "I'm not going to be caged up and kept in the dark. Starting right now, I'm not a prisoner or a lab rat—I'm a willing participant who expects full disclosure not only about the operations but about anything else that's going on here. If you can't do that, then I walk—and I'd love it if you tried to stop me."

Corvus said nothing, holding Auriga's gaze with a measured look. Auriga saw no hatred in the expression, only quiet contemplation. Surprise was absent as well: the psionic man was already aware and accepting of his presence here at Fornax. Auriga released the officer's arm, and the man rubbed his wrist with a pained frown.

"We can have this conversation later, Mr. Auriga," Vulpecula said. "In the meantime, if you're not happy with the arrangements here, whether we can stop you from walking away is a moot point. Even if we can't, I'm sure *they* can."

She gestured to one of the security monitors, and he stepped closer to study the grainy image. A camera on the building's roof was zooming in on a ragtag convoy of vehicles that dragged curlicues of smoke and dust behind as they raced toward the laboratory. Auriga thought of his Resistance brethren but saw that this was impossible: although hardy and reinforced, these were solar-powered city construction vehicles, not the rough-and-tumble diesel transports used by the nomadic desert folk. He watched as the smaller pickups and vans fanned out, dropping back to defer to a giant dump truck that edged its way to the front of the pack. The assortment of speeding transports looked like a lopsided chevron, an ironic parody of the one embossed upon his own shirt.

"Who are they?" he asked.

"Four days ago, a demonstration by the Anti-Augmented Foundation ended in a bloodbath," Corvus supplied. "About a dozen people were killed by a cybernetic after they cornered and confronted him on the Thoroughfare. It was just the kind of thing the AAF is always up in arms about: to them, it confirmed how dangerous, even how murderous, augmented individuals can be."

Vulpecula studied him, and again Auriga thought of a circling predator. Comprehension encircled Auriga's reeling mind. "This cybernetic—he wouldn't happen to be..."

"A sandy-haired teenage boy, wearing dark clothing, with a cybercomputer on his left arm," Corvus finished.

Auriga exhaled. "The muchacho's had quite a week."

"As secretive as our operations are, Fornax Enterprises is still the leading name in genetic engineering and human augmentation," Vulpecula said. "It's an obvious target for retaliation. Even though Orion Danes has never had the slightest connection with this facility, it hardly matters. The AAF's propaganda machine could garner a lot of support after a public massacre like that."

"What kind of security does this place have?" Auriga asked the Protectorate officer.

"Reinforced barriers at the perimeter, but nothing that would hold up to a convoy like that. Eleven officers, counting myself, with tactical gear and an assortment of semiautomatic ballistic weapons. Electronic locks and sally ports throughout the facility."

"That's it?" Auriga stormed.

"This is a genetics laboratory, not a military stronghold," Vulpecula said.

"What about escaping? You've got to have aerial transport on the roof, at least for medical emergencies."

"Our pilot is on loan to the UCO headquarters to assist with the aftermath of the attack you caused," she said. "Can you fly a helicopter?"

Auriga didn't answer but turned back to the bank of screens. The camera panned outward now, revealing the scant distance between the facility's outer barrier and the rampaging dump truck that was spearheading the charge. The Protectorate man left them and hurried up the corridor, barking orders into his comlink.

"Give me a weapon," Auriga demanded.

"Out of the question," Vulpecula shot back.

"I know there's not a lot of good faith here, but I trusted you to screw around with my insides. You should at least let me pick up a weapon in my own defense."

"It would be too easy for you to play the turncoat," she said. "Your scars from the surgery are minimal, so you don't appear to be enhanced. You have a prolific history of attacking the UCO and its various causes. Don't act like it hasn't already occurred to you to shoot me in the back and escape with the AAF. I'm not putting my life's work in jeopardy to take a chance on you."

"What do you expect me to do, then?"

"Get back to your quarters and stay there. You're wasting precious time as it is."

"You're going to need help fighting," Auriga said. "Don't cut off your nose to spite your face."

She locked eyes with him, resolute and unflinching even when the horrendous squeal of crumpling metal announced the flattening of the perimeter fence. The blaring of the alarm changed to an intense Klaxon, and the overhead floodlights switched to a deep crimson. Outside, the clatter of small-arms fire rose above the angry roar of the convoy's engines.

It was Corvus who spoke up. "He's right, Noreen. If we don't give him a *chance* to fight with us, he won't have a *reason* to fight with us. By treating him like a captive, he'll only work that much harder against us."

Auriga smirked. "Listen to the guy. We all know I'm not going to sit in my room like a good kid. You might as well put me to use."

Vulpecula's eyes flashed before she broke the stare. In a swift motion, she cast her white lab coat to the floor, revealing a black knee-length dress with the gold Fornax logo embroidered over the left breast. She retrieved a lockbox from beneath the counter and opened it with a silver key. She equipped a compact machine pistol and slung a black canvas haversack diagonally over her body. The doctor then stalked to the weapons rack on the wall, unlocked it with her key card, and hefted a carbine rifle out of its housing. She thrust the gun against Auriga's chest; he caught

151

it in both arms and quickly racked the slide.

As she piled loaded magazines into her bag, Vulpecula spoke to him over her shoulder. "It looks like you're going to get the excitement you wished for, Mr. Auriga. Get ready for your first field evaluation."

Chapter Thirteen

T he rifle bucked in Auriga's arms, spitting tapered shells one at a time from the ejection port. His bullets splashed into jagged metal blossoms on the convoy vehicles, which were circled in a tight defensive posture just inside the ruined fence. He could see only fleeting snatches of the attackers who clustered in the safety of the makeshift barricade. Someone screamed accusations and indictments through a bullhorn.

An incoming round snapped into the exterior wall of the building just at his six, and Auriga crouched farther behind the stone pedestal that supported a twisting and mesmeric modern statue. He reloaded. Several meters to his left, Protectorate men clustered at the front door of Fornax Enterprises, peppering the trucks with leapfrogging bursts of gunfire. Someone screamed orders and commands through a bullhorn.

Auriga waited several seconds before sneaking a peek back over the upper edge of the pedestal. The sun blazed off the hoods of the black trucks, ripples of desert heat wafted from the scalding metal, and sand whipped through the courtyard in opaque clouds. The hulking vehicles obscured the hostiles, hiding any telltale signs about their outfitting and intended tactics. He observed their tight grouping, and wished for some kind of explosive ordnance. Then a muzzle flash glinted against the sunlight and a pockmark appeared in the statue five centimeters from his right eye, showering his cheek with chips of metal. He ducked again: he'd have to do a better job of staying hidden.

From his makeshift cover, he analyzed the tactical situation in the courtyard. The Protectorate men stationed behind deployable shields near the front door blasted away at the barricade, their salvos unfruitful but effective in keeping the hostiles pinned down. On the other hand, the attackers weren't unloading a barrage of fire—rather, they were picking and choosing their shots. Auriga had seen several near misses.

"They're trying to wear us down!" he shouted to the lieutenant, distinguishable by the white stripe at his collar. The officer shook his head, not understanding. Auriga tried again, cursing the fact that he hadn't been given a comlink. "They're luring us out, making us go through our ammo! Conserve the ammo!"

A penetrating clack sounded from the flattened fence, and Auriga shaded his eyes to track a glittering orb rising in a fast trajectory against the blinding sun: LITEs, or "long-range incendiary torch explosives." He lay back to get a better angle on the sky, popping rounds off while taking care to remain in cover. His fourth attempt connected, and the sphere bloomed in a vibrant orange flourish. Another clack, and another; sun-colored balls the size of cantaloupes soared in a speedy arc toward the building.

"Shoot the LITEs!" the security men shouted. Gunfire rose to the sky, and more beautiful flourishes opened, bringing flame down to the earth. The incendiary munitions burst short of their intended targets, and Auriga returned his focus to the mobile black barricade. The unseen men behind the trucks had to be up to something, and he needed to get a better vantage point.

He spotted a more favorable position: twenty meters away, a

vacated brick guardhouse stood next to the drive at the neglected and barred front gate. The sentry within had pulled back to the main building, but the square shack would provide adequate cover and a better line of sight to his enemies, if Auriga could get there. It was time to move, while their attention was consumed in launching the LITEs or in counteracting the bulk of the Protectorate men at the front door.

Auriga summoned a jolt of adrenaline, and inhaled. His body hummed with energy, and he launched from behind the pedestal, covering ground in a dead sprint. The landscape blurred for an instant, and he was in cover against the brick wall in no time. Futile pops sounded as bullets kicked the dust where he had been—he had moved faster than the reaction time of his opponents, who were shooting at an indistinct shape that had already passed by.

He stepped along the wall to the far side of the security post. The barking reports of gunshots continued sporadically behind the trucks. He should be able to flank them now, but he wouldn't dare a glimpse around the corner this time: it would be a monstrous gambit to betray his position. Instead, Auriga shunted his head and rifle together past the edge of the brick, lined up the sights, and fired upon the first black-clad man he saw hiding at the barricade. The figure flailed against the side of a truck as Auriga snapped off multiple rounds—but the dust billowing off his dry, bulky sleeveless shirt betrayed the tactical vest underneath. Auriga notched his aim a bit higher and scored a head shot, punching a scraggly hole into the man's balaclava.

Even as the attacker's corpse slid down against the side door of the vehicle, return fire popped in Auriga's direction. He retreated into cover, ejecting his magazine and slamming a fresh one into place. Only a few bullets struck the side of the brick wall, though:

155

no more than a single operative seemed to be shooting back at his position. Instinct nagged at Auriga, asserting that something was wrong—an unwelcome distraction in the midst of a firefight, but Auriga could not disregard its subtle insistence. *Where is everyone? Several trucks can't be driven by only a couple of enemies.*

Then, like a second adrenaline jolt from within, his thoughts caught up with the reality of what he had seen: it wasn't waves of heat that he had noticed near the hot metal of the vehicles.

Auriga sidled back along the wall to get within sight of the Protectorate men at the front door, staying on the leeward side that kept cover between himself and the barricade at the fence. He waved an arm, signaling the lieutenant again. "Active camo!" he screamed. "Watch your flanks, they have disruptors!"

The officer caught Auriga's movement, but his words of reply were drowned out amid the gunfire. Auriga tried again: "Active camo! They'll get behind you!"

Now Auriga saw the ripples moving through the courtyard: in plain sight, yet so easy to miss, looking for all the world like curls of hot air in the sweltering sun. He fired at the blurred apparitions, guessing at the positions of the men, but his efforts were inconclusive. Some of his shots may have connected, but he had no way to tell: the photostatic disruptors hid their users much too effectively. Auriga sprayed more bullets into the rippling horizon, hoping that his inexplicable choice of target might attract a change of tactics from the officers.

Now the lieutenant seemed to understand: Auriga watched as he redirected the gunfire from his men. Lead rounds chewed up mists of sand as the Protectorate men saturated the area to their left with a hail of fire. The wind stirred forth its opaque clouds again, and this time, Auriga spied silhouettes, ghostly and indistinct, in the choking fog. He fired until his weapon ran empty, connecting a few times: some of the shapes bucked and faded into the earth, but there were still more men moving to a dangerous and deadly position past the deployable shields.

Gunfire erupted from nowhere, cutting into the Protectorate men at their left flank. Four of the officers went down as a barrage of bullets tore through them. The lieutenant and three others wheeled back into the shelter of the doorway, returning blind fire. Auriga hastened to reload and distribute more covering fire, but the shell casing from his third shot jammed in the ejection port amid an obstruction of sand and dirt. He tugged at the slide release, trying to force it all the way open, but the jam didn't loosen. Instead, he dug the shell out with his index finger, slicing it on the fiery metal, burning a pink crescent into his flesh. He jerked his hand free just before the bolt snapped closed on the empty chamber like a pair of hungry jaws.

He racked the slide again, chambering a fresh round. Another of the Protectorate men had fallen in the onslaught, and he winced at the delay that had cost one defender his life. He shouldered the rifle to resume the attack, but the rippling shapes were now absent, and the Fornax soldiers retreated backward to the front of the building.

The absence of gunfire was surreal after the brutal exchange. With the hollow silence weighing on his ears, Auriga repositioned for another look at the barricade—but as he turned, keeping his back to the baking bricks, he saw a dark figure at the corner of the wall. The other enemy from behind the vehicles had snuck around the guard shack, pistol in hand, while Auriga's attention was diverted.

Auriga twisted and lurched as the loud reports began again. He'd been flanked; there was no cover, and a desperate surge of speed was his only defense. He flew away from the wall, diving acrobatically, tumbling in the air as shots zipped past his body. His rifle toppled into the sand, and he used his empty hands to push against the scorching ground in a forward roll, tucking his legs and then launching up with a powerful push. A bullet ripped against his left shoulder, tearing a gash that splashed dark blood on the nearby wall. Jolts of painful fire mixed with the adrenaline coursing through him.

He'd covered a lot of ground with the maneuver, and flown to within arm's reach of the black-clad man. Auriga's hand shot out, gripped the enemy's wrist, and twisted it. His other hand wrapped around the man's pistol-wielding hand in a controlling position. The assailant's struggles were like those of a child in Auriga's unyielding grasp, and he felt wrist bones crunch before forcing the muzzle of the gun under the operative's chin and slamming down on the man's trigger finger.

The report was muffled by the point-blank pressure of the barrel, and sickening spray cascaded as the body fell lifeless onto the dust. Auriga took a step back, the pistol now in his own grip, and examined his shoulder. The shot had merely grazed him along the top of the bicep, and as he watched in amazement, the ruddy drips slowed in their course and then halted altogether. Beads of sweat sparkled on his brow, and his shirt was soaked. He swept the desolate courtyard again and discerned that no one else was there—even after scrutinizing the waves of humidity he saw all around. This time, he felt sure they were only ripples of heat.

Auriga raced to the scene of carnage just outside the facility's front entry. There was nothing to be done for these men, and everyone in the laboratory was now in danger. He snatched a comlink from a corpse's jaw, folded it over his right ear, and squeezed the transmit button. "Attention, the hostiles' positions are unknown and they may be in the building, equipped with tactical weapons and photostatic disruptors. Five officers down at the main entry. Please respond. Over."

He snatched a smoking submachine gun from the ground. The pistol had to be tucked into his waistband for lack of a holster—an arrangement he disdained for its lack of sturdiness, but Auriga loathed the prospect of being unarmed much more.

The comlink had still given no reply as he nudged one of the double glass doors open. Broken glass littered a cramped foyer; bullet holes and bloody splotches on the next set of doors were a grim herald, but he saw and heard no signs of other combatants. He threw the next door wide and hustled forward into the hallway, pausing for cover in a laboratory door's recess. It was tempting to charge forward headlong into the fray, but caution prevailed; although it had been scarcely a minute since he'd lost contact with what was left of the Protectorate group, Auriga could not be certain of anything that had unfolded in that time.

Shell casings littered the floor; there had been plenty of trouble, but silence alone now occupied the halls. Auriga was thankful for the brass shells: they would crunch underfoot even if a potential attacker was concealed from sight. It would be better if the entire hallway were carpeted with them. He would not be anticipating an abrupt muzzle flash from nowhere and the painful shock of a bullet whistling him to oblivion. His head would not be itching, worrisome, a fateful harbinger of execution by an invisible foe. He would not be thinking of failure, of the unexpected end of life... He would not be afraid.

It was doubly afflictive, grappling with this insistent apprehension, so soon after he'd been ready for the final curtain. He had not feared death when the Protectorate had stormed his hideout—he had thought only of the task that remained to him. Now the task of slaying Corvus was deferred. Uncertainty was the villain that prevailed over a sure demise: even if his actions were those of a man running on a treadmill and gaining no ground, even if the path was difficult to tread for all the brass casings upon it, it was a thousand times preferable to having no action available at all.

Auriga edged out of the doorway, sweeping the submachine gun across the empty corridor. He kept his eyes peeled for distortions in the light as he tiptoed to the security station where he'd met with Corvus and Vulpecula before the siege had begun. The rattle of weapons fire echoed elsewhere in the building, and the comlink awoke in his ear. Instead of confident orders and appraisals, though, what he heard was panicked screaming. He yanked the headset out and cast it away, then hustled toward the sounds of the disturbance.

The unmistakable scent of smoke now reached his nostrils. The harsh pops grew sporadic and intermittent and mixed with the muffled crackling roar of flames somewhere in the building. The Klaxon alarm wailed on. Rounding a corner, Auriga fell in beside Corvus, who also hurried—albeit with a pained stagger—toward the sounds of distress. Auriga had no time to reflect on the unlikely pairing before the psionic's arm gripped his left bicep, drawing him up short. Corvus gestured with fury, and a dazzling spade-shaped knife streaked from his fingers. The blade hung in midair, stabbing into nothing, but deceptive ripples shimmered around an invisible man's form. Weapons fire went wild, punching crooked dots in the ceiling and further delineating the enemy's hazy silhouette. Auriga's gun clapped four times, and blood burst in thick springs from thin air before the ghostly form crumpled.

The photostatic disruptor fizzled, revealing the dead operative sprawled on the tile. Corvus's phosphorescent dagger remained lodged in the man's forehead for a few seconds longer before shattering apart in a kaleidoscopic array. Auriga shot a dire look at Corvus, who surveyed the hallway before nodding once in satisfaction.

"How did you see him?" Auriga demanded. "He was standing perfectly still—there were no ripples."

"I can see their auras," Corvus explained. "The disruptors don't mask those a bit."

Wonderstruck, Auriga turned his gaze to the corpse. "There's no way these guys are AAF," he said.

"I think you're right," Corvus said. "They're too well equipped and organized. This isn't an angry mob we're dealing with."

"Yeah—if they wanted retribution for what happened in the city, they could just burn the lab to the ground with everyone in it. They've got plenty of LITEs; why even bother coming into a burning building?"

"It only makes sense if they want something—and don't plan on leaving any witnesses." Corvus rolled up the sleeves of his black dress shirt; Auriga noted the slender hands were now empty, but deadly nonetheless.

"Where's the doc?" Auriga asked.

"When the building was breached, she said she wanted to secure the things that were most important to her work."

Auriga frowned. "You let her go off by herself?"

"I saw an intruder, and after I dealt with him, she was gone. I was trying to find her, but I ran into you first." Corvus turned dark eyes on him, obsidian pools that were tinged with weariness. "You may not like this idea any better than I do, but I think we should stick together until this is over."

There was so much Auriga could say to him. *No, I don't trust you. I think you'll kill me the first chance you get. I don't know if you're telling the truth about Vulpecula. You know more than you're letting on.* A storm raged inside him. Time was ticking, action must be taken, and Corvus probably sensed these unsaid questions all the same. *You're lucky, to know if something is truth or deception with nothing more than a simple glance. How can I know if we're on the same side? I don't even know what side I'm on myself. You're a weapon that might blow up in my face—but to stay alive, I need all the weapons I can get. And aren't you thinking the exact same thing about me?*

Instead, though, all Auriga said was, "Try to keep up."

Corvus nodded once, then stepped over the dead man to continue down the hall. Auriga took care to avoid the slick blood that was spreading into a ruby-red lake, and hurried after him. Side by side, the pair scoured the building, peeking into darkened laboratories and scrutinizing the pathways ahead that were from time to time bedecked with shell casings or a fallen Protectorate officer. The smoke grew thicker, screening their efforts with dark clouds, bringing with it an urgent heat rivaling that of the desert outside.

At one corner, the psionic man called for a halt, and Auriga stole a glance around the bend with caution. A side doorway was open, and as he watched, the shaft of light that stretched into the hall was broken by shadows from movement within.

"What room is that?" Auriga whispered.

"Supply closet," Corvus said.

Auriga's eyebrows angled, but he held his tongue. Gesturing with his chin, he crept to the far wall and then sidled over toward the occupied room. Corvus stayed close, bent forward with his fingers splayed. The Resistance man reached the threshold of the door and ducked inside, raising his weapon; his companion followed with a small, shimmering blade sparking to life in his fingers.

Shelves lined the sides of the modest room, stocked with powered-down cleanerbots and an assortment of parts and office supplies. At the opposite end, Vulpecula stood with one hand on the steel bars of a ladder, the other cradling the haversack to her side. Auriga glimpsed a pair of datapads and a hard metal carrying case peeking out of the bag. Next to the doctor, a black-clad commando held the doctor's machine pistol while her hands were occupied. Sunlight blazed down on them both from the open hatch in the ceiling.

The masked man trained the weapon on the newcomers. "Hold it. Don't do anything stupid," he warned. Auriga kept the barrel of his gun pointed at the operative, but Corvus's eyes, narrowed to slits, studied Vulpecula.

"I should have known," Corvus growled.

The doctor kept still, ready to ascend the ladder, while leveling a hard gaze at the psionic. "Why the surprise? I told you exactly what I was doing: making sure my work was safe." She cinched the haversack tighter to her body.

Realization dawned on Auriga like the sunlight that poured down from a doorway above. "You hired mercenaries to kill everyone and destroy Fornax Enterprises. Now that you know that the procedures behind your theory are sound, you were going to take your work and disappear, and let everyone blame it on the AAF."

Her question seemed to echo in the room. *Why the surprise?* Auriga's anger blazed—mostly at himself. What had he expected from Vulpecula? Yes, he'd made a deal with the devil when he'd agreed to the operation. Power always came with its price. What stung him was not that he might have died on Vulpecula's operating table but that she had declared him expendable after he hadn't.

Vulpecula's mouth pursed. "You have no idea what I've gone through to make this happen. The years of work, the sacrifices—"

"Sacrifices?" Auriga said. "Your test subjects have all sacrificed their lives. I'm the first human subject who survived the operation. I put my life on the line just like you did. Don't tell me I don't understand."

"You're not going to make me feel bad about this. There is always a price to pay for progress—and usually that price is measured in human lives. *That's* something I know you understand."

"What I don't get is why you would throw this all away," Auriga said. "You have everything going for you here: the equipment, the funding, the secrecy. Why burn down your own lab?"

"Because she wants to be off the grid," Corvus said. "Away from the UCO and anyone else who knows what she's doing. Were you going to sell these procedures on the black market, Noreen? Surely you won't be content with just elevating mankind's raw potential in the name of altruism."

"Your foolishness is astonishing, Josiah," she snarled. "How dare you cast those sanctimonious judgments at me. You're a puppet for the architects of humanity's downfall—nothing you've ever done has expanded mankind's potential."

An explosion thundered nearby, followed by a second. Tanks of oxygen and propane were bursting in the neighboring laboratories, and the cannonade brought a flinch to everyone in the room. Startled, the commando tightened his hand, squeezing off a burst of rounds. Corvus staggered back through the door, bullets ricocheting from the invisible wall of his mind, but Auriga heard a grunt of pain from the psionic as one round found its mark. Auriga jerked backward and lost his balance in escaping the assault; his own shots went wild, hammering into the shelves. He crashed to the floor on his back and saw Vulpecula take the ladder in a single bound, flying four meters straight up to disappear through the hatch in a blink.

The commando stood over Auriga and brought the machine pistol down to finish the job. Auriga bucked with a vicious kick, connecting the heel of his boot into the man's kneecap. Bones crunched, and the man's agonized squeal of pain was swallowed by a third detonation. The submachine gun hit the ground at the same time as the crippled enemy, and Auriga's searching hand found the pistol that had fallen from his waistband. Auriga climbed to his feet, casting an ominous shadow over the gunman who writhed and cradled his shattered knee, and shot him to death with three judicious blasts.

Smoke swallowed the tiny room, and the torrid, dry air made Auriga choke. Corvus came limping out of the sweltering billows, clutching a blood-slicked hand to his stomach. Auriga vaulted up the ladder, gripping the fiery metal rungs with one hand and the smoking pistol in the other. He rolled out onto the baking roof amid rising black plumes. Here on top of the building, something large and powerful beat the air, whipping the pillars of smoke into rising veils.

Auriga circled the hatch, moving to get a better view, as Corvus clambered out onto the roof. Fifty meters away, Vulpecula pulled the door closed from inside a sleek black helicopter as its blades whirled into invisibility. Already it was beginning to rise, the skids leaving the concrete surface and climbing into the heat-soaked air. From the pilot's seat, a familiar face peered at him, half obscured by dark driving goggles.

"*Canalla,*" Auriga said, raising the sidearm and moving forward. He fired several times, but from this distance, the bullets missed widely. The slide locked back on an empty chamber.

The helicopter lifted away. Auriga tensed for a sprint but hesitated. Giving it everything he had, he might catch the lower rails with a flying leap, but to what end? He would then be a sitting duck, dangling from an airborne craft and easily picked off by its occupants. He dropped the spent pistol onto the smoldering concrete and shaded his eyes to watch the fugitives depart.

High above the building, the helicopter turned toward the west. The nose dipped as it set a course into the desert and sped away from the hellish chaos of the blazing facility. As Auriga looked on, watching it vanish against the reddening horizon, a slight wobble shook the craft; it jerked and pitched with tremors. In seconds, the lurching intensified—and soon, the chopper quaked in the air. It careened in a dangerous spiral, losing altitude, whipping in ever-tightening circles as if tumbling down a drain. The helpless craft plunged to the earth and was lost to sight for a moment, until a languid drift of smoke rose to mark its grave.

Auriga turned to the psionic man beside him, whose soot-streaked face was awash with concentration and effort. Then the intensity left Corvus's features, and he faltered, sagging on his feet, nearly collapsing before Auriga bore him up with a sturdy arm.

The concrete was broiling now; the rubber soles of Auriga's boots were melting, and thick, stifling clouds buffeted him. Another explosion rumbled within the building, larger than the others, shaking the entire structure and almost toppling him.

"We've got to move it," he screamed, but Corvus, leaning against him for support, gave no reply. Auriga wrapped the man's arm around his shoulders and hustled to the east side of the roof, half dragging Corvus. Ripples of heat and sun obfuscated the courtyard at the front of the building as they reached the edge.

The Illuminatus was barely conscious. Auriga hoisted Corvus over his shoulder in a fireman's carry, then planted one foot on the brink and leapt off into the choking waves of smoke.

Chapter Fourteen

The compound loomed ahead, a skeleton standing bleak and bare in the dust. The simple chain-link fence cut diamond patterns into Auriga's vision. As he staggered through the gate, he avoided eye contact with the sentries, whose scowls were half hidden behind bandanas. Beside him, Corvus still leaned on his shoulder, taking uneven steps with one hand pressed to his stomach, but managing to match Auriga's pace.

The Resistance youths, armed with AK-47s, withheld their customary demands for identification; Auriga was known here, of course, although the circumstances surrounding his arrival were certainly unusual. They'd have been watching the visitors approach on foot through the wasteland for two kilometers.

One of the stone-faced guards asked in a muffled voice, "Anyone else with you?" When Auriga shook his head, the reinforced gate was pulled closed.

The pair made its way through the courtyard, past the sandbags and trenches to the Depot. The setting sun dyed the building's bricks a splotchy mauve. Corvus settled onto a waist-high fortification with care while Auriga pounded at the dented metal door. After a few seconds, it swung inward with a rusty creak.

The frowning, mustachioed Warden leaned on the doorjamb, blocking the entry. "*Qué quieres*, Auriga?" he barked. "I ain't in the mood for you right now."

Auriga was parched, but this wasn't the reason the words stuck in his throat. "I need help," he said.

The man folded his arms in expectation, and said nothing. A smirk grew beneath the dark mustache.

"We got into a lot of trouble with the UCO and barely made it out," Auriga began. "We escaped from one of their facilities when it was attacked. We got a pickup truck that belonged to the attackers and tried to drive here, but we ran out of gas. We had to walk the rest of the way."

A weighty pause unrolled. A trickle of dirty sweat crawled down Auriga's forehead, and he wiped it away with a grimy hand. The Warden kept his silence, and Auriga tried again. "I need some gas, amigo. Just a few liters—this is the closest place. I'll leave my friend here and walk back to the truck, then I'll come back and get him. I'll come back and pay you, I swear."

"No." The Warden sneered. "Gold up front, or you don't get nada. And I want double the price."

Auriga's skin prickled in a chill, but he continued to sweat. "I don't have anything on me, man. We just jumped off the roof of a burning building, okay? I don't have a gun or nothing. I just got the clothes on my back. *Por favor*. Please. You know me, you know I'm good for it. I got a wounded man here, we have no water. Help us, amigo, please."

"Yeah, I see you got a wounded man," the Warden said. "I don't know his name, but I know his face—he's UCO. Look at that shirt you're wearing: Fornax Enterprises? That's UCO too, ain't it? I always knew you had cojones, Auriga, but this takes it to a whole new level."

The rusty door began to close, but Auriga slammed his palm against it. "I'm not UCO, you *idiota*. This is just a shirt. And it's complicated, but I need him alive. There's a girl's life depending on this. I need water, rest, medicine, anything. Don't do this."

"What about the guys you were traveling with before, Auriga? I know they're dead."

A figure moved inside the outpost, behind the Warden. Auriga could identify the man with the gold tooth, peeking through the doorway. When Auriga caught his eye, the man turned sheepishly away.

"One of them was a mercenary," Auriga explained, fighting to stay calm. "He was trying to get close to me, and he killed one of my men. He paid the other to chicken out—that's how you got the story. I hate that it happened, but it wasn't my fault."

"That ain't what I heard."

"What you heard wasn't how it happened." Rage was bubbling to the surface, but Auriga pushed it down. "Don't listen to that *mentiroso* in there. He's just trying to save his reputation. I'm not with the UCO. I got arrested, but I escaped. That Fornax place is history, and everybody's dead. Just let us stay here for the night. Give us a bottle of water, anything. I'm begging you."

"I don't want this to get ugly. I don't want to see you get shot or nothing, so I think you better go, *vato*. Don't come back here again."

The Warden pushed the metal door closed, and a latch clicked from inside. Auriga's palm remained on the hot surface for several seconds before curling into a fist. He turned back to Corvus as the sentries from the gate formed a semicircle around the two of them. The Resistance men held their rifles at a low-ready position in an indelicate nonverbal command.

Auriga helped Corvus to his feet, slung the wounded man's arm around his shoulders, and walked with him to the gate. On the way out, one of the young soldiers handed him a one-liter bottle of water. It was lukewarm and two-thirds full, but

Auriga accepted it gratefully. Sand eddied and swirled against the setting sun, muting the dusty colors that spread through the blank landscape that lay hungry and dormant, ready to swallow them whole.

***

The fever of the daytime had broken, and the desert was now a serene tone of midnight blue. They marched west, Corvus's steps faltering at times but not slacking in their progress.

"There's a *vaquero* across the river who will help us for sure," Auriga said. "The sun's gone down, so the hard part's over. We can make it."

Corvus smiled weakly. "Staying positive, I see."

"*Sí*, keep your spirits up—no need to make this walk any longer than it has to be. What I wouldn't give for your hovercar right about now."

The smile widened. "Me too, but it's a hundred and fifty klicks south of here, in a place called Fort Davis."

"Really? Shoot, I thought the muchacho was going to take the tracking device out."

"He did, but I'm a psionic. I know where my car keys are at all times."

Auriga chuckled. "Why couldn't you make the Warden change his mind about helping us?"

"I was trying the whole time you were talking to him," Corvus admitted. "It's a taxing effort, and I'm not at my best right now." His face had a rosy flush in the moon's glow.

"You took out that helicopter with no problem."

"I wouldn't say that. It already takes a great deal of blood and oxygen to fuel the human brain—and much more so at the increased level of a psionic."

"So if you overexerted yourself, you'd fall into a coma like Lyra did."

"Yes. She's gifted, but she wasn't ready to use her powers so aggressively. I couldn't allow Vulpecula to escape, so I did what I had to do. I probably would have never made it off the roof if not for you, though."

The corner of Auriga's mouth twitched, and he wished for a cigarillo, a shot of mescal, something to mask the poignancy of the conversation. He had to settle for a sip of stale-tasting water. "Well, I shot you in the neck. I think I owed it to you to get you out of there."

"Indeed. I hadn't forgotten that." Corvus's response was mirthless. "I never ordered you to be taken alive, you know."

"I know." Auriga breathed his thanks to Lyra, and passed the water bottle to Corvus. The Illuminatus drank sparingly. Warm wind stirred the silence around them.

"Is she going to be all right?" Auriga asked after a beat.

"Of course," Corvus said. "I have confidence in the Greys. There's no better place for her to be."

"I don't see how you can have such faith in those sadistic freaks."

"I know the Greys better than you do, Auriga. Suppose that a surgeon were to perform a painful operation on a child, saving his life. Suppose that the surgeon and child did not speak the same language. The child, not understanding what was going on, would merely think that the surgeon was sadistic and cruel."

"This isn't a question of a language barrier, man. The Greys aren't saving our lives. That's just UCO propaganda, and I'm surprised you still believe it."

"What's untrue about it? Humanity is a stagnating species on a dying planet. The rate of damage we were inflicting on Earth over the past hundred years was unsustainable, even before the war against the Lacertas—a war we would have lost without the Greys' intervention."

"We would have beaten the Lizzies. It wouldn't have been pretty, but we would have done it." Auriga's voice had a forlorn edge.

"Even if mankind had managed to win against the Lacertas, the cost would have been too great to bear. The casualties from the war itself, and the secondary casualties afterward. The radioactive fallout, the supply shortages, the utter breakdown of societies—it would have pushed us to the brink of extinction. Now man is resurgent instead. It was all planned to be this way, so that we would survive and thrive."

Auriga cast an alarmed glance at Corvus. "What are you talking about?"

"You remember what I told you before about the Roswell incident," the Illuminatus said. "The aircraft recovered at the crash site was nothing more than a weather balloon that was pioneering an experimental attempt to intercept Soviet communications. However, the publicity surrounding this event, when it was believed that the remains of a genuine flying saucer had been found, led the authorities of the day to ask themselves what would have happened if that had actually been the case. President Truman launched a secret organization called 'Majestic 12' to track and investigate paranormal activity, specifically that concerning UFOs."

"Obviously those efforts paid off."

"Yes, right away. I told you before that the Greys have exhibited influence and have bestowed gifts upon humanity since before recorded history. It's not that they ever intended to keep their presence here a secret—they were just highly selective about with whom they shared this information. They wished to make contact with humanity's leaders, but it wouldn't do to park a flying saucer on the White House lawn and come inside for a chat."

"Majestic 12 gave them a chance to make contact."

"Yes. They could reveal themselves, with discretion, to those humans who were actively looking for them: humans who could, in turn, pass along information about the Greys to the appropriate world leaders."

"How did they get around the language barrier?" Auriga questioned. "I'm guessing that since they had studied humans for so long, they could understand us, but we couldn't communicate with them."

"That's correct. It was time for another, much older, secret society to come to the fore: one that had studied the mysteries of the world since ancient times."

"The Illuminati." Auriga saw the pieces coming together.

"The Illuminati was, and is, a collection of the most gifted minds on Earth: savants who were capable of perceiving worlds and concepts beyond this plane. Almost every psionic who ever lived was either a member, or felt its influence. These men and women could communicate with the Greys and share their secrets—and they quickly found that there was something of great importance the aliens...wanted us...to do."

"And what was that?"

Corvus didn't answer right away. Auriga let the silence hang, crediting the Illuminatus with reluctance to reveal the more sensitive information about his brotherhood. When the seconds ticked on, Auriga cast a sideways glance at the psionic, and stopped in his tracks. The wounded man's skin was ashen and drawn, his lips blanched; he swerved on his feet and pitched forward in exhaustion. Auriga caught him as he collapsed, and helped to recline him on a slope of smooth sand.

"Corvus, stay with me here," he coached, fetching the water bottle. "Talk to me, hombre."

Corvus took only a little water, and struggled to swallow. The bandage at his neck was soaked through with blood, as was the black shirt that now looked glossy in the starlight. Auriga removed the bandages to examine the first wound, applying gentle pressure and frowning at the red streaks that had appeared near the bullet hole, which was black and inflamed.

"It's infected." Auriga sighed. "You didn't have access to any antibiotics with everything that's happened today."

Corvus was looking past him to the sky, a dark blanket sprinkled with glittering specks. His expression was so curiously entranced that Auriga couldn't help but follow his gaze, becoming lost for an instant himself in the imponderable cosmos.

"I had hoped...I wouldn't have to...use this."

When Auriga looked back to Corvus, the wounded man had pulled a small cylinder out of his hip pocket. It was narrow and black, with a shiny metal band and a round button on the end.

"No, wait! What is that?" Auriga reached for it, distraught, but the other man's bloodstained thumb had already closed on the button. A sapphire light blinked with steady insistence.

"What did you do?" Auriga exclaimed, leaping to his feet and backing away.

"It's not a weapon," Corvus said, stretching back upon the sandy incline, his breath and words becoming incrementally more certain. "Don't worry...it's a transponder. The Greys..."

Auriga paused, dumbstruck. He took a tentative step closer, trying to examine the device from a distance. His insides were hollow, and he searched the sky, then the desert around him. What good would it do to run? There was nothing for kilometers, and soon a spaceship would be on top of them.

Corvus now lay with contemplative ease, cradling the cylinder to his chest with his right hand. "You'll be safe... They won't hurt you," he said. "You'll see that I'm right. You'll see them...the way I do."

Auriga approached, seating himself beside the wounded man. He grasped Corvus's left hand with his own.

"Corvus, there's nothing I can do," he said. "We got no supplies and we're in the middle of nowhere. If they don't come for you, I can't help."

"They'll come." Corvus's voice was serene.

The sacrosanct calm of the wilderness was captivating. Auriga, humbled by the borderless expanse that swallowed his senses, forgot his cravings and concerns, and he fixed his eyes on the infinite solitude of space. The heavens were pure and supreme; the darkness was simplicity itself. Beneath the awesome sphere that wrapped the planet like a shroud, they waited together, watching the skies.

The sapphire light blinked like a beacon, a faithful countdown to some undetermined outcome. The stars twinkled cryptically in answer.

"How long will it take for them to get here?" Auriga asked after a time.

"It takes as long as it takes. Most people wait their entire lifetime to be rescued from this world by the Greys. I'm certainly willing to wait for the rest of mine."

"Corvus..." He hesitated, wondering if it was right to speak what he was thinking. Somehow the openness of the setting beckoned him to forge onward. "I don't think they will come.

They turned their back on you in the skyscraper. They left you to die."

Feverish eyes pierced his own. "Your Resistance friends did the same thing at the Depot two hours ago."

Auriga nodded, examining the irony, tasting the truth of these words. He could no longer call himself a member of the Resistance, but that hardly drove him into the arms of the UCO. He still believed in the rebels' cause, but he now realized he no longer wished to be counted among them. The world was more complex than he had ever imagined—a battlefield with numerous fronts. It was as if he had experienced one flat plane for the entirety of his life and had only now glanced up to perceive the sky above.

"Everything I am, I owe to the Greys," Corvus went on. "How loathsome, to live and die a mortal man on this stinking rock, forever a slave to nature. How much we can learn from an entire race devoted to envisioning what *could be* instead of what *is*—that would subjugate life itself and open new horizons..."

Auriga touched the Illuminatus's forehead; it burned underneath a sheen of perspiration.

"Corvus, what was the secret task that the Greys wanted humanity to perform?"

The red-rimmed eyes were searching the heavens, and Auriga wasn't sure if the man had heard him. Then the cracked lips parted, and words came with dulcet reverence. "They wanted us...to travel to the stars..." He drew a shallow breath. "But they wanted us...to be ready first."

The sapphire beacon blinked a final time, then went dark. Clouds moved over the moon. When the Illuminatus spoke again, his words were faint and fleeting. "I'm ready now," he whispered. "I'm ready to leave the world behind."

Auriga's gaze moved from the man's flushed, upturned countenance, to the dormant transponder, to the grandeur of the limitless sky above. In the darkness left by the moon's absence, a curious glow developed. He fixed his eyes on it in shock.

Auriga lurched to his feet, staring at the strengthening light. It was indistinct but unmistakable: a soft, oval-shaped effulgence that contrasted against the starry band of the Milky Way. In a scant few moments, a flying saucer would appear in the desert, and unearthly beings would decide his fate. He had never expected them to appear. He envisioned horrendous experiments, terrible perversions. Would Corvus intercede for him? If he did, would it matter?

"It's so beautiful," Corvus murmured from behind him. "I knew they would come for me."

Auriga sweated despite the coolness of the night. He studied Corvus's enraptured face, devoid of its fever in the glow. Words failed him, and he listened.

"I was a young man when I first saw them," Corvus confessed. "I'd displayed the raw potential that they were looking for—the psionic aptitudes, the scholastic abilities. The world didn't yet know that they existed, but I could see beyond the shroud. They chose me...to journey beyond the stars..."

The light paled, and Auriga looked back to the eidolon in the sky. The ghostly cloud of light was waning: gossamer, apparitional. Again, he fixated upon it, gaining a sudden recognition.

"It's the *gegenschein*," he said. "It's not the Greys. They're not coming."

The lunar gleam now returned as the clouds thinned, defeating the spectral luminance. Auriga watched the soft oval light dissipate and die.

"It's the sunlight backscattering against cosmic dust," Auriga continued. "You can see it if it's dark enough; if you're away from the city and the time is right, the sun lines up opposite a cloud of fine particles in space, and the light gets diffused..." He trailed off, and the stillness returned. He brought a hand to his eyes, wiping away the blurriness before turning back to terrestrial reality.

Corvus lay in repose, his features solemn and quiet. His half-closed eyes mused upon the unending magnitude of the darkened heavens; Auriga reached out and drew the man's eyelids down to rest.

∗∗∗

Auriga put his shoulder against a half-buried boulder and heaved, wrenching it from the ground. The massive rock tumbled end over end a few times before settling, leaving a bowl-shaped depression in the loose, crumbling earth. He laid the slim, still body inside and used flat rocks to scoop the sand and dirt back over it.

Hunting in the silver moonlight, he retrieved an assortment of colored stones and boughs with desert flowers to arrange as an altar upon the grave. A short distance away, he was aware that a Lacerta was watching, but the ritual was not disturbed. By and by, it withdrew back into the night.

Auriga gazed at the black cylinder in the palm of his hand before wrapping his fingers closed around it. He set off to the west, leaving swirls of dust drifting in the hot, windless air. A thin trail of cinders crawled behind him, wispy with the smoke of dreams, and settled back to a landscape that belied any signs of life.

Chapter Fifteen

The entire front wall of the dilapidated shack rattled when Auriga knocked at the door, which was flimsy and rotten. He couldn't help thinking that a sharp kick would send the hovel crashing down. He angled his head to where the late-afternoon sun was denied by the brim of his black Stetson, and called out in a low voice, "Muchacho, open up, it's me."

"I can't believe you're alive," came the discordant croak from inside.

Auriga glanced over to where the black horse stood, its reins looped incongruously around the door handle of the motionless hovercar parked nearby.

"Yeah, neither can I. Let me in already." Auriga remembered that the teenager had a computer grafted into his arm and had probably scanned him from a few kilometers away. It would have the convenient effect of making Orion very difficult to sneak up on, if he wasn't otherwise distracted.

The shoddy door groaned inward, and Auriga peered into the shadows. The boy looked haggard, still wearing the same black loose-knit sweater and olive cargo pants that Auriga had last seen him in. His right hand held the lower assembly of an M16, which was angled to the ceiling.

Auriga himself was freshly shaved, wearing a brown short-sleeved button-up shirt and black denim jeans. Orion stepped back to admit his visitor; when Auriga entered the humble house, unloading the gunnysack from his shoulder, there was nowhere to set the bag that wasn't covered in pulverized debris.

"Where'd you get a horse?" Orion said. "How did you make it? What happened to Corvus?"

"The *vaquero* past the river helped me. As far as Corvus... Man, it's a long story. Here, I brought you something."

Orion grasped the leg of a small stool, tipping it to dump the rusty machine pieces occupying it onto the floor. Auriga produced two flat clay pots, lifting the covers off: one held a stack of soft flour tortillas, the other a generous helping of chicken mole. Kneeling, the boy set upon the dishes with vigor.

"You okay, muchacho? When's the last time you ate?"

Orion was chewing, and offered a noncommittal shrug. Auriga surveyed the little shack: in its ruined condition, the centerpiece of the room seemed to be the large workbench crowded against one wall. Yellow light from a dingy metal lamp painted over puzzling curiosities, and he noted an impressive collection of tools that was worth more than the house. Some indefinable object lay on the soldering pad, like a short scepter with many branches; it looked so outlandish that the sight of it set Auriga ill at ease.

"Have you heard from Lyra?" Orion paused before reaching for another tortilla.

"No. As far as I know, she's still on the ship."

Orion nodded solemnly and returned to his meal.

"Corvus is dead," Auriga said, leaning against a wall. "So the inside of your head ought to be a little safer now. I thought you'd be glad to know that."

He saw the young eyes close in relief for a moment, and the

teenager smiled. Auriga set a plastic bottle of water next to the stool, and continued. "He had something that you might want to take a look at. It might be dangerous, though. I don't want it, and I wouldn't feel right letting anyone else have it."

When Auriga produced the transponder, Orion's eyebrows shot upward, and he abandoned the food to reach eagerly for it. Plucking the cylinder from Auriga's fingers, he scrutinized the odd device with a wild expression.

"This is Grey technology," Orion said.

"So Corvus was telling the truth. He said it would call the saucer to come help him... They didn't come, but I don't think it was because the thing doesn't work. I think they let him die," Auriga said.

Orion didn't respond. He stumbled over to the workbench and donned an optivisor.

"Anyway," Auriga said, "I need a couple of things. Let me trade you this for the M16." He removed a large revolver along with its holster from his belt and set it by Orion's elbow. "It's old school, but a mag round will still blow a Lizzie's head clean off. Just watch out for the recoil." He stacked two boxes of ammunition against the gun and then helped himself to the carbine rifle.

"Uh, okay." Orion was still hunched over the alien object.

"Also, there was a UCO lab that got burned down, and one of the doctors is a pretty hard case. I'm going to go back and make sure she's dead." He took the car keys from the corner of the workbench. "I need the car. There's a horse for you outside."

Orion laid down the transponder and swiveled on the stool. "A doctor...at a UCO lab? In the desert near here?"

Auriga nodded, his eyes crinkling with concern. "Dr. Vulpecula? What do you know about her?"

"She's inhuman."

Auriga closed his eyes. "Are any of us human anymore?"

Stillness cloaked the shanty.

The doctor's words came back to Auriga as he looked around the dim hovel. *Powerful yet expendable...twice as bright, half as long...*

Auriga opened his mouth to speak but found himself, for once, at a loss for words. *The clock is ticking. How much longer does he have? How can I tell him?*

And would it matter if I did? If I didn't have much time left, I'd want to spend it with the people who meant the most to me.

"Do you really have to go?" Orion asked.

"I still have things to do," Auriga said softly. "I'm working against the Greys, too, in my own way."

"You can stay here," Orion said. "If Corvus is dead, you don't have to go. We can still help Lyra. It's not too late for her."

"Listen to me." Auriga laid a hand on the boy's shoulder. "I think what you're doing is...the best anyone can do for her."

Orion's eyes, magnified by the optivisor's lenses, looked enormous, and Auriga gently removed the scavenger's headgear before continuing.

"Since the last time I saw you, some things have changed. None of us are the same as when this all started."

"You don't have to tell me that. I can't think of a single thing that will ever be the same again."

"I hope that thing helps you," Auriga said. "I hope you can get her back, and soon."

Orion turned back to the transponder and selected a tool from the bench.

Auriga opened the front door. "*Vaya con Díos*, muchacho," he whispered.

Orion already wasn't listening, lost as he was in an unending microcosm of artifice.

***

Fornax Enterprises had stopped smoldering, and the ugly dark smudge that remained of it was difficult to discern in the twilight, even at an altitude of thirty meters. Auriga steered the hovercar into a sloping descent, circling the compound while he examined its environs. His maneuver disturbed a flock of buzzards, which vomited and flailed about clumsily before rising into the air. The stench of charred remains assaulted him, and he spied corpses baking in the heat.

He moved on in the direction of the vanishing sun, picking out the darkened, crumpled heap of the helicopter in the gray stretch of sand. The wreckage bore closer examination, and he settled the vehicle with a skittering stop nearby.

His shadow stretched over a burned body that was half buried in the rubble. A wide pair of driving goggles were melted against the incinerated face; carrion birds had gnawed away much of the remaining flesh. Auriga nudged the carcass aside with a kick and fished through the twisted fragments of metal, plastic, and glass.

There was no mistaking it: a second corpse was conspicuously absent. Vulpecula had walked away from the wreck.

"*Lo supe,*" he muttered to himself, returning to the car. Vultures settled back in to continue their despicable feast; he considered blasting away at them with the rifle for catharsis, but it wouldn't do to waste bullets.

***

Auriga picked up the trail by tracking the Lacertas in the region: a single traveler, on foot, would normally be an easy target for the carnivorous aliens, and he would follow their prints as they sought their quarry. Auriga recalled the unexpected strength that the doctor possessed—her superhuman qualities were surely responsible for her escape from a fiery death in the helicopter—and wondered how many of the reptiles it would take to overwhelm her. He suspected that if she weren't badly injured from the crash, they'd have to earn their meal.

He spotted two of the ambling lizards in what remained of the western light. Grating snarls reached him as he passed over them, steered for a vantage point, and set the hang-brake at a height of twenty meters. A rushing breeze blasted from the sides and bottom of the hovercar as it parked, motionless in midair. However, the vehicle rocked as Auriga leaned over the center console to fetch the rifle and then lay the barrel on top of the passenger door to steady his aim. One alien leapt for the car, and the rifle cracked several times: the bullet-riddled monster's corpse pitched back to the ground from an interrupted arc, plowing a furrow into the sand with its snout.

The other alien opened fire on the vehicle—as he ducked for cover, Auriga cursed his foolishness for not having seen its weapon. He had instead focused on the Lacerta who had behaved as he'd expected. Plasma fire splashed on the sides and undercarriage of the vehicle, and it plunged down at the nose. Auriga smacked the hang-brake and held on tightly in the sudden gut-wrenching dive; the evasive action put his heart into his throat but kept him from being blasted out of the air.

The vehicle stabilized just before hitting the ground, and the Lacerta adjusted its aim, but not soon enough: Auriga centered his sights on its chest and slammed the trigger several times. The alien careened into a faltering backward dive, spurting black blood from a half dozen places.

Auriga wrestled with the controls, trying to regain altitude and move on, but his efforts were rewarded only temporarily: moments after rising a few meters in the air, the car would founder, pitching back to the ground from an interrupted arc, spurting black smoke from a half dozen places. He pumped the pedals as the car groaned in protest. After several attempts, it would no longer even hover above the earth's surface, and settled into the sand with a final rattling cough.

Auriga pressed the black Stetson firmly on his crown and slung the rifle and his knapsack over one shoulder. After abandoning the vehicle—*a lucky find for some scavenger,* he thought—he perused the two dead Lacertas and found nothing. The plasma rifle carried by the second alien was, of course, ergonomically designed for the lizard-men and would be too cumbersome and unwieldy for a man.

The sun would plummet soon, and he'd lost his biggest edge against Vulpecula: he'd intended to confront her at gunpoint from the air. Now he wished in vain for a scope, something to give him an advantage over the plain iron sights on the rifle, but the old *vaquero* had had none. It would take time and ammunition to sight one in anyway, and Vulpecula would either be close enough to hear her pursuer and be warned, or far enough away to gain a commanding lead on foot. The desert seemed determined to set them on an equal playing field. He kicked dust and sand with derision over the fallen pair; sightless eyes stared from the sides of their heads. Auriga set off to the north: a predator, hunting one of his own kind.

A contemplative hour's walk, and he was greeted with the sight of a silhouette in the distance, swimming in and out of the haziness on the horizon. Auriga quickened his stride, slogging through the sand at a rate that sapped the energy from his legs until he remembered to flood them with a jolt of strength from his hyperactive glands. The fatigue melted away. He closed on the other traveler, who was traveling north as well and hadn't seen him.

Auriga broke into a run, leaping over the deadened terrain. He jumped from a flat rock and sprang over an ocotillo, sliding to a stop on one knee as he landed. He unslung the rifle from his shoulder and brought the sight up to his eye in a smooth motion: he spied the fluttering black dress, framed by the rails of the gun's sight, and the compact, careful gait less than a hundred meters ahead. He squinted one eye, zeroing in on the doctor with crisp focus; his finger touched the steel action of the gun.

Vulpecula heard or sensed something, and turned. Seeing the predator close behind, she crouched in a defensive posture—but Auriga saw that her hands were empty. Auriga moved the barrel in a slight adjustment, aiming at the nearby Lacerta as it pounced toward Vulpecula. He released his breath and held it for a moment before squeezing the trigger.

The Lacerta's head ruptured into a spray of gore, and it stumbled grotesquely amid its halted momentum. The dead reptile crashed into the sand a few meters from the doctor, throwing up a thin cloud that drifted over her. Vulpecula straightened with care, still on guard and aware of the crosshairs invisibly marking her form.

Auriga now approached, training the weapon on her with businesslike callousness. She remained still; he studied the streaks of soot and dust, and the minor scrapes that marred her normally immaculate skin. Still, she hardly looked the worse for wear. Desert winds rippled the knee-length dress where it was not held in place by the strap of the satchel slung across her body. He glimpsed the same two datapads and the metal carrying case peeking from it: so they had survived the crash intact as well.

"Looks like we can continue that conversation from before," he called from ten meters away. The doctor could cover ground in an instant, and Auriga didn't dare lift his finger from the trigger or let his aim stray from the dark figure. *Remember, she's more dangerous than any alien you've ever encountered,* he thought. *All the more so because she doesn't look like it.*

"Very well," she said easily, as if they were sharing a pleasant discourse over drinks. "I'm glad to see you've escaped from our prior entanglements, Mr. Auriga."

He snorted. "That's an interesting way to put it. You blew up a laboratory and tried to kill me, and now you're glad to see me again."

"I never tried to kill you," she corrected. "I'm certainly responsible for putting you in a dangerous situation, but we both know you're capable of taking care of yourself—especially with the augmentations I gave you."

"So why did you go to so much trouble? You destroyed Fornax and now nobody in the world knows you're alive. What's your next move?"

"Mr. Corvus was on target, as he usually is. After the success with your surgery, I'd gone far enough with the resources of the UCO, and it was time to go dark. I couldn't allow a breakthrough such as this one to be shared with the Greys."

"And now you're heading back to the city," Auriga said. "I take it you have a hideout there where you can finish your work in secret. You've been planning this for years."

"I could use a good lab assistant, you know. You're more

familiar with the procedure than anyone."

"That's because your previous assistants are all dead. You should be sure to mention that in your 'Help Wanted' ad. Full disclosure, you know."

She switched gears, untroubled. "Speaking of Mr. Corvus, I take it he didn't fare so well."

Auriga shrugged. "Corvus chose the wrong side. I do agree with you on that: humans should be ruling this world, not the Greys."

Vulpecula's eyes were triumphant. "I knew you didn't come out here to kill me."

"I haven't decided yet," he said.

"Of course you have. You know that if you pull that trigger, you doom your race to a future of enslavement. What I have is the precursor to mankind's resurgence—not just in this satchel, but in my head. One is useless without the other."

"I can't argue with you. If I kill you, the Greys win. We continue along in chains until the next visionary rises up with the means to overthrow them. Maybe by then, it will be the right time. Or maybe people will shoot her too, and resign themselves to the cycle yet again."

"And if you don't...?" Her voice was alluring, but he ignored the seductive tone.

"If I don't kill you, what can happen? Suppose you were to accomplish it all. You develop a means to elevate us above the Greys, like you've promised. But you're cunning and ambitious—would you use it in the right way? You could be no different from them. With an army of super-soldiers answering to you, you could be *worse*. And even if you weren't, these new surgical techniques don't guarantee anything. So what if we're stronger and faster? We're already stronger and faster than the

Greys are, and it hasn't helped. This struggle can't be decided with hand-to-hand combat."

"You're absolutely right: it's decided with the willingness to fight. A thousand men and women like you and I could overthrow the Greys, where a hundred million others would not find the strength to even try. Our procedures would breed soldiers—not just in body, but in mind. Humans who have the potential for action."

Auriga smiled grimly at the words. "As an incidental result of the surgery, right? Like what you said about Orion and Lyra: behavior is influenced by the choices that are available, therefore, augmented individuals are more likely to pursue violent objectives."

"Of course."

"But at the same time, we could be playing right into the Greys' hands by giving them a stronger race to control."

"Maybe the human race should remain shackled, then." She pulled the collar of her dress wide, exposing a curvaceous décolleté that glistened with perspiration. "Pull the trigger, and it will happen."

His dark eyes strayed for a moment, and then pierced hers. "You know that I would never really consider that an option. People like to talk about their available choices, but there are so many things you never have control over. So many things that you didn't even realize you had a choice about until the time has already passed.

"That's why this situation is unique: I can recognize the gravity of the choice I'm about to make. I can dimly envision a world where you've achieved your goals, but I can clearly envision one without you."

He shifted his focus back to the weapon's sight. It was time to choose. Here in the lifeless desert, set apart from the rest of the world, one man could make a choice that would redefine mankind. He knew the path he would take: it was wholly his own, as one who travels through the desert has no road before him and must make his way as he will, without guidance. Clouds of dust might obscure the path ahead, but they were not solid: although he could not see through, he could penetrate them by walking resolutely forward.

"You're a decisive man, Mr. Auriga. A man of action. It's not like you to waffle."

He couldn't suppress the boyish grin, even though he knew it let her see that she had prevailed. "One of the things you love about me, eh, Doc?"

A half smile creased the corner of her mouth as she released her collar. "You had to hold me at gunpoint to get me to admit it."

The barrel lowered. "You're right, you know. I never really intended to shoot you. Don't make me regret that I didn't."

"Words to live by."

Chapter Sixteen

Auriga bounded to the top of the five-meter-tall wall and landed in a crouch next to the mounted holostacker. It had a hard transparent case around it, rendering it bulletproof. He rammed his fist through it with a grunt, and the housing cracked apart, metal crumpling. Plastic bits exploded, and he wrenched the assembly off of its guide pole and cast it into the desert.

Still ducking, he surveyed his surroundings: inside the wall, rough, cobbled streets threaded between grime-striped concrete houses. Dirty streetlights feebly battled the gloom, and dark shadows pulled at each other, twisting together in the late evening. A few residents sidestepped into their homes, careful not to make eye contact with the burly man scowling down from the wall with his nose and mouth buried inside the raised collar of his shirt.

Vulpecula had directed them to the least desirable area of the city to make their illegal entrance, since documented ingress for either of them would raise an alarm. Auriga was wanted by the UCO for a variety of transgressions, and it was also important to maintain the fiction of Vulpecula's death.

"All clear," he called.

The doctor stood off to one side, in the lee of the wall with Auriga's black Stetson pulled low to cover her face. The holostackers employed in the city used facial-recognition software, but this was not hard to overcome. The aliens seemed to display a rare instance of overconfidence in their technology when it came to the study of human faces; after all, the Greys' own features were identical, and Auriga supposed they falsely believed the humans' diversity was an Achilles' heel. Someone had once told him that if everyone in the city were to go around with a bandana over the lower half of their face, the Greys' holostackers would think it was the same person over and over again. He doubted that was the case, but it was a rare thrill to find an exploitable chink in the aliens' armor.

Vulpecula pounced atop the wall, alighting next to him. Handing the rifle back to him, she whispered some general directions. "It isn't far away," she added. "We can stick to the roofs most of the way to stay out of sight."

Auriga wrapped the weapon's sling across his shoulder and gestured for her to lead. He watched in curious anticipation as she gathered strength for an instant. When she shot away in a mighty leap that covered half a city block, he raised his eyebrows. He leaned forward, training his eyes to pick out the slight shadow that dropped to the roof of a house forty meters away.

"*Madre de Díos*," he said to himself. "No running start either. Well, here goes..."

He surged pure liquid energy into his powerful leg muscles, compressing his body like a spring. He launched up and out with every ounce of force he could exert, and flew from the wall's surface, rocketing above the tenebrous slums with astonishing speed and height.

The house where Vulpecula stood grew nearer with silent alacrity, and he crashed upon the flat concrete roof next to her with a shock that spread into a spiderweb crater. Below them, someone within the dwelling screamed.

The doctor smirked at him. "Nice job, but work on the landing."

She jumped again, soaring in another impossible arc, one hand pressing the Stetson down upon her head. He sailed in a wide arc through the sky after her, noting the continued absence of the Grey spaceship. Without its silent sovereignty, they were the gods of this realm. His boots crunched onto the next building's roof without cracking it this time. He tasted the stale urban air and knew that his collar had slipped down, but he was not concerned: the city's holostackers were predominantly aimed at the streets and not at the tops of buildings.

Beside him, Vulpecula winked. "Now let's take it up a notch."

Her figure became a shadowy blur, flying across the city's landscape with such celerity that she threatened to leave him behind altogether. He alternated hurriedly between tracking the doctor's wild flight ahead of him and the all-important placement of his lightning-quick footsteps on the roofs and ledges. When at last she halted at a nondescript bunker, he was still with her, both of them breathing hard from the exertion. As Auriga assayed the plain concrete building, his energy returned at once—and likewise, the doctor recovered in no time.

She placed her palm on a plain metal plate, and the door swung open. Auriga followed her through, and the portal closed as lights flared overhead. The main room was a laboratory, with polished tile floors and a high ceiling. A steel operating table was the centerpiece of the large chamber, and an impressive array of tools and equipment lined two of the walls. Auriga recognized the attractively utilitarian features of human-Grey hybrid technology among many of the consoles. Beakers and vials stood pristine and ready on a neat row of shelves, and he marveled that the room was just as immaculate. Not a speck of dust marred the surroundings; the room must have been air-cycled with the efficiency of a spacecraft, and it was apparently sterile enough for surgery. A sleeping medibot in one corner of the main room lent credence to this observation.

"Not bad at all, Doc. I have to wonder, though…"

"Did I rip this stuff off?" she finished his sentence using uncharacteristic vernacular, eliciting a broad smile from the Mexican. "Of course not. The equipment belonged to a colleague of mine with a private practice: an augmentation clinic. He decided to sell it to me very cheaply, and in a hurry, amid concerns over competing with the UCO in the medical field. It was a perfectly legitimate transaction."

"You're really something else. Where is he now?"

"He disappeared before the deal was finalized. I'm afraid the legal registration for the equipment was never transferred to my name."

"Did he regret having gone into competition with the UCO when that happened?"

"He didn't say."

Auriga circled the room. "But that's just the equipment. This is no place for a private augmentation clinic—it's a modest stockroom in the middle of a slum. You bought the property a long time ago."

She rested her hands on her shapely hips. "I bought it at auction. So what?"

Auriga gave her a knowing look. "Auction, eh? I'm guessing the owner died unexpectedly and had no heirs."

Vulpecula tossed the black wide-brimmed hat onto the counter and walked to the back room. "I'm going to take a shower and change clothes. You can play detective out here—dust for prints or whatever you like. Let me know if you crack the case, Mr. Auriga."

When she was nearly to the doorway of the bathroom, she pulled the dress over her head and dropped it to the floor. He glimpsed black lingerie over mocha skin before she disappeared through the door, and then he heard water running.

Auriga rummaged in the cabinets in the tiny living space in one corner of the main room. He found a half-empty box of saltines that was out of date by almost a year and several packages of instant ramen. He washed a large Pyrex beaker, filled it with water, and set it on the hot plate to boil. After scouring the living area for silverware and finding none, he returned to the laboratory shelves and retrieved a pair of steel surgical forceps.

He heard the water in the next room stop, and Vulpecula reappeared moments later, wearing a white lab coat that was buttoned all the way up in front. She cackled at the sight of him sitting on the narrow cot, winding long strands of steaming noodles around the forceps.

"Looks like we're out of forks," she said.

"Looks like we're out of bathrobes too," he answered, passing the beaker to her.

She seated herself on the cot. "Actually, I've always been quite comfortable wearing these."

"I don't doubt that a bit," he said.

"We should be able to pay a local kid to run to the store for us. It shouldn't trigger an alarm if the holostackers caught sight of you for a short time, but the Protectorate would be out looking for you soon nevertheless. It will be best for us to stay indoors as much as we can for the time being. Of course, we have plenty to keep us busy."

"So what's the plan?"

"We now know that we can successfully administer remarkable upgrades to a human's raw physical potential using the same techniques that you and I have gone through. However, while the procedure is worth every ounce of the risk that comes with it, it's expensive, time consuming, labor intensive, and unfortunately still carries a very real threat of failure or even mortality if the subject's body should reject the invasive procedures. These are challenges that can be overcome in a research laboratory, but not on the front lines of a battlefield." She handed the noodles back to him.

"I'm with you so far. You and I can't recruit and build an army of super-soldiers one at a time, performing endless surgeries in this hideout with limited resources—especially once the Protectorate and the Greys actively begin trying to stop us," he said.

"Right. Surgical enhancement will continue to be crucial for our very best candidates, but in the meantime, we will need to build the ranks much more quickly."

"You're saying that the Greys are making shock troops, and we should fight fire with fire."

"Mercenaries are not difficult to come by," she said, "but we've recently seen their shortcomings. What we need are soldiers with more capability as well as loyalty."

"And the manner in which we get them has to be more expeditious than surgery, and more reliable than bribery."

"Absolutely right."

Auriga grimaced. "You're talking about synthesizing another drug."

"It's by far the most effective way to achieve this goal. By leveraging some of the Greys' own work using action potentials,

I've done some preliminary work on a compound that will have the effect of a metabolic steroid regimen, although the cycles will be much more powerful and transitory."

"So the subject will have brief periods of unbelievable performance while the drug is in his system. Have you tested this yet?"

"So far it hasn't been pretty," Vulpecula said. "The demands on the metabolic process are rigorous, and it leaves the subject's musculature completely ravaged. My next round of testing will need to introduce an agent to replenish the muscle tissue as it's being consumed by the massive amounts of exertion."

"It sounds like you're talking about stem cells, but it takes time to assimilate them and build up the tissue—"

"Not when they are benefitting from the heightened rate of the action potential catalyst," Vulpecula said.

"Okay, so there are many types of stem cells. Which type are we talking about?"

"Obviously this is experimental, but I'd like to start with amniotic stem cells due to their propensity for stimulation of tissue growth and zero risk of host rejection—so we'll need a pregnant female," she said.

"That's the lousiest way to proposition a man that I ever heard," Auriga replied.

"I didn't mean *me*," she said amid their simultaneous laughter.

"So you expect me to run around the city with a mask on, find a pregnant girl, and convince her to let me bring her back here and jam a needle into her stomach for the sake of science?" He was still laughing, but it had an undercurrent of sarcasm.

"I have plenty of capitals," she said. "Take some with you, and stick to this side of town. You'll find someone who needs the money. Just as long as she's healthy." Lifting a corner of the thin mattress, she revealed a futuristic-looking handheld weapon. She handed it to him butt first. "And don't take no for an answer."

"Good grief. Want me to stop by Memorial Park on the way back and dig up some bodies for you, Doctor?"

Vulpecula blinked. "Why would I want that?"

Auriga rose, muttering to himself. "Just when I was beginning to think you actually had a sense of humor."

***

It was the early hours of the morning when Auriga knocked on the door. Vulpecula admitted him and his guest with no delay, and he was struck by the thought that very few people would open their homes at this hour to a man with his appearance. With the Stetson's brim pulled low and a black kerchief tied around the lower half of his face, showing only his eyes, he knew he looked like a train robber in the Wild West. Instead of a six-shooter, though, he used a compact, satin-finished plasma pistol to nudge the blindfolded young lady into the room. The door swung shut on weighted hinges.

Vulpecula had donned a clean knee-length black dress; her lab coat was unbuttoned over it like a jacket. A surgical mask hid most of her face; Auriga supposed that perhaps she had wanted to already be prepared for the procedure, but it was more likely that she had simply anticipated the reluctance of their guest and was hiding her face.

"Have a seat, please," Vulpecula said, indicating the operating table as Auriga removed the blindfold.

The young woman had dark hair and almond-shaped eyes that were heavy with fear. She was slender except for a round, swollen belly; her feet were rooted to the floor. Auriga stowed the pistol in a holster at his belt, and took her by the arm, escorting her to the table. She walked woodenly, repeating Spanish phrases in a whisper. Auriga helped her onto the smooth metal surface that was covered with a thin length of sterile white tissue; as he coaxed her to recline, Vulpecula secured the girl's wrists into the metal manacles that were affixed to the table.

Auriga gave a sharp look, but the doctor turned her attention to an assortment of instruments on an adjacent tray.

"We're not going to hurt you or the baby," he said to the girl in Spanish. "I'm sorry, I know you're scared and you don't understand, but this has to be a secret."

Vulpecula pulled up the woman's oversized T-shirt and placed the bell of a stethoscope against her skin. The patient flinched; the doctor wrapped the drum in her palm, locking eyes with Auriga, and breathed on it deliberately to warm up the metal.

After listening for a minute, Vulpecula unequipped the instrument and draped it over her shoulders. She nodded at Auriga, reaching for a bottle of rubbing alcohol and a stack of large cotton pads. "Ready to proceed," she said.

He caught her wrist. "How about an ultrasound to confirm the position of the infant? You don't want to hit it with the needle."

She slipped on a pair of magnifying bifocals and studied him with a detached gaze. "Does this look like an ob-gyn lab to you? I don't have an ultrasound, and I wouldn't need it if I did. I just checked the heartbeat, and I know where the fetus is. I don't need your help if you're just going to second-guess me at every opportunity." Despite her irritation, Vulpecula had taken care to refrain from using his name in the presence of the patient.

Auriga released the doctor's wrist, and she soaked a cotton round with isopropyl alcohol before swabbing it in circles near the woman's navel. Auriga took the patient's hand, staring at her ballooned stomach. Somewhere within, a silent being floated in the darkness. He imagined its bulbous head, frail body, and dark, analytical eyes. An unpleasant miasma encased him; he envisioned a Grey in the fetal position suspended in a murky cocoon.

"Syringe," the doctor prompted.

Auriga swallowed, then took the hypodermic needle from the equipment tray. His hand shook. The patient's skin was cool, but sweat shone on her forehead. Again he shuddered at the mental image of a diminutive, hairless being: a large head atop a slender body, swiveling to stare at him with huge onyx eyes.

Vulpecula reached across the table to pluck the syringe from his hand, a crinkle etched into her forehead above the glasses. Auriga turned the patient's chin to look at him and not at the long, gleaming needle; she inhaled sharply when the hypodermic punctured her skin but remained still. The reservoir swelled with a cloudy yellow liquid. When it was nearly full, Vulpecula withdrew the needle, laying the syringe on the tray before attending to the wound with more cotton and an astringent. After applying a small bandage, she nodded a second time.

"Simple as that," she said. "Blindfold her again and escort her back to where you found her. Give her some money too."

Auriga assisted the girl down from the table, supporting her at the elbow while they crossed the room together. His nightmarish fancies had evaporated, leaving him with only the perception of a frightened young mother and her helpless infant. This, however, unsettled him in a different way. His final thought before the steel door banged shut was that not all monsters came from outer space.

Chapter Seventeen

Orion placed his palm against the reader and fried the access circuits. Sparks blasted from the console in a pyrotechnic array, but he did not shield his vision. The South Point Salute entry gate was in chaos; the Protectorate men stationed here fled farther into the city, their guard lights casting conflicting stripes on the smooth pavement of the Thoroughfare as they retreated.

The electromagnetic portal fizzled, and Orion strode through. Some of the officers fired their weapons behind them as they ran, but he vaporized the incoming rounds with outstretched fingers. Gunpowder and lead dust scattered across his body in a glinting haze that sparkled in the sun. His black boots left craters of dust in the road; static crackled at his fingertips. He swept the Thoroughfare with electric-blue eyes, marveling at the scene of unbridled lawlessness.

Panicked civilians scrambled in the street, stumbling over one another in desperate surges. Trampled men and women moaned in the gutters, and abandoned children wailed from the alleys. Protectorate men in riot gear struggled to form ranks, but the throngs overwhelmed them in an unthinking swell. Above the city skyline, the sun was the great ruby-red orb of early evening, but it shrank as a gigantic flying saucer moved to dominate the sky.

"Now hear this," a dominant voice boomed from the public loudspeakers. *"Routine selection processes are underway. All citizens are hereby mandated to comply with the selection operations. Do not resist the actions of the Greys."*

Skirting the crowd and sheltering for the moment in a narrow doorway, Orion readied the Vinculum device. He studied its dark, exotic contours. The object was thirty-five centimeters long, the width of a broomstick handle, tapering to a blunt point at the bottom and widening to a knobby sphere on the top. Patterns of circuitry crawled vertically along its surface like dancing hieroglyphs. Two small winglike protrusions flared from the wand, and the creeping sigils scrolled up across them as if on a screen.

He read the arrays: the device was close enough to detect and recognize the Grey ship but still too far away to make use of its operations. The massive disc was evidently at a greater distance than it appeared to be—and he'd have to traverse a significant portion of the frenzied city district to make his approach. The streets boiled with hysteria, so a journey through this environment would be far more treacherous than the desert Orion had always called home.

Orion set his face in a determined frown, stowed the Vinculum in the large buttoned pocket on the side of his cargo pants, and plunged into the bedlam. The throng pushed and shoved without mercy, and he steadied his will, controlling the rising prickles of skin that would lead to tragedy in this cramped setting. He resolved to stay in command of himself, a bulwark of restraint in this flailing ocean of panic. Hisses and pops sporadically sounded, and canisters sailed overhead, trailing plumes of pale, translucent smoke. The Protectorate was firing gas to control the crowd—people nearby choked and coughed, some even doubling over and retching, but Orion, who did not have to inhale, was hardly affected. His eyes watered and stung a bit, but his progress through the horde was facilitated as other men and women retreated. He inched through the crowd, pressing forward to come to a street junction where the mob had thinned.

Through the partially obstructed vista that was now and then compromised by the shifting of the crowd, Orion watched as a girl of perhaps eight fled through the square, a thickly knotted black braid trailing behind her bobbing head. His view was blocked for an instant, and he heard a sound like the sonorous lowing of some great underwater beast. When the people in front of him had parted again, the child was sprawled on the pavement, half paralyzed and dragging herself along with her hands.

Orion could see more of the square now, and although he had steeled his nerves against the coming shock, the awful sight sent shivers of revulsion through him nonetheless. Two Grey aliens marched through the vacant intersection, staring callously at the throng of panicked men and women who dared come no nearer. Each alien held a bizarre pistol in one spindly hand, and one of them lowered its weapon after the debilitating shot that had struck the child. They approached her without a sound—fifteen meters away, then ten.

Orion swallowed a scream in his throat and shoved harder against the multitudes. He could progress no further; people were packed together, struggling to flee from the presence of the invaders. He dug his shoulder between two squealing vassals, barreling through to get a better vantage point of the street beyond.

A man and woman were now in the intersection, several meters behind the aliens who stood between them and the wailing child.

The girl crawled toward them; the woman strained to rush to her child, but the man held fast to his wife's wrist. The roaring din of the streets swallowed their fevered exchanges, but Orion could read the scene plainly enough without the need to hear their words.

The mother continued to struggle, but the father insisted on holding her back. He caught her other arm in an unyielding grasp but could not succeed in dragging her away. Screaming and almost hysterical, she fought all the harder as the pair of aliens advanced on the girl. Orion knew what the father must have been saying to his wife: that nothing could be done, that resisting this ordeal, awful as it was, would only make it worse. The woman's screams broke, and she tore herself away from the man, sobbing.

One of the Greys had turned to take in the pitiful scene. Its cold eyes and expressionless features guarded any possible motive from the multitude of witnesses, but Orion alone understood. The helplessness of watching a tragedy about to unfold cloaked him, and he thrashed against it with both mind and body. He lifted his baggy sweater with his left hand and reached for the gun at his hip, but the press of the crowd was too thick. The alien faced the stricken mother and father, raising its weapon, and Orion jammed an elbow into the person next to him, trying to gain enough space to draw the pistol. He managed to clear the gun from the holster, and he brought it up to chest level, close against his body as he kicked and shoved his way to the front of the crowd.

People shrieked as they noticed the enormous revolver in his hand, and struggled to get away from him. Orion's eyes locked on the Grey as it aimed its pistol at the man and woman; the girl's father shielded his wife's body with his own as he

205

stared remorsefully at the child lying in the street. A piercing screech cut the air, and a yellow shock of light struck the man: for one brief instant, dazzling rays transfigured his silhouette, and then the radiance exploded, scattering dark, gritty ashes in a morbid bloom. The woman gasped and choked, ashes caking her form; she was a colorless wretch, overspread with the powder of her husband's remains. Her dry, agonized wail mingled discordantly with the gun's second earsplitting blare, then blazing light overtook her and heaps of ashes again littered the street.

The crowd was going truly berserk now, and the tide bore Orion off his feet. He landed on his stomach and rolled among the lashing feet. Weapon in hand, head ducked low, he crawled toward the cleared intersection; boots bashed his ribs and neck, and people tripped over him and fell in the street. The roaring chaos of an unthinking mob swallowed his senses. Through the parting forest of limbs, he spied the black-braided girl now sitting up, scurrying backward, her eyes wide with terror. The Greys were upon her now, wrapping their gangling fingers around her wrists.

Orion emerged at last from the brutal storm of limbs and took aim while lying prone in the street. As he did so, the outline of the two Greys and their captive became distinct and sharp. Contrasting waves emanated from them, surrounding the trio with a confusing aura of distorted space: the aliens were being transported back to the ship. Orion paid no heed to his aching, battered body and lined up the gun's sights on the slender form of one alien. The gun boomed like a cannon, bucking in his hands, and although he knew his aim was true, the bullet did not pass through the twisted waves. Instead, it disappeared from this reality to be transported to some random time and place that no one could guess.

Another moment, and they were gone. Orion rubbed his eyes and stared again at the empty place where the Greys and the young girl had just been. It was not quite empty after all—a small metal object marked the place where the horrendous crime against sanity had just occurred.

Orion scrambled to his feet and hastened to the spot. The air was feverishly warm, like walking past an open oven. Holstering the revolver, he stooped to retrieve the dull black item: one of the Greys' disintegrator pistols, dropped from distress or neglect during their departure. It scorched his hand, but he could not bear to release it from his grip. The weapon seemed to hum with synergy, and when he held the sight up, the familiar yellow crosshairs appeared in his vision.

The streets cleared of the unthinking mob at last, and he was afforded a clear view of the Thoroughfare. Shops were closed or abandoned, and the holostackers in front of them had been commandeered by the city to broadcast announcements and instructions. Protectorate men moved to restore order as the gas dissipated, sweeping the highway in teams of five and six. One such group was less than thirty meters from Orion, and he was spotted before he could act.

"Hands up!" the point man yelled through his rebreather. The barrels of six submachine guns trained on Orion at once.

Orion winced at the bad timing; he let his left hand hang at his side near the pocket containing the alien wand. If the Greys were within range of the ship's biotransporters, perhaps he could use the Vinculum to access those systems and escape as well. With his right hand, he positioned the disintegrator in an unthreatening orientation, waving it back and forth so that that the motion would attract attention. He began fiddling with

207

the first button on his pant pocket's flap.

The officer saw through the ruse, however. "Don't do it! Put your hands up now!"

Orion resigned to obedience, and moved his hand away from the pocket. As he raised his left hand over his head as well, movement attracted his attention from farther down the Thoroughfare. The gate he had entered through was now alive with Lacertas; several of the bipedal green menaces poured through the abandoned and disabled entry portal. With a vicious swipe, a Lacerta disemboweled a responding officer, and the lizard-men charged into the city streets.

"Watch out," Orion cautioned, pointing to the gate—but as he'd feared, the officers were suspicious of his attempts at diversion, and were taken aback by his cybernetic voice as well. The Protectorate men shouldered their weapons, inching toward him, and safety switches disengaged with a snap.

A cadre of Lacertas bounded down the Thoroughfare, which was blessedly more vacant than it had been only minutes before. Straggling civilians still wandered the streets, whether wounded, bereft, or curious—and these were set upon with furor. Orion watched the approaching rampage, helpless: he could not convince the officers to intervene, and any move to ready and use his own weapon to aid the citizens would surely cause the Protectorate to shoot. He could terminate a good deal of the incoming bullets, as he had done at the gate, but with this many weapons arrayed against him, some of the rounds were certain to get through.

"There are Lacertas coming," he tried again. "I'm not kidding, they're right behind—"

A growling snarl drowned out his words, and one of the beasts overtook an officer on the end of the line. The Protectorate man went down with an agonized scream as the giant jaws locked around his head. The other officers swiveled, opening fire. More Lacertas pounced; some fell amid a barrage of bullets, while others dragged black-clad operatives down to the bloody pavement. The air ignited as panicked shouts mingled with panicked gunshots.

Orion turned to run. His intuition urged him to flee, to distance himself from the chaotic scene as two factions of enemies set upon each other—and yet he tarried, reluctant to abandon these men who stood in defense of the city. How many tens of thousands of lives depended on these beleaguered soldiers, now that the worst had happened?

The South Point Salute gate still teemed with lizard-men. The influx of beasts would overwhelm the Protectorate forces in this section of the city. Responding officers would be delayed by the panicked mobs, and lives would be needlessly lost. Nor was there aid forthcoming from the Greys themselves; the saucer was nowhere in sight. The aliens were false gods, extending an illusion of security. The vassals who had forsaken the turbulence of the wastelands in exchange for peace, shelter, and subjugation were now beset by this deadly pandemonium all the same.

The enemies had always been at the gate, and a moment's opportunity was enough for them to capitalize upon. And although Orion had indeed disabled the portal to the desert, was he culpable? It could have been a doorway to freedom for the vassals just the same. The Greys had done this to their helpless charges, but there were men and women who were steady and strong. The city dwellers needed to be reminded of this.

The disintegrator pistol was awkward, even repulsive, in his hand, but his aim was true. A sunbeam pierced the brutal melee and pelted one lizard-man's upraised arm; Orion expected to

209

see the alien wholly crumble into gritty dust, but only the one appendage was consumed. Fiery golden eyes bored into his, and the creature pounced at him with killer instinct. Orion's next shot connected with its chest, and a gaping burn opened in the Lacerta's torso, powdery with ashes that fell from the outer fringes. Still the monster charged, though, and it was the third pistol blast that decayed it completely at last.

Orion pressed the attack, casting the yellow crosshairs through the boiling, bloody fracas. With each pull of the unwieldy, wedge-shaped trigger, a Lacerta was smote with an amputation or a burning cavity in its body. Even so, their hardiness and numbers made it a grudging battle, and it was not until heavily armed Protectorate men responded with reinforcements that the conflict was won.

As the last of the Lacertas fell or retreated from the fray, the point man who had demanded Orion's surrender approached the teenager. He lifted a black rebreather to unveil a clean-shaven face, with a marengo-colored gaze that was hard and reflective like polished marble. Orion's HUD employed facial recognition, and a semitransparent flag titled "DET HARLOW F" fed him what appeared to be the UCO's dossier on the detective.

Harlow appeared to have confirmed Orion's own identity as well. "I know who you are," he said, but his submachine gun's barrel remained lowered.

Unsure, Orion balked at further discourse—but the Protectorate man had information that he could not do without. "You're not going to arrest me, are you?" he asked with suspicion.

"I'd like to, but I can't spare the manpower or the time," Harlow growled. "If you're fighting the Lacertas for us, then I have better things to do."

"What could be more important than keeping the Lizzies from

eating us all alive?" Orion asked.

Wails and shrieks still wafted on the ash-laden air, but Harlow seemed oblivious to them. "Determining my orders, and following them."

"And people think *I'm* a robot," Orion sneered. "What do you mean, 'determining your orders'? Don't you know what your orders are?"

The blue-gray eyes danced as the man debated before speaking. "Two hours ago, the UCO went dark. Our last transmission advised us that there would be a fluid situation developing in the city over the next several hours, and directed us to await further orders."

"You mean no one's in charge?"

"The Greys are in charge," Harlow said.

The hair on Orion's arms rose, forming thousands of tiny antennae to a past that was not yet buried. He shook his head. "No, they're not. The entire city is on autopilot."

"Now hear this," the city's public address forum cut in. Orion flinched: the soulless, automated recitation was more unnerving than his own gravelly, artificial voice could ever be. It underscored his conviction that the rudderless metropolis had begun to flounder.

"Routine selection processes are underway."

A terrible ruckus exploded from the streets several blocks away, in the direction of the city's slums. Orion and Harlow both wheeled in the direction of the uproar, then eyed each other. The detective hoisted the unequipped mask back to his lips and barked an urgent query.

"All citizens are hereby mandated to comply with the selection operations."

Orion listened, certain that there would be no reply. The

radio silence, itself speaking volumes, reflected in Harlow's smooth visage as he let the rebreather dangle from his collar once more. The sounds of pandemonium intensified, and Orion took tentative steps away from the detective, backing up toward the unknown maelstrom. When the scavenger abandoned pretense and broke into a full run, however, Harlow raced alongside him, followed straightaway by a cadre of black-clad Protectorate men.

"Do not resist the actions of the Greys."

Chapter Eighteen

"They've begun building their army. Listen: it's like a war zone out there," Vulpecula said.

Auriga and the doctor were drinking coffee after dinner on the roof of the concrete bunker housing the laboratory. Groceries had been procured, and Auriga was satisfied at the doctor's employment of the hot plate to make pasta—prepared with water boiled in a Pyrex beaker, of course. Auriga himself had never before used a Bunsen burner to toast and butter garlic bread, but again, the results had been pleasing. Now, as they sipped a strong and bitter brew in the cooling evening air, the sun waned as turmoil surged.

"It's worse than you think," he said to the doctor.

"How so?"

"The Greys need a new Illuminatus now. They know that Corvus is dead, and Lyra isn't working out like they had hoped. These 'selections' are how they're going to find the next candidate."

Her lip curled in distaste. "I believe you're right about that."

The day had been spent in crawling conjectures and setbacks. Vulpecula's ministrations with the ill-gotten amniotic fluid had been stymied again and again, and despite many diligent hours and repeated attempts based upon the most solid grounds, not an iota of actual progress had been gained. Vulpecula had grown downright choleric, rejecting Auriga's assertions that undertakings such as these were necessarily characterized by bitter strings of failure interrupted eventually by triumph; and it was only upon the stipulation that they redouble their efforts through the night that Auriga's insistence upon rest and provisions was finally heeded. Furthermore, he had no illusions about what the intense disturbances within the city would do to her already expedited timetable.

The doctor fortified her mug with a refill from the steel carafe. "I think we've been taking the wrong approach. What we've found is that amniotic fluid is invaluable for its anti-inflammatory properties and could be equally impressive with respect to the treatment of grievous wounds and the regeneration of scar tissue, but this has limited applications for us at the moment."

"We've been on the path to making combat medics when what we need is front-line infantry," Auriga said.

"Once again, you've grasped the situation with perfect clarity. I'm going to discontinue the amniotic-stem-cell research."

Relief and apprehension washed over Auriga simultaneously. He welcomed the prospect of ceasing their existing research, with its unwholesome experimentation regarding the pregnant and unborn—but comfort continued to escape him. What callous and yet unassailable scheme had replaced the doctor's prior designs? What macabre tasks could he now be called upon to effect?

"You wouldn't pull the plug on one approach if you didn't already have a better one lined up. Let's hear it," he said.

Vulpecula set the ceramic mug down on the rust-streaked patio table. "So far we've been operating with the intention of perfecting an injection, or a series of injections, that would drastically increase the subject's physical capabilities. I've come to believe that there are many drawbacks inherent in this approach. For one thing, syringes are fragile, making them difficult to transport safely. Injections of any sort can be dangerous if not administered with care, and we need to remember that these augmentations will sometimes be carried out in certain high-risk circumstances."

Auriga rolled his eyes. "Such as being administered to people against their will."

"Yes. But the Greys are abducting people as we speak, which means we don't have time to perfect an approach of this sort. Distributing shots to a large population of people one or two at a time just isn't going to work. I still have the synthetic compound based upon the aliens' own groundwork with action potentials that we discussed before, but it may become necessary to abandon our attempts to make it more sustainable within the host's body."

Auriga closed his eyes. "You said that it placed an extraordinary amount of strain upon the subject's musculature. What's the point in augmenting someone if they end up being worse off afterward?"

"I'll isolate and add an increased amount of myoblasts to compensate for that effect. It won't be perfect, but we're talking about a first line of defense that will buy the human race more time. All I'll need is a subject with very healthy muscle structure."

Auriga stretched his arms behind his head. "I'm flattered, Doc. I'd like to think you wouldn't do anything to hurt your only lab assistant, but in light of what happened to my predecessor, I think I'd better ask you how you plan on extracting these myoblasts."

Vulpecula shook her head. "Not from you. I'm not talking

about existing muscle tissue, which you admittedly have to spare. A myoblast is a progenitor cell from which actual myocytes—muscle cells—originate. Myocytes grow and produce muscle fibers, called myofibrils, when they're exercised, but they can't divide on their own to produce more cells. To put it simply, muscle cells come from myoblasts, and you have much more of the former than the latter."

Auriga cringed. "I'm not going to like this, but I have to ask anyway: Where do we get someone who has a significant amount of myoblasts?"

"A newborn infant, or at the least a small child. They have a much greater number of myoblasts than adults, due to their need for prolonged and accelerated muscle growth." Vulpecula took a long sip, but her brown eyes remained on Auriga over the rim of the mug.

Auriga stood up, the metal legs of his chair scraping against the concrete. "No. I draw the line here. Abducting an infant to experiment on? No. It does not happen."

"Calm down. I've come to expect these outbursts of righteous indignation. Must I remind you again that the Greys have no conscience and no remorse, and that anything we can do to stop them is not only justified but absolutely necessary?"

"All of your moves are straight out of their playbook. How can you condemn them for having no conscience and no remorse when you're adopting the exact same methods?"

"I shouldn't have to justify myself to you. You're well aware of the need to act on behalf of the greater good."

"What happens to the child?" he demanded, his raised voice eliciting a guarded glower from the physician.

"The child will be more scared than hurt. We're just going to collect some tissue samples: myoblasts and osteoblasts. It will be just fine."

"Osteoblasts?"

"For bone strength—the subject's skeletal structure will have to endure the demands of increased performance as well. Small children have an abundance of potent osteoblasts in their bone marrow."

"Bone marrow extraction is one of the most agonizing things a person can endure," Auriga said. "Only a monster could kidnap a baby and perform a procedure like that—"

"I'm not happy about it either. Do you think I would intentionally harm a child?"

"If it meant achieving your goals, yes, I do."

She stood as well, upsetting the table with the coffee carafe. "My goal is to *protect* the child we're talking about, and a billion others, from a lifetime of slavery. I'd undergo the procedure myself, or use you instead, but it wouldn't do any good. Stop seeing things in black and white."

"That's ironic," he said.

"What do you mean?" she snapped.

"You want me to see things in shades of *gray?*"

"Your puerile outlook is growing tiresome."

"I'd better watch out, then. If I start to remind you of a child, you might use me in another experiment."

"That's precisely the behavior I'm talking about," Vulpecula said.

Auriga strode the length of the roof and back again. Her challenging posture dared him to escalate the encounter, but he summoned the effort to control his rage. After several moments of tense silence, he turned to point an accusatory finger at the doctor.

"There's another way, and I'm going to find it. You're just not looking in the right place."

"You're a sentimental fool," she said. "Go ahead and waste your time."

Auriga turned from her and stepped off the edge of the roof, dropping down into the dusky tumult of the city streets.

***

Auriga marched the sidewalks, seeing red. The thoroughfares boiled with rushing crowds, people who were trapped in the evening's madness without shelter. Roadblocks had been set up by the Protectorate in many places to corral the swarms, directing them into channels to be preyed upon by the collection efforts of the Greys, and many people could not reach their homes.

Auriga skirted the barricades by climbing fences and traversing rooftops when it was possible, and by shoving against the flow of the crowd to escape to an unpatrolled street when it was not. He could not say where he was going, only that it was absolutely necessary for him to be alone with his thoughts rather than in the company of that maniacal, cruelly obsessive genius. The streets of New Zaragosa were hardly the place to cool his anger, however; the swelling hysteria and close, crushing press of bodies did little to soothe his agitation.

Auriga snatched the padlock off of a barred metal gate with a hooked finger. The steel housing squealed as it gave way, and he kicked the turnstile off its mainspring. As he emerged from an alley into a wide boulevard choked with trapped vassals, the herd of people formed an unthinking influx into the newly opened gate, threatening to drive him back the way he had come.

Auriga pushed forward more roughly; he was a man among

sheep, and this sentiment was doubly painful in the realization that he had argued to Vulpecula against her treating them as such. He surveyed the faces around him twisted with fear, mindless and numb with panic. Was even one of them worth saving? Would a single man remain behind so that his fellows might escape the danger at his own expense? No—they clawed and fought, lashing and wailing to advance before each other into the false security of a darkened and steam-shrouded cavern. Disgust rippled through him.

He broke through the multitude by force, leaving bruised and howling livestock in his wake. The crowds on the Thoroughfare had thinned out, and there was enough open space to view his surroundings. He stepped into the middle of the street, taking in the unfolding events of the urban arena.

The Protectorate had erected a massive barricade at either end of the city block. Titanic steel sawhorses, bristling with thorny shafts, were arrayed before neat rows of black-masked officers. Wounded and bloodied bodies lay in scattered positions all around; only some of them twitched and groaned. Gritty heaps of ashes swirled in a morbid frolic upon the promenade. Small groups of vassals cowered together, seeking futile and illusory safety from the sticklike predators that stalked supreme among them.

Greys shambled among the people, scrutinizing the trembling members of the herd. Many people were ignored, some were more closely examined, and some were instantly conscripted. The aliens fell upon their victims piecemeal, seizing a wrist, shoulder, or throat with clammy fingers. The afflicted humans gasped, winced, or whimpered, but they did not dare deny the dark approbation. Their outlines grew distinct, disharmonized against the waning light of the sun, and bizarre spatial waves emanated from the joined figures. In an instant, they vanished. As fast as they disappeared, more Greys would materialize in the avenue, and the horrible nominations would begin anew.

Witnessing the sanity-shattering selection processes of the Greys shocked Auriga out of his mounting rage. His disdain was lost in an urgent call to action, and he reflected that, despite the differences with Vulpecula that he had dwelled upon, her inability to tolerate these abominations was to remain a concrete bond between them. It was not possible to save all the humans, but together they would make it possible to destroy all the Greys.

Auriga started forward, reaching for the plasma pistol. The Greys and the Protectorate had grown accustomed to the mute docility of their human vassals, and he would even the prodigious odds against him with a furious first strike, followed by a retreat into guerilla tactics. Before he could join battle, though, a Klaxon blared, freezing him with sudden and guarded apprehension.

"Now hear this. A wanted fugitive has been sighted."

Auriga's heart sank: in his departure from the laboratory, he'd forgotten to gird himself with his kerchief and hat. His face was uncovered, and he'd been identified by the city's passive scanners. The public address loudspeaker continued with citations of his identity and his crimes, and instructions for himself and for nearby citizens. But Auriga wasn't listening. The marauding Greys froze in their apprehending, and scowled at him with leering bug-like eyes before evaporating to the waiting refuge of the ship. Auriga expected the ranks of Protectorate soldiers clustered at the barricade to advance upon him, but instead they withdrew, hurriedly vacating the fortified barriers to melt into the relative shelter of the intersection's perimeter.

Puzzled, he turned his attention back to the loudspeaker, but its further directions were now surmounted by a steady, sonorous crashing. The drumming footfalls of a colossal beast drowned out everything in the street: he saw vassals screaming, but heard nothing. All was swallowed by the heavy sound of steel-laced doom slogging to meet him.

The Demistrider rounded the corner and towered in the middle of the street, knocking aside the metal sawhorses with a clattering cacophony. Auriga stared up the length of its bulk, a ten-meter-tall metallic war machine standing on massive jointed trunks that terminated with three circular pads in arrays that served as flexible feet. The spheroid torso housed several formations of missile weapons, which were clustered in ordered rows within rectangular assemblies. One giant arm split into two barrels—a pair of energy cannons mounted vertically one atop the other—and the second arm sported an immense belt-fed ballistic weapon with an ammunition box at the elbow joint. Crowning the artificial behemoth's shoulders was a sleek, mirrored dome from whence the pilot could administer untold computer-augmented destruction while protected inside a fortified sanctuary.

The left arm erupted with orange flame, and bullets sprayed the pavement in a frenzy. Auriga rolled to escape the chips of stone as an endless stream of hot, leaden rounds disintegrated the street. Biting flecks of lead and rock stung his arms and legs as he raced ahead of the onslaught. There was no cover in the open street, especially none that would stand up to the hail of large-caliber bullets that whirred from the fire-breathing minigun at astonishing speed—he was forced to zigzag inexorably toward the monstrosity. His own superhuman celerity made the entire backdrop a blur, and the seconds crawled by in sluggish feebleness even as the rest of creation danced in hyperventilating chaos.

At last the whining of the massive gun died, and was replaced by the clanking ratchet of the reloading action. Despite the seeming interminability of the assault, it had taken scant seconds to deplete the weapon's ammo, and there would be only an equally brief period before it was replenished.

The laser cannon fired before Auriga had the chance for further reflection, and a piercing beam of superhot red energy sent him leaping for asylum yet again. The laser's scorching trail followed him so closely that the searing air brought forth scalding blisters on his skin. This time he was forced to run up the walls of nearby buildings to evade the deadly rays, and the Demistrider's path of devastation hurried right behind. After a few seconds, the laser's glowing cannon was forced into remission, and he kicked away from the side of the building, finally seizing on a tiny, desperate window in which to counterattack.

Aiming the plasma pistol from the hip as he fell through the air, Auriga pumped the gun's trigger. Conical orange bursts washed over the Demistrider's massive frame. He kept it up until the gun grew blazing hot in his hand and the thermodisplay at the top of the backstrap protested with a flashing red circle. He hit the ground rolling, then sprang into a leap that carried him to the opposite side of the street. The Strider fired rockets from its chest in a rapid chain; explosions erupted throughout the boulevard in rippling lines like the path of a stone skipping across a pond.

Agonized shrieks now carried through the street: the groups still cowering in the boulevard were taking fire from the indiscriminate bursts. Chunks of debris pelted some, while others were caught in the wake of the actual missile blasts. Crimson blood stained the streets and sidewalks; prostrate forms lay blackened and incomplete.

Auriga coughed in the rising gales of white dust, choking for air but thankful for a momentary smoke screen. He knew the pilot would switch to infrared vision, and hoped that the sensors would take a few precious seconds to reset: if his earlier bombardment with the superhot streaks of plasma had done its work, the giant machine might be close to overheating. He stumbled through the smoke for a new vantage and emerged only meters away from the massive legs. The striations of burned metal were only surface deep, and the exposed areas were bright with heat; Auriga could see that the actual damage was minimal, but a more adroit offense might open the Achilles' heel of the merciless thing.

The Demistrider's torso was still angled to aim farther up the street, close to where Auriga had been when the fallout of the missile strike had overtaken him. For an instant, he admired the effective ruse, and he crouched, raising his pistol again—it was nearly cool enough to use. An insistent *thunk* drew his attention, though: something bounced off the Demistrider's torso and crumbled to the pavement. A second smash was even louder, and he saw what was happening: people were pummeling the war machine with rocks and chunks of pavement picked up from the devastation in the street. Auriga expected that the heavily armored Demistrider would shrug off the ineffective assault, but as the hail of bricks and concrete intensified, small dents and hairline cracks began to show on the besieged vehicle's chassis.

The Demistrider took two steps backward, lengthening the distance between it and the puny, ill-equipped challengers, and opened fire with the giant machine gun. A tongue of ghostly flame spewed from the flying barrels, and the smooth, streaming whir of the constant ballistic assault blended beneath the horrifying shrieks of a death visited en masse upon the pitiful crowd. Auriga did not look back, not wanting to see the gruesome pink mist settling over the street in a fine spray. He dared not take his eyes from the Demistrider as he blasted it with a new barrage of plasma. The orange jets tore into its armor plating a second time, not penetrating into the deeper levels but thankfully dissipating heat across the machine's surface once again. Auriga leapt and rolled to dodge the answering burst of the laser cannon, leveraging his reserves of adrenaline to bring him back into close proximity with the Strider. Smoking black trails traced his progress, dangerously close, and he smelled burnt hair as his skin reddened with an instantaneous sunburn.

He was within five meters of the enormous legs, battering the limbs and the chassis's underside with feverish pulls of the trigger in his sweat-soaked hand. The air was like a furnace; heat radiated from the war machine, from the discharging pistol in his fist, and from the red-hot cannon that traced patterns of scorching agony, burning thousands of degrees in an ever-expanding strip of hell.

The Demistrider's laser cannon and his plasma pistol over-heated at the same moment, and both weapons halted in sudden complaint. Auriga could barely touch the fiery metal of the overtaxed weapon, and flung it hard into the glowing-hot barrel of the great broiling gun. It rattled deep into the open, waiting mouth, and vanished into the calescent tunnel. The scalding foreign object would now interfere with the weapon's cooling operation, preventing the gun from firing safely. Auriga leapt to position himself closer to the giant three-toed feet—the machine gun would not angle so sharply as to fire at the Strider's own legs, and the mech's pilot would not be so foolish as to risk a rocket attack that would catch himself in the splash radius. It was the safest place to be, if he could avoid being stepped on.

A decisive *clank* announced the completed reload of the machine gun, and the Demistrider continued its rearward pace in an attempt to get a firing angle. It sapped Auriga's strength to time his leaps with the great strides, and the close proximity to the overheating machine was sweltering. His muscles burned, and sweat drenched his body, but a misstep would be fatal. At length, a deafening *snap* came from the laser gun's barrel, and Auriga exulted at the sound of the laser's heat coils splitting open. As he'd hoped, due to his interference, the cannon had stayed too hot for too long and had suffered a catastrophic failure.

Auriga was not prepared, though, for the fiery, walloping punches that shook his form without warning. The mech's pilot was indeed launching a battery of missiles at the ground directly before it, and while Auriga was not close enough to be torn apart by the actual blasts, he was burned and battered by the dangerous proximity. Deadly red flowers bloomed in the heat of an artificial sun, and he screamed aloud at the anguish that enveloped his world.

When the bloodshot blossoms died to a hazy char of smoke, pregnant with the stench of burnt hair and flesh, further damage to the Demistrider was apparent. The cracks and dents in the aggrieved chassis had worsened—its inner mechanisms could be glimpsed in small places where the armor had breached, and the obsidian dome's smoothness was now marred by a jagged white spiderweb. Sparks shot from its joints, and billows of oily black clouds now mingled with the charnel-gray smoke of the street.

Auriga's body was exhausted and in agony, and his reserves of strength were nearly spent, but the mech's vulnerability was at last exposed. Auriga channeled a last burst of vigor and leapt upward. When he rested one boot on the Strider's right leg, the sizzling metal melted the rubber sole. He vaulted higher, taking care not to touch the chassis with his hands; this time, his other boot met the great machine's left forearm, and the slipperiness of the dissolving sole almost sent him toppling back to the ground. Before he plummeted, Auriga righted his balance by kicking fiercely off of the metal frame, spiraling upward in a violent cyclone of fists and feet. At the zenith of his leap, he brought his right leg around in a wide arc and drove the heel of his boot against the failing glass of the cockpit in a ferocious kick.

A sharp, gratifying *crack* accompanied the drastic widening of the fractures. Silvery forks chased each other across the glossy surface, and a hundred malevolent reflections of a barbarous madman leered against the background of a hellish, smoke-filled twilight sky. He rebounded from the devastating strike, preparing a follow-up attack; Auriga's descent now carried him past the centrum of the cockpit, and he punched it with all his might.

The mech's ruptured windshield shattered, and Auriga's fist continued forward into the Strider's sanctum. The pilot recoiled, his features hidden by a large black helmet; Auriga seized the front of the man's jumpsuit, and jerked him bodily from the control seat. The man's thin body slipped from the safety harness, and tubes and cords snapped, severing the pilot/vehicle interface. Gravity did the rest: as Auriga landed with a jolt before the mech's feet, the pilot collided with the crumbling pavement in a clumsy, twisted heap.

The Demistrider now sagged wearily, its arms lowering, its torso slouching, a crippled beast in need of rest. Auriga towered over the operator, who was also immobile. The cracked black helmet had slipped off and rocked in the street. A tangle of limbs hid the pilot's head from view, but Auriga stared in alarm at the

226

unnatural physique. He reached out with a half-melted boot and nudged the injured operator onto his back.

A dry wheeze escaped from the ashen, lipless mouth. The bulbous black eyes were closed, but the lids fluttered. The large, hairless cranium rocked once, and was motionless again. Auriga stood alone in the street, contemplating the wild scheme that struck him with the pinpoint precision of a laser cannon. He could hear other people returning to the scene, perhaps Protectorate officers; the time for hesitation was past. Auriga scooped up the flimsy body, draped it over one shoulder, and hurried away from the approaching men.

Chapter Nineteen

"*Have you lost your mind?*"

Vulpecula stood back from the steel door to admit Auriga and his unconscious captive. He carried the alien to the center of the room and deposited it on the operating table. The built-in manacles were too large for its skinny wrists and ankles. He busied himself with removing the torn and burned jumpsuit from the limp form and smiled grimly when he noticed that his own clothing was in even worse shape.

The doctor was already examining Auriga's injuries, although he wasn't sure how she was able to keep her eyes off the unfolding exploit. "You've got some pretty bad burns here. You need first aid or you'll get an infection."

"Yeah, I know. In a minute."

She hurried to assist him in undressing the creature, then placed a stethoscope against its puny chest. "It's unconscious, but we need to make sure it stays that way. I have no idea what to give it or what the dosage should be, though." She began unbuttoning Auriga's shirt with nimble fingers while guiding him to a metal stool. When he was seated, she delicately pulled the charred garment away from his skin, watching his face as he winced in silence.

As Vulpecula employed a medibot to help attend to his wounds, Auriga studied the prostrate form on the table. "It's going to be a challenge," he agreed. "While the central nervous system of the Greys is presumably similar to our own, we have to assume that the cerebral cortex is different enough to pose some challenges in supplying anesthesia."

"I have an idea: I stole some sodium thiopental from Fornax when I was preparing to go rogue. It's not normally used for general anesthesia, but with the subject's extraordinarily low amount of body fat, I'd say it would keep it under for quite a long time."

"Good, but we also need a respirator in case the muscles become too relaxed to keep its airways open," he said.

"I have a child-size breathing tube that I would have used if I had gone ahead with the operation we discussed," Vulpecula said. "That should fit it."

Auriga turned to look at her, but she placed a hand on his shoulder as the medibot continued working. "*If* you had gone ahead?" he asked.

"I'm not going to do the surgery," she said.

"Why not?"

"You know why not," Vulpecula answered. "It's hard enough doing this *with* your help. Despite what I thought, I'm not ready to be alone yet. I still need you here."

An uncomfortable silence followed, and Auriga took a deep breath as the doctor began applying gauze to his burns. "That must have been hard for you to say."

"Well, I would say that it must have been hard for you to come back here, except that you were burned half to death and packing an unconscious alien on your back." She smiled. "Where else could you have gone?"

Laughter dissolved the tension, and Auriga's eyes strayed to the workstation near the steel door. An array of beakers, dishes, and utensils were aligned near a blinking, humming console. "What were you working on?" he asked.

"I was attempting a method of stimulating myoblast and osteoblast growth using synthetic ligands instead of concentrated doses of the real thing. It normally takes at least thirty days to see significant results—which is why I didn't initially consider it as an option—but some of the Grey equipment appears to be highly specialized in promoting cellular division. I think it's going to be a viable alternative."

"You found another way after all," Auriga said.

"We'll see." She sighed. The medibot finished its work, and rolled to the tableside in order to attend to the Grey. Vulpecula switched it off and placed her hands on her hips. "Now it's time for me to ask: Why exactly did you bring it here?"

Auriga pulled his ruined shirt loosely back over his shoulders, leaving it unbuttoned so as not to chafe his raw skin. "You wanted a vehicle by which to introduce further genetic therapy to ourselves and our candidates," he said. "I'd bet my right arm that the problem has been solved for us already. We've gone this far by leveraging the work of the Greys—so let's see how they've done it."

"But we don't know if this creature has been augmented in any way."

"If it has, it's been at the genetic level—I don't see any cybernetic enhancements. And what is this thing obviously missing?"

Vulpecula nodded, catching his train of thought. "It has no reproductive organs, so it must have been grown in artificial conditions. A test-tube baby."

Auriga stood at the foot of the operating table. "Right. It's got to have an enhanced cellular structure, something that we can get ideas from, if not use outright. Let me get washed up... Is there any coffee left?"

When Auriga returned from the washroom, having donned a surgical gown and mask, Vulpecula's preparations were complete. "We'll start with fifty cc's of thiopental, and prolong unconsciousness with desflurane and nitrous oxide," she said, readying an intravenous line. "Then we'll take some tissue samples—"

At the instant the needle touched its skin, the alien twitched on the table, and an invisible force tore the needle from Vulpecula's grasp. The thin metal spike shot through the air toward Auriga, who jerked his head to the side just in time to avoid it lodging in his eye. The needle left a shallow scratch across his cheek before plinking against the far concrete wall.

Auriga bounded to the table, where the Grey was sitting upright. With a balled fist, he delivered a solid left cross to its narrow, pointed jaw, and the slender being collapsed back to the steel surface with a vanquished groan.

Vulpecula stood staring at Auriga with raised eyebrows. The IV line in her fingers was spurting clear fluid, and she pinched it shut.

"I found another way," Auriga said, "and I think it's going to be a viable alternative."

***

The room was quiet and still but for the soft purr of the various consoles. Reclined on the cot, Auriga began rolling a cigarillo, but Vulpecula remonstrated him with a shake of her head. "I know you're not going to smoke that in here."

"Seems like I hear that a lot. Okay, I'll be out back for a minute."

He rose, placing the cigarillo between his lips, and clamped the Stetson down with the wide brim hiding his eyes. Three strides carried him to the back door, and then he froze, craning his head in attention. "Someone's out there," he whispered.

Vulpecula looked up from her work, scowling. Quiet returned to the laboratory, and the pair listened for several seconds. Auriga stepped to the foot of the bed to retrieve the carbine rifle propped against the wall, then eased back to the door, with the doctor approaching as well. At a nod from him, she flattened her palm against the metal plate, and the door swung outward. The darkness was thick, overlaid with the continued sounds of unrest in the city. A muted blue glow was visible just outside the exit, casting eerie light upon a tenebrous silhouette, and Auriga snaked his arm outside the door to arrest the intruder.

He jerked the visitor into the room; Vulpecula slammed the door, and Auriga shoved him up against it in order to cover him with the rifle. Auriga then stared in astonishment at the sandy-haired boy; the blue glow he had seen was caused by the display of the youth's cybercomputer as he had lurked outside, studying it.

"Muchacho?" he exclaimed. "How did you find us?"

"When I got to the city, the abductions had already started. I was trying to help people, and I heard this massive disturbance, so I went to check it out," Orion said. "Turns out that it was somebody taking a Demistrider apart. Not too many people who could do that, but I figured you were one of the ones who could, and I tracked you here." He paused. "And by the way, the Protectorate is still out looking for you too." As he finished speaking, the young man eyed Vulpecula with unease.

"Tell me something I don't know," Auriga said.

The doctor extended a hand in greeting, and offered a thin smile. "I'm Noreen Vulpecula," she said. "We haven't met, but I believe we—"

"We met a long time ago," the raspy voice broke in. "I'm not surprised you don't recognize—" This time his own words were interrupted as he inspected the surroundings. Auriga watched as the teenager moved through the space, his wide eyes flitting over the arrays of machinery and paraphernalia. He stumbled to the room's macabre centerpiece with its immobile occupant, and he asked with a whispering croak, "What in God's name are you doing here?"

Auriga moved forward, speaking calmly, slinging the rifle over one shoulder. "It's okay, we have this under control. Look at me."

Dumbstruck, Orion stared at the comatose Grey. When Auriga rested a hand on his shoulder, the scavenger flinched and shook it off. Vulpecula approached as well, stone-faced and intense.

"Our work is going to turn the tides of augmented warfare," she announced. "We're finally going to be able to overcome their advantages. The next generation—*your* generation—will be on equal footing with the Greys, technologically speaking."

"You're abducting Greys and experimenting upon them, just like they do to us. I can't believe how perverse this is." Orion backed away from the operating table and walked woodenly to the door. "Auriga, you told me you were going to make sure she was dead."

"Don't let him leave," Vulpecula snapped. "He's seen too much."

For a moment, Auriga stalled. The laboratory was thick with portent, and inaction paralyzed him for a matter of seconds. Then, resolve flooded over his hesitation; the choice had been made, and he crossed the room with quick strides.

"Sorry, amigo," he said as he blocked the exit. "I know what I said before, but she's right. We don't have the luxury of worrying about the moral high ground, and I have to do some things I'm not proud of. You'll understand later, but we can't risk anything happening; it's too important. You have to stay here."

Vulpecula was now behind Orion, and with a quick gesture, she relieved his holster of the giant revolver. Too late, he spun to interfere, but Auriga reached out to hold him in place. The doctor continued to search the scavenger, and soon she hefted the wand-like Vinculum device in her opposite hand. Its displays were dark, and she spied it with suspicion.

"What is this?" she demanded.

Auriga's hands grasped both his shoulders, and Orion glowered at the woman. "It's called the Vinculum," he said. "I'm going to use it to get back on the flying saucer and help Lyra, but it has to be within range of the ship."

Further searching revealed the dull black disintegrator pistol. Vulpecula pursed her lips but did not ask what this item was. She handed the revolver to Auriga and laughed dryly. "You're trying to use Grey technology to defeat them, and yet you condemn me for doing the same thing."

"You have no idea how I came to have this thing," Orion shot back. "It would blow your mind if I told you."

"I'd love to hear all about it, then. We're going to be here together for a while." Vulpecula opened a tall steel locker, placed the Vinculum and the alien gun on a shelf inside, and fetched a pair of powerbinders. She compelled Orion to a cot in the corner of the room, seated him upon it, and clasped one bracelet around his right wrist. His left arm was positioned in a debilitating crossed position that held him pinned while the other bracelet was fastened around a steel pipe affixed to the wall. A soft and steady buzz reported the restraints' active employ.

In a world where many criminals chose augmentation in order

to become more powerful than the average man, conventional handcuffs had become obsolete; as their chainless replacements, a set of powerbinders were linked by an electromagnetic bond so powerful that a silverback gorilla would be helpless against them.

Orion sat, sullen and icy, as his captors returned to their tasks. After only a few moments, Vulpecula appeared to be breezily unaware of the visitor, so engrossed was she in her work; Auriga, on the other hand, cast frequent glances to the figure in the corner but fell just short of looking the boy in the eye. Two quiet hours crawled by.

Auriga's attention was commanded, though, when Vulpecula called him to the live cell microscope. "This is amazing," she said. "I believe we have something significant here."

"What is it?" Auriga hurried to the eyepiece but was stymied by the Stetson's brim. He cast the hat to the floor and looked again.

"These are live cells from one of the Grey's tissue samples. It appears certain that this cell structure would be a suitable vehicle for introducing further genetic therapy to you or me."

"It looks somehow familiar, but I can't say for sure," Auriga said, twisting the dials. "I'm not a scientist, Doc. I'm afraid you'll have to explain it to me."

"It meshes with the work we've already done, almost like two different parts of the same project," Vulpecula said. "The cell structure of the Greys should be thoroughly compatible with our purposes; in fact, it might be the backbone of the agent we're synthesizing."

Auriga looked up from the microscope. "We've always heard a lot about the Greys and humans being distant cosmic cousins. I always dismissed that as crazy. Could there really be something to it?"

The doctor shook her head. "No—I was a skeptic too, and, in fact, I'm less inclined to believe that now than ever before. The cells that make up the bulk of the Greys' vascular structure are compatible to bond with the myocytes found in humans, but are by no means the same thing. The cell structure—insofar as I can call it that—is so radically different that it's more akin to a virus, albeit an artificially engineered one."

"Well, we already knew this thing was a test-tube baby."

"You're still not following me. Yes, in vitro fertilization, like what you're referring to, is rather mundane, and tells us little about the organism or its race as a whole. Even creating a life-form from *ex vivo* methods is no more spectacular than, say, cloning an already living being found somewhere in the universe," she said. "This, on the other hand, is proof that the Greys themselves are *artificially engineered life-forms*."

Auriga stared at the sleeping alien. "Like a race of robots, but organic instead of synthetic. A brand-new form of life that was...created from scratch. By another race."

"Yes." Silence enveloped the lab, which suddenly seemed frigid and raw.

Vulpecula walked to a different workstation, her footsteps making precise clicks like the inexorable ticking of a clock. "I believe that combining this creature's stem cells, for genetic coding, with the action potential catalyst, along with myoblasts for improved musculature and osteoblasts for bone strength, would create a 'virus' that would propel humanity to the next level."

Auriga slowly nodded. "All right, I think you have a sound premise. Where do we go from here?"

"Some of the work that still remains is in finding a more

236

panoptic delivery agent—as it stands now, the strain is not particularly virulent and would have to be centrifuged and introduced directly into the host organism for its effectiveness to be assured," she said.

"In other words, you don't think it's contagious, and we need to fix that."

"Yes. I had initially intended for the final product to be air based, for ease of distribution, but this would present its own difficulties: we couldn't be as selective with the recipients, and not everyone might be agreeable to its effects. Furthermore, not everyone who *was* affected might respond favorably toward us." Vulpecula said, using a pipette to incorporate a number of clear fluids into one reinforced Pyrex vial. "Those who did, however, would become heroes capable of astounding feats—slaying the monsters that have plagued mankind, and finding the divinity inherent within themselves. I shall call this strain the 'Perseus Agent.'"

Orion spoke up. "This is even worse than I thought. You intend to unleash a virus on everyone, and you call it a gift to humanity?"

She cast a dismissive gaze to the youth. "There are several types of viruses, some of which are beneficial to the host organism. Don't presume you know anything about my work."

"I know a lot more than you think."

"Well, maybe you'd like to become even more closely acquainted with it. I'd love to use you as a volunteer for the prototype…" Here she paused, her hand hovering over a sterile syringe for a long moment. Then, she picked up a rubber stopper instead, clamped it over the vial's mouth, and taped it shut. "But I don't believe we would get a clean reading because you're already so heavily augmented. I'll have to look elsewhere for a suitable control group."

"What a shame." Orion's throaty rasp was laced with scorn. "Why don't you just drug the whole city's water supply?"

She looked back at him, unperturbed. "Maybe I will."

"Well, in that case, you've got a long night ahead of you," Orion said. "If you'll unlock these powerbinders, I can get out of your hair."

Vulpecula turned to Auriga. "We won't be needing him. You should just get rid of him instead."

The outlander and the scavenger locked eyes for an instant, and Auriga looked away. He took a step toward the corner, opening his mouth to speak—but as the first word came, brilliance erupted from the Vinculum on the locker's shelf. All eyes flew to the curious device as it blazed with an electric-blue light. Its displays activated with glyphs and numbers that flowed down from the wing-shaped screens through the tapered handle.

"What's it doing?" Vulpecula asked with urgency.

"The ship is in range. It's linking with the Greys' applications and accessing their systems." The youth shifted back and forth on the cot. "Give it to me. *Please.*"

Vulpecula was a few paces away from the locker. Her features portrayed mingled wonder and suspicion as she stepped closer to the device. She reached out one hand—and a spire of awesome physical power carried her off her feet. The vial flew from her grasp, and she hit the wall behind her with such force that the cinder blocks pulverized, collapsing in broken fragments as she sailed through into the night outside.

Auriga wheeled around in alarm, first suspecting that the Vinculum itself had discharged this unworldly energy. The gadget trembled and then lifted off of the metal surface. Then Auriga saw that the Grey was sitting up on the table, one of its spindly arms outstretched to the locker. The Vinculum swept through the air toward the alien's waiting grasp. Auriga jumped into the object's path and slapped it away; the wand clattered to the corner, subject to the laws of terrestrial physics once more.

Auriga was distracted for a moment, hearing several blips that signaled some technological function, and glanced to where the teenager had twisted his left arm into a painful position that allowed him to access his cybercomputer with his captive right hand. An awful buzzing pulse sounded, and the powerbinders released with a clack.

The Grey had swung its legs off the side of the platform, and it continued to gesture with its empty hands. Beakers and utensils now hurled themselves from countertops, raining down on Auriga. Broken glass, sharp metal contrivances, and a myriad of liquid solutions showered him; he could not tell if any were caustic, but his already damaged skin flared anew with blistering agony. Shielding his face with one forearm in the midst of this terrible hail, he seized the pistol's butt with the other hand and leveled it at the slim, ghastly frame. When he focused on the alien, it was pointing the black disintegrator gun squarely at him, having retrieved and equipped the weapon while he was occupied with the hail of glass.

He did not hesitate. Three devastating explosions hammered from the revolver's barrel; the Grey's torso shook in a horrendous trio of convulsions, and silvery ichor splattered the room. The alien toppled from the operating table and crashed to the floor in shambles.

Auriga brushed broken glass from his clothes. Streaks of blood raked his arms. He shook rivulets of unknown solutions from his hair. Orion had risen from his makeshift prison, and dove for the floor in the corner: the Vinculum wand and the vial containing the prototype agent lay within centimeters of each other.

Auriga lunged for the precious items as well. The two tussled on the floor. The vial was closer to the youth, and his hand wrapped around it first; Orion raised it to smash it against the concrete floor, but Auriga tore it from his hand. The cybernetic scrabbled for the Vinculum, and Auriga knocked it farther out of reach. Orion responded with a sudden jab to the face that stunned him for a moment; the vial rattled precariously to the floor again, and rolled away.

They were fighting in earnest now. Auriga's commanding size and speed enabled him to thrash the younger combatant with flurries of punches and kicks; when Orion was weakened, Auriga initiated a clinch that pressured and immobilized his opponent, but an excruciating current of voltage soon detonated from the underdog that forced him to release his captive. Orion tumbled and twisted on the floor, handing out fierce cyber-assisted strikes with deadly precision. With each well-targeted blow, Auriga felt his power sapped and his muscles stiffen, as if he were being needled by an electric stiletto. Before the youth could secure the upper hand, though, Auriga mauled him with a vicious haymaker that sent Orion reeling, and the brutal melee began again.

They rolled and fought in the broken glass and equipment of the ruined lab. Auriga grabbed Orion, planted a foot in his stomach, and rolled onto his back to hurl him into the row of lockers. The metal shelves caved in with a squeal, and Orion slumped facedown onto the tile. Auriga had just climbed to his feet when the cybernetic pushed himself up to lash out with one electrically charged hand that wracked the larger man with twisted blue forks; when Auriga stumbled backward in suffering, his foot nudged a forgotten object. He looked down to see the revolver lying abandoned in the detritus of unwholesome scientific pursuits. The agent's vial was centimeters away.

People outside screamed, their voices carrying through the ragged hole in the concrete wall with a clarity born of urgency and proximity. A battered figure dragged itself up to the broken cinder blocks; as she rose in torment to her feet, Auriga saw that Vulpecula was limping terribly, and her once-pristine lab coat and dress were torn and bloody. Her wild eyes fixed on him.

Orion scrambled for the Vinculum again, its sapphire-blue beacon still blazing in a heralding call. Auriga stooped, reaching for the object at his feet. His body seethed with pain; as he gritted his teeth, his hand passed over the revolver and landed on the vial. When he straightened, the doctor held out her hands.

"Hurry, they're coming. Give me the agent!"

He tossed the Perseus Agent to her; as it traveled in a gentle arc, he saw in its airborne journey the very destiny of mankind: a soaring climb, a brief pinnacle, and a harrowing descent. So fragile, so uncertain. The vial flashed with a prismatic shimmer in the fluorescent lights, and then the shadows of the doctor's outstretched hands harbored it. Another moment, and she fled, crippled and limping, but soon lost in the howling, hungry night.

Auriga saw Orion stand with the Vinculum finally in his grasp, and the carbine rifle as well. His own fists were empty, and the drive for pugilism had drained from him. The shocking white eyes of the teenager carried a mixture of camaraderie and sadness. Auriga yearned for the right words to convey his thoughts, but he was straddled between two worlds. Conflict tore him open within and surrounded him without; at last, all he could manage was an earnest smile.

"I told you before that none of us were the same since this all began," he said.

Auriga turned to follow the doctor through the hole in the wall and into the chaotic city; Orion began to reply, but the gravelly croak was enveloped by a louder, harsher sound.

Both of the laboratory's metal doors burst inward under an influx of Protectorate operatives. The black-clad commandos streamed into the room; Auriga hurried to the decimated pile of cinder blocks but found that avenue also bristling with the barrels of submachine guns. A swarm of masked officers packed the ravaged room, yelling out a rising and overlapping chorus of instructions and demands. Auriga raised his hands, backing toward the center of the room with his eyes on Orion.

As the scavenger twiddled the odd controls, already the blue glow bathed his form in a marvelous haze; his outline grew acute and ultra-distinct, and sparks of glittering cobalt danced around him. The officers screamed and challenged, but Orion ignored them all. He was blessed, rising to a celestial place; his eyes locked upon the Auriga's as the holy blue light embraced and then swallowed him.

The officer at the forward position strode up to Auriga with a grim expression on his unmasked features. Leisurely, Auriga moved his hands to rest on the back of his head and interlaced his fingers as he knelt. Broken glass crunched beneath his knees, and he fixed his attention upon the name "Harlow," which was now at eye level on the Detective's breast.

Someone was behind him; the hum of powerbinders overtook his senses. His arms were positioned behind his back, and his wrists were constricted and immobilized. He was damned, falling to an infernal place; the dark shapes moved in as one, casting him in shadow, lining his view as if some total eclipse of reality had consumed all the light in the cosmos.

Chapter Twenty

Orion stepped from the pedestal, and the gentle illumination dissipated. He readied the rifle and brought it to shoulder level, but a sweep of the curvilinear room revealed that he was alone. Aboard the bewitching alien craft once again, his mind fluttered in a ballet of recognition and revulsion. Earthbound experiences now melted from his thoughts; even the aches and injuries of his exodus from Vulpecula's laboratory were supplanted by a wondrous and hideous peace.

He moved into the hallway, a gentle curve that pulsed with ambient light. The wand-like device in his hand still glowed blue, but it beat in rhythmic harmony with the ship's serene gleam instead of blazing with solid ferocity as it had done down below. He stowed it in the wide pocket of his cargo pants as he advanced down the corridor.

Spindly figures gazed at him through viewing bays to either side. Their heads moved on stalklike necks to track his progress, but the aliens made no attempt at intervention. Presently, he came upon other Greys in the pathway; his finger curled against the gun's trigger, but the ashen beings deferred to him, offering no resistance.

Orion continued through the weird pathways of the ship, reluctant to initiate any offense against the aliens for fear of what they might do in retribution to the captive Lyra. It was best to find her first—with her and the Vinculum, he would have the upper hand. He quickened his pace. God only knew what the aliens' intentions were; he had limited time to rejoin Lyra and escape from this vehicle.

The hallway's arc led him through various branches and past mystifying side rooms and window bays, but he relied on instinct and his sense of direction to thread his way closer to the heart of the saucer. The aliens in his path now followed him in an unsettling discipleship. He scowled and postured at them, thinking to frighten them away, but, like submissive dogs, they retreated for a moment only to resume their disturbing pilgrimage. Anticipation hung heavy in these narrow halls, and when Orion at last reached a corridor that terminated in a blank wall with a closed door to its left, he checked his weapons and summoned a tranquil focus before stepping up to, and through, the sliding portal.

This chamber was circular, and less than fifteen meters in diameter. Viewing bays, lined with impassive black-eyed faces, circled the bulkheads. One door stood within the far wall, and before it, the room's single, horrendous occupant waited. Thrashing metal limbs whipped from the ghoulish man's bifurcated torso. Veins and fetid rot mottled his bloated purple flesh. A thick tongue swelled in his throat, gruesome milky eyes rolled in their sockets, and it gargled hellishly. The thing staggered forward on stiff legs, driven by some mysterious perception of the young invader who now backed against a door that slid shut, preventing escape.

Orion took the initiative, raising the ballistic weapon and rattling a short burst of rounds at the monstrous thing. The projectiles clanged and sparked, deflecting from the thrashing metal tentacles that provided effective defense as well as a formidable threat. The beast clambered close enough for Orion to see that each tentacle terminated in a different tool: a narrow blade resembling a pike, a grasping claw, a knotty club, and so on. Keeping his distance, Orion skirted the outside edge of the room while searching for some weakness in the disgusting abomination.

He couldn't put together a plan before it charged, although the lopsided, drunken tripping that the monstrosity displayed was more reckless than any coordinated attack. Still, the lashing metal tentacles kept Orion hard-pressed to stay clear, and as he fired the rifle again at the stumpy legs, trying to buy some breathing room, the writhing arms nullified his shots once more.

A wild appendage knocked Orion sprawling, and he cried out in helpless rage. As he rolled onto one side, his skin prickled, and his ruffled hair grew static-suffused and fuzzy. He tore into the monstrosity with a storm of sizzling current, but again the flailing limbs absorbed the brunt of the attack. Forks of electricity danced around the tips of the terrible metal arms, arcing from one to the other, but what little voltage reached the disfigured body was shrugged off by the uncommon fortitude of a rambling creature that exhibited little sentience and felt little pain. The bolts of current withered and died.

Orion dodged and rolled to reach the opposite end of the chamber, and the mindless aggressor shuffled after him from the far side of the room. The cramped locale filled with the sickening, ceaseless gargle—the awful noise would drive any victim mad, if they weren't dismembered by the fetching claws first. Orion shut out the sound with a fierce effort of will and cautiously turned partial attention to his cybercomputer's display.

The thing was not a cyborg or a machine, and yet it was not

wholly organic either. There was no centralized processor to combat on the virtual battlefield—Orion could not hack into it or shut it down. Still, he perceived some circuitry patterns in the unholy augmentations, and he assembled a wild plan. He continued his careful sidestepping of the constant assault while keying urgent instructions into the computer.

It did not take long, either a testament to his technical or tactical superiority or just blind luck. Orion's computer displays flickered and danced, establishing a resonant frequency with the circuits in the twitching metal arms. He pushed the coupling power to a balefully intense range; his own augmentations kindled in protest, but the abomination's wicked limbs overloaded in frenzy.

The metal appendages surged with uncontained energy, and all semblance of command or hindrance fell away. A fascinating, suicidal tarantella ensued as the tentacles whipped in horrid circles, beating at the air and at their proprietor's flesh indiscriminately. The arms bashed the lolling head over and over and ripped chunks of bloody tissue from the noisome torso. Void of direction or cognizance, the deadly arms flailed and spun like a deranged propeller. Soon the appendages were beating too fast to be seen as anything beyond a whirling blur, and the stinking spray of blood drenched the walls and floor in a tapestry of horror. Gushes of crimson, rolling in thick streams, blotted the faces of the Greys watching from the windows.

The mangled monstrosity tottered and plunged to the deck. The pummeling tentacles still hammered at the twitching trunk and struck violent tattoos on the floor, but the nauseating gargle had ceased. Orion edged around the gore-bedecked chamber to find the door opposite where he had entered. He withdrew from the ghastly room into a corridor and headed farther within the ship.

Another minute, and he came to a curving wall that led him around to the left. Orion was near the center of the flying saucer now; the next chamber seemed to be a perfect circle, and he passed occasional windows that revealed nothing despite his careful scrutiny. The next door was locked, but a moment's attention with the Vinculum, and it slid smoothly open.

This great chamber was indeed circular and domed. A series of platforms piled one atop the other in concentric rings; colored light cascaded down the lateral surfaces of each dais. Around the perimeter of the room, illumined lenses were arranged on the floor, each large enough for a man to stand upon; Orion guessed that these were avenues by which to access other floors of the ship. On the topmost dais, a contoured throne revolved in prismatic coruscations. By degrees it swiveled to face him, and Orion gazed into the august visage of the throne's occupant.

It was a Grey, that much was certain, although its cranium was decidedly larger than average, and was shaped more like a heart than an inverted teardrop. The massive brain was divided into two distinct lobes that, although hidden by folds of wrinkled, pallid skin, pulsated now and then in a revolting series of rippling twitches. Likewise, its body, while sharing the sickly, hairless anemia of the other aliens' physiques, was built more sturdily, and Orion fancied that the increased musculature was a necessary byproduct of supporting the immense head. It wore a flowing robe of purple and gold, which carried the sheen of fine silk. The lustrous garment draped generously over the throne and much of the topmost section of the dais, leaving Orion to wonder at the actual size of the puzzling, regal being beneath it.

The sovereign's intrusive leer seemed to bore into Orion's beleaguered consciousness from the instant that the chair's crawling rotation afforded the opportunity. There was haughtiness and contempt in that cold, withering gaze, but nothing of real hostility. And though the youth's heart raced and his blood chilled, he stood his ground and stared back in defiance.

"I am called Pyxis," spoke the being into Orion's mind. The voice that he perceived—rather than *heard*—was balmy and ethereal in timbre, and superior in inflection; it manifested as neither masculine nor feminine, neither mortal nor divine. It soothed and unnerved at once. *"This is my ship, and you are welcome here. We have things of import to discuss."*

"This isn't a social call, Pyxis," Orion said aloud. "All I want is to get my friend and go home." He forewent the meaningless posture of equipping the rifle at his shoulder; ballistic rounds would never reach a creature with this kind of psionic power, and they both knew it.

"You insist on communicating via those vulgar human means," the voice in his head observed, *"despite your hatred of the sound of your own voice."*

"I don't care," Orion answered. "This is the way I sound. I have to deal with it, and so do you."

"Very well, I will accommodate you," the being said aloud. Now the voice was dry and wheezing, no longer beautiful, like an old man pronouncing curses on his deathbed. "But it is not a fitting manner with which the new Illuminatus to speak."

Orion started, drawing his head back in surprise. His words were almost reflexive. "No. No way. I'm not an Illuminatus. Even if I were suited for it, I would never—"

"No one is better suited," Pyxis explained in a patient tone. "You are familiar with our race and display some of our prominent successes in your very physiology. You are adept with our technology—you even boarded this ship by your own devices.

248

Your gifts allow you to bridge the gap between man and Grey. You will be an ambassador to your race on our behalf."

A troubling question emerged in Orion's thoughts. "Corvus served you with such enthusiasm. Why did you throw him away?"

"His failures were evident, and they were not mitigated by his zeal. You faced him and defeated him. Does this not make you worthy to take his place?"

"Just like that awful thing with the metal tentacles, Pyxis? Will I be taking its place? If I'm welcome here, why did it try to kill me?"

"That wretched thing was simply a failed experiment," the alien pronounced. "I am entitled to a guardian, but you've proved your superiority over that unfortunate creature, as I expected. Thank you for disposing of it—you continue to please us with your performance."

"I'm so glad to be the one experiment that actually went right," Orion said. "You guys don't have much of a track record: my parents, the Lacertas, and everything else you've ever screwed around with has been the worse for it."

"We are patient beings, and know that each failure brings us closer to success." The sovereign smiled, a sight that Orion found more unsettling than its prior impassivity. "It is not a simple task, after all, to rewrite the laws of evolution and elevate an entire race."

Orion's body tingled, except for those areas where machinery was grafted into his skin—those were numb. "It's difficult with good reason. Technology isn't a substitute for real life."

"You are more right than you know," the alien replied. "Your race has stagnated its development with technology, rather than using it to strengthen its potential."

"I've heard the sermons on the evils of video games, but you're barking up the wrong tree. Those are for rich vassals in the city," Orion said.

"Actually, we Greys do use technology for entertainment—especially on long spacefaring voyages. Our senses are stimulated by rich, vibrant patterns of shapes and colors, and we enjoy viewing them by electronic displays for extended periods of time."

"So you're speaking of the development of the species as a whole. Evolution."

"I am." The alien folded its spindly fingers across its chest. "The Greys use technology to bolster our strengths; humans use it to prolong their weaknesses. Useless pursuits such as keeping the old and feeble alive longer, or supplementing the forms of the crippled and infirm, have stunted your evolutionary progress. As a technologically enhanced race, humans have stagnated, failing to honor the natural concept of 'survival of the fittest.'"

"Dr. Vulpecula might disagree with you." Orion offered a mischievous smile.

The alien frowned, its skin wrinkling into deep furrows. "This leads us to Lyra," he said.

The impish grin melted from Orion's features, and his chin rose with a start. "What's wrong with her?"

"She remains in a coma," the wheezing voice pronounced. "Her psionic gift is a flawed one. She is a prototype, you must recall: the first human to receive a psychoactive regimen of this intensity."

"Her mind is still active; it's just her body that needs help," Orion said.

"Mind and body are not separate concepts; they are codependent. Her abilities are prodigious, but her body appears unable to support the immense power required to use them."

"Let her go. I know there's some way to help her. I'll do anything."

"I find your priorities to be quite puzzling," the alien said. "You say that all you want is to return to Earth with this human. Why limit your existence to a backward, mundane planet? Why help only one human by staying, when you can grant a boon to your entire race by becoming an Illuminatus?"

An action potential could not go back the way it came...

"That would serve you more than it would serve mankind," Orion corrected severely. "And besides, she means more to me than the rest of the human race put together."

"This is foolish. One human cannot be more valuable than the entire race." The Grey leaned forward in the coruscating throne, its inky eyes searching for revelation in the young man's face. "The irrational notion of individuality that humans insist upon clinging to is one of the foremost reasons for their decline. Explain it to me."

Orion stood silent, groping for defense and justification. The sovereign waited for a response, but argument had abandoned him. He could only think that if Lyra were here, she would have an answer. She would know how to explain the concepts of humanity to this unearthly being—indeed, she would illuminate Orion on these things that he could only dimly grasp himself. He smiled at the rueful irony that he could better understand what it was to be human only with her aid. It was as though the alien were correct and incorrect at the same time.

At last he could only say, "People value individuality because they are all different. If you don't know, then I can't explain it to you." He laughed at his own helplessness.

"Hmph." The sovereign frowned, sinking back into the throne.

"As absurd a statement as I could ever imagine. With over three billion people on the planet, how could anyone claim to be unique? All of you have the same motives and goals: to acquire wealth, to acquire a mate, to prolong your health and life, and to experience that feeling of diversion that you call 'fun.'

"To whatever extent that you *are* different can be objectively measured: Talents are quantifiable. Intelligence is quantifiable. Motives are either logical or they are not. Humans themselves can be objectively measured, and they are each suited for one purpose or another, but this does not strengthen your claim that individuality is to be prized—these purposes are only valuable insofar as they advance the interests of the collective.

"Suppose that a man were a superlative speaker. What good is that without other men to hear him speak, and thereby receive inspiration? Or suppose that he were a skilled craftsman. What were his labors, without others to agree upon their value? Can a man create something, and then say, 'I deserve wealth in exchange for this,' without another man to substantiate that exchange?"

"There are different kinds of wealth," Orion answered. "On Earth, I would not be considered wealthy at all—but if I could live there with Lyra, I would consider myself rich. Some men have great possessions, and are sad because they have no one to share them with. Other people might disagree, but a man can choose his own life, unlike a Grey. By our very nature, we espouse different values than you—even from each other—and that is why we must prize individuality."

He would have said more, but an indelible miasma now seemed to grip the peregrine craft. His movements were not sluggish or uncoordinated, but the surprise of this unheralded transformation halted his train of thought.

Then the revelation opened as with a gentle glow in his brain: the saucer was moving. Not in the sense of gliding over the city but rather accelerating with true purpose. Whereas the propulsion systems of conventional human design increased gravitational force to an immobilizing extent, the Greys' craft seemed to produce only a mild disorientation. Still, alarm took precedence over wonder, and Orion moved to fetch the Vinculum from the side pocket of his cargo pants. The device would be able to tell him the projected trajectory of the ship, and allow him to interfere if it was unsatisfactory—but the Vinculum tore from his grasp and sailed across the room to rest in the outstretched hand of Pyxis.

"I'll help myself to this fascinating invention," the alien hissed. "As it is attuned to the applications of my ship, I hereby claim it as my rightful possession."

"Where are we going?" Orion demanded.

"There is no reason to stay on Earth any longer," Pyxis said. "Our mission here has been completed. We are returning to the home of the Greys, called Ios. It is a magnificent city in space—the capital of this galaxy—and its grandeur will appeal to you. It has long been my intention to introduce the race of man to galactic society, and you will be the first to receive this privilege."

Orion's rage was mounting. "And what's expected of me when I get there, other than being paraded around like a poodle at a dog show?"

"On Ios, you will learn your new duties and become...acclimated to them."

"Why bother mincing words? I know what that means, you bug-eyed fascist."

The sovereign continued as if Orion hadn't spoken. "Meanwhile, another diplomatic vessel is arriving on Earth soon to take our place."

The scavenger was horrorstruck. "All of this butchery, these countless atrocities—this is what you call a *diplomatic* mission?"

The alien blinked at him, still impassive. "These are peace-keeping operations agreed upon with Earth's leaders years ago. You're aboard a scout-class saucer, which has the power to level a small city. The people of Earth have never even laid eyes upon our warships."

Horrible realizations unfolded before Orion. He was truly leaving Earth and everything in it for the world of these enigmatic masters of the unseen. He had done little more than deliver himself into their clutches—what a fool he was! Chills prickled his body anew, and he closed his eyes against the tears that started to brim.

"It is time to show you to your quarters," Pyxis said. "The journey is not inordinately long, but you will want to be secured in your travel harness before we initiate the faster-than-light jump. You may find the astral plane to be quite disorienting."

When Orion opened his eyes, a Grey had entered from one of the side doors and was approaching him with mute insistence. He sneered at it, this contemptible, supercilious weakling; his scowl deepened when the alien stretched out a beckoning gesture and projected two words into his mind: *"This way."*

This way, indeed. Humanity would go whither they were bid, as they had done ever since these sadistic shepherds had led them by the nose into the very abyss of slavery. Down crawling paths of stultifying decrepitude man would hurl himself, reveling in the worthless ashen-gray blessings of nameless beings. In that instant, he hoped that Vulpecula would succeed, no matter what the cost. In that instant, he wondered if he would ever feel human again.

Orion ripped the rifle from his shoulder and clubbed the head of the gesturing Grey with the butt of the weapon. It recoiled with a squeal, bringing its puny hands up to splay across its wide forehead; silver blood trickled from between its fingers. He reached out, gripping the creature's skull with an open palm. It convulsed with minute jerks as its skin and brain fried; wispy smoke rose in curlicues from its seizing form. With a powerful jolt, Orion blasted the sizzled corpse away. It shot through the air in a headlong arc and bounced off the far bulkhead before smacking the ship's deck and lying still.

Orion backed away from the circular daises and floundered toward one of the illumined lenses near the room's periphery. The sovereign watched him, frowning with curiosity and re-pugnance, as Orion stood upon the colored platform, keyed instructions into his cybercomputer, and descended through the floor to the level below.

Chapter Twenty-One

C harging through the curving corridors of the ship, Orion peered into viewing bays on his right and left. Now and then an alien came into view ahead of him in the hallway, but these would scamper into some side room that sealed shut after it. The lower level of the saucer appeared to contain those subjects who were awaiting, or recuperating from, the operating table, and he supposed that the upper levels, by contrast, housed a higher population of the Greys and the ship's administrative chambers.

Many of the rooms Orion passed were dark; some were pristine laboratories whose cleanliness belied the gruesome truth that lurked within. As he passed other viewing bays, insensate faces that were too stolid to be called human leered back at him. His inadequacy in helping these ill-fated wretches tore at his heart; still, he had no choice but to move forward.

With a skilled ballet of his fingertips, he synced his cybercomputer to the positronic centrum of the spaceship. The computer sapped juice from the ship's channels, and his cybernetic components converted it to bioelectric energy, supercharging his body. A power surge in the craft—such as the upcoming one to initiate faster-than-light travel—would overload his body and kill him instantly, but he considered the reward to be worth the risk.

Short-lived electrical events...

He burned with severity and vigor. Each stride, every move-ment, was perfect in its intention. This was what people must experience in their final seconds of life: such crystalline exactitude, such raw and primal purpose. His life was either about to end, or truly begin.

His senses lit up in premonition—as he wheeled around, two aliens rounded the bend behind him, raising their weapons in tandem. Orion flicked his left wrist, and with a twisted motion of his hand, massive streams of lightning jetted from his fingertips. The mingling forks of arciform energy crashed against the pair with an audible concussion; after the sapphire flashes subsided, charred remains rested against a scorched bulkhead.

He resumed his advance through the maze of corridors, projecting a schematic of the craft from the ship's centrum onto his HUD. Expedited in this manner, he soon stood before the room he sought. The locked door yielded to a savage heave that ripped it right out of its housing. Orion forced the dismembered portal into the bulkhead's vacant pocket. The unfailing motion of the ship's engines, and the accompanying sensation of gentle ascendancy, sparked an urgency within him—but he could not enter the room without pause.

Lyra reclined on an oval-shaped padded platform that resem-bled a daybed. Her torn and stained desert clothes were gone, and she was dressed in bottle-green slacks and a black tunic that crested with the cowl indigenous to the Illuminati. The hood that covered her shorn head did not hide her beauty; beneath the pink, circular scar, her eyes were closed in neutral repose. Her hands lay clasped at her stomach, and though the serene pose spoke of calm and quietude, Orion obeyed a tangible magnetic pull that drew him to her side.

Her mind is still active. It's just her body that needs help.

Well, between the ship's power and my own, I think I know just how to do it.

Purposeful strides carried him across the room. He marched to her bedside and placed his right hand under the base of her head, lifting it up. He moved closer, settling his left hand on her smooth jawline, and bent to kiss the pale, carnation lips with long-deferred ardor. Lightning branched between their lips as he drew near, connecting them with a torrent of newfound spirit, and when he met her in a kiss, bolts of current flowed freely and joined their mouths with a sparking flux.

She remained motionless, however, and he pulled away. Frantically, he examined her placid face. *Nothing's happening. If she doesn't wake up...* Oaths of vengeance screamed through his mind. He would allow the Greys to take him to Ios, and then he would make them regret having done so.

Then Lyra trembled, and her lovely gray eyes opened. Her eyebrows lifted, and she drew a yearning breath. With both hands, she grasped Orion's face and pulled him down to her lips again in a fervent and impassioned kiss.

The current surged anew. Orion surrendered to the flow of vitality between them, a passage that invigorated her with a profusion of bioelectric energy, resetting and strengthening her action potentials to accommodate the increased demands of her brain's unprecedented potency—but what held his senses captive was the bliss of joyous communion with her. The air around them danced with static; he could easily have forgotten the fetters and constraints of time, the impending reckoning with their ever-present peril.

At last she broke away and rose to a seated position on the platform. "We have to get off the ship," she said.

Their predicament resurfaced in Orion's thoughts, but he

could hardly bring himself to shift his focus from Lyra. Only by reminding himself that her life was still in danger could he turn away the urge to forsake all the world and remain here with her.

"Yes, we've got to leave now. The ship is rising through the Earth's atmosphere, and when we're clear of the planet, we're going to jump." The lights on the ship flickered, and Orion looked around in confusion. "What was that?"

Lyra bounded from the mattress with a nimble movement. She bowed her hooded head, closing her eyes, and the ship shuddered in response. Again, the meager illumination faltered. When she locked eyes with Orion, a smile spread on her sprightly face. "The Greys use their own psionic energy to direct the craft: Pyxis, or a team of other navigators, probably steer it and engage other controls just by using their thoughts." Her face glowed; she was vibrant, flush with unbounded vigor, just as he was. "And now that you've given me the increased potential that I needed, I can too. Keep siphoning as much power as you can from the ship, and I can struggle with Pyxis for control of it. If we can force the energy channels into a dearth, the systems should crash."

"And so will the ship," Orion said, looking at her roguishly. "I could kiss you again, if that would help."

She laughed. "Later. I want us to be able to take our time."

Four Greys rushed through the broken door, opening fire as they entered the room. Orion twisted into a dive, hitting the floor with the carbine rifle readied; Lyra stood firm, extending a palm that deflected the incoming bolts. The heated stripes of orange streaked along diverted courses to end as ragged burns on the surrounding walls. Orion fired back, snapping rounds from the rifle with breakneck pinpoint accuracy. Silvery holes opened three of the bulbous foreheads in rapid succession; the fourth alien twitched and sent the bullet careening out of its trajectory.

Lyra pushed the air in front of her with both hands out, and the Grey flew back with sudden violence, impacting against the bulkhead behind it with such force that bones snapped over the sound of the metal wall crumpling. The broken body tumbled to the deck in a jumble of twisted limbs.

Orion regained his feet, leaving the spent weapon on the deck with its bolt locked open. As he joined her, Lyra resumed her look of deep concentration. This time, the saucer convulsed with such pressure that Orion was nearly deposited on the floor a second time. He kept his footing with the aid of the daybed, and the tremors built to a furious degree. Consulting his computer's display, he confirmed that he was still greedily drawing power from the ship's cortex, which was approaching failure. The shuddering intensified further, and when Lyra slid on the uneven surface as well, he wrapped an arm about her waist to hold her closer to him.

The sensation of gliding movement dissipated and was lost. They reached the teetering apex of a weightless sublimity; their ascent to the heavens had slowed and stopped. For one interminable second, the sum total of existence hung in vivid, breathtaking stasis—and then the lights throughout the ship dimmed into feeble vestiges against the encroaching shadows, and the plunge began.

The room tilted askew, and Orion braced himself in the gut-wrenching freefall. He was buoyant and light in the abruptly rescinded gravity; his feet were not pulled from the floor, but maintaining his balance required constant readjustment. The sense of casual airiness, at odds with his dire surroundings, was almost enjoyable until he considered that they were now trapped within a flightless metal disc hurtling toward the earth at terminal velocity.

"Let's get moving," Lyra said, wavering on her feet also. "What's the fastest way off the ship?"

Orion checked the relevant schematics. "Escape pods are on the uppermost level, where the navigation rooms, and most of the aliens themselves, are located. I don't think that's going to work—they'll either have used the pods themselves by the time we get there or assembled an army for us to fight through, and we don't have that much time. The ship doesn't have enough power for us to use its biotransporters either. We'll have to get the Vinculum back from Pyxis; it's the only option we have."

Her eyes narrowed. "All right, then. We have to hurry."

Orion pitched toward the exit, but progress was more harried than he had supposed; the room tilted at least twenty degrees laterally in relation to the door, and he walked a tottering, uneven track, free of any support other than Lyra's hand. "This isn't working. Jump—we can cover ground quicker."

A coordinated leap brought them both close to the open door; they misjudged the center of the portal, but Orion caught the doorjamb with his free hand. The aliens' corpses slid in a twisted pile toward the lower end of the room, leaving a wake of silvery blood smeared across the floor. It cast a hypnotic sheen in the failing light.

In the sloping corridor, travel was easier: Orion could bolster his balance by walking close to the bulkhead. Still, it was an upward climb to return the way he had come, and the sleek walls offered no handholds. He trudged on with determination and reached a bend where the hallway curved to the right. From this point, the slope allowed him to walk with one foot on the bulkhead itself, and he now raced forward with Lyra close behind. Such resistance as they encountered was easily overcome—the narrow, blood-slicked halls channeled them onward, an inexorable harbinger rising sharply in voltage, with a single, clear task ahead and no way in which to retreat.

They reached the colored lens signifying access to the next floor and found it a sickly yellow instead of the usual vibrant orange. Still, motes of light swirled in the vertical avenue between the floor and ceiling, and it appeared to be operational. The pair halted for the briefest respite, exchanging solemn looks of determination before proceeding: Lyra first, and then the scavenger.

The psionic shot up through the floor of the room above. When Orion followed, planting his boots on the tilting deck, he saw that she had never landed: Lyra hovered a full meter above the floor, her arms out to either side as they gathered imbued energy. The otherworldly look in her stormy gray eyes was transcendent.

The command chamber had darkened, but the lateral surfaces of each dais were a deranged assortment of hypnotic displays. Colors bled in nightmare collusion, and the shifting patterns were eerie and unsettling. Atop the summit of this chaos, Pyxis now rose from its throne, its long robes trailing in cascades from its indiscernible form. It ruled a scene of frightening cosmic majesty: its own grandiose brain a crown and the Vinculum a scepter. As the alien stood, it continued to ascend until it, too, was levitating under its own power; the raised platforms receded into themselves, sinking into the floor like a primal continent disappearing into the sea.

"You are powerful," the alien intoned in its baleful, shriveled voice. "I would rather have guided you to the grandeur of the stars—but you have chosen to remain earthbound. This is foolish."

"Hand over the Vinculum," Orion implored. "Once we're gone,

you still have time to save your ship."

"No," Pyxis wheezed. "Power and foolishness is a combination I cannot allow in the race of men. You must be destroyed."

"Now you're being the foolish one. If we go down, you're coming with us."

"That is preferable to you leaving with the device."

Orion balled his fists, which crackled afresh with lightning. Then he realized his folly: he dared not attack the sovereign in such a manner. The risk of shorting out the Vinculum was too great. The alien returned the scavenger's look of consternation with one of triumph, and pierced him with a debilitating wave of mental agony—Orion's mind crumpled against the invasive devastation of the psionic attack.

There was no recourse against the madness that tore his diminishing sanity apart. The world around him evaporated, leaving him abandoned and unaided, veering hopelessly through the desolate cosmos amid a screeching cacophony of wretched lost souls. Orion lashed out with his mind, willing himself to break free of the enveloping despair, struggling to project himself back to the ship. Alas, all around him was cold and eternal death, a prison with an absence not only of walls but of reality itself. He railed against the mounting enervation of the barren void, and to his utter stupefaction, the universe responded.

Something cracked through the infinite space: a doorway opened, flooding light and warmth into the Acheronian waste. Blinking his eyes in the dawning light, Orion perceived Lyra at the threshold of the dimension, reaching a slender arm out to him. He seized her hand as a drowning man grasps at a lifeline, and was pulled through.

Gravity, now restored, forced his body downward with an

insistent pull. He was back on the saucer, and the abrupt shift in equilibrium, along with the perilously slanted deck, threatened to cost him his footing. The chamber was almost dark, with glimmers of that same maddening prismatic display, and Pyxis and Lyra whirled about the room in a cyclone of psychic conflict. Their deadly midair dance seemed to thicken the very atmosphere as they hammered and buffeted one another with unseen and eternal forces.

Strident pops and clacks now sounded from the upper levels of the craft; Orion could identify them even before his diagnostic display confirmed the responsible event. Escape pods were launching from the navigation deck—the Greys were scuttling the ship, which was certain to crash at any moment. Meanwhile, the commander was going down with the ship, while making certain that the humans would do the same. With Pyxis engaged against Lyra, the scavenger had one last chance to regain the Vinculum.

Orion dashed in a furious hustle down the slope of the deck, and continued up along the curvature of the bulkhead. He gathered speed through the trough formed by the dip in the lowest end of the wall, and mustered all the fervor he could, aided by the dwindling energy of the ship, to race up the ascending side. Fighting to compensate for the drag of gravity against his momentum, he timed his lurching steps to carry him as near to the apex as possible, and then leapt off with a maneuver that spent the dredges of his remaining technologically enhanced energy.

Orion dove downward through the center of the room, stretching to his limit to coincide his fall with the levitating alien as it passed beneath him. One grasping hand latched on to the wand-like device, and he dangled precariously in the midst of his arrested flight.

Taken aback, Pyxis halted its own movement and glared down at the unexpected challenger. The alien prepared to deal yet another telepathic blow, but a moment's break in its concentration against Lyra's unending assault left Pyxis unable to finalize the action. The two hung in stasis, falling precipitously from the sky. Orion reached up with his right hand to the keys of the cybercomputer on his left forearm—centimeters below the ashen hand that clung with tenacity to the Vinculum.

With nimble commands, Orion uncoupled from the ship's positronic centrum and linked his system to the Vinculum itself. Exquisite spates of energy and pain frazzled his already overwrought senses, but he found access to the defunct saucer's biotransporters and flooded them with power. He held out his hand for Lyra; as she flew to him, the scope of his world grew crisp and hyper-distinct. The device was slipping from Pyxis's attenuated grasp, and malice and rancor spread across the alien's pale features.

Orion watched with distinct accuracy as the thin, curled fingers gave way from the metal shaft at the instant that Lyra reached his side. Her hand entwined with his about the device that surged with an electric-blue beacon. Orion's right arm clung to her waist; his left hand seizing the hard-fought prize, they plummeted together toward the deck's unforgiving surface. His strength failed. In the sudden drop, he couldn't hold on, and she tumbled free of his arms as he braced for impact.

Epilogue

Gentle bites of cold brushed at his face before he opened his eyes. Snowflakes had settled on his skin, and the delicate feathers melted away as he pulled his weary body to a sitting position. Halcyon white flutters cascaded down from the gunmetal-gray sky, and stormy clouds of smoke floated heavenward from the gunmetal-gray earth. He stared in bewilderment at the breadth of smoldering wreckage littering the frost-tipped tundra.

Debris was scattered over a considerable area, although the majority of it lay within the crater blasted into the frozen earth. The saucer had stayed intact until the final instant, and had hit the ground with overwhelming force, shattering it into a million twisted hunks of detritus. The Vinculum had succeeded in transporting him off the craft; nothing could have lived through such a monumental disaster.

Orion scanned the wreckage for any sign of Pyxis or Lyra, and found none—they had both been spirited away to some unknown place by their proximity to the Vinculum as well. He envisioned weird and lurid realms to dominate a freedom so recently, so grudgingly, won, and then reflected on the very real possibility that he was now more in need of aid than Lyra was, wherever she might be. These phantasms promised only to highlight callous injustice and despair, and so he shut them from his wearied mind. As he surveyed the area, his cybercomputer detected no bioelectric signals from anything larger than a field mouse in the vicinity of the crash site. A distinctive signature lured him with its bright beacon, and he recovered the winged, wand-shaped apparatus among the rubble not far from where he had awoken. He stowed it in its familiar pocket and was buoyed by the relic's return.

His optimism was tempered, however. He was ill equipped for the cold, and unaccustomed to such a climate. He had no food or water, no shelter or transportation, and the harsh tundra sprawled in every direction. He thought to identify his active GPS coordinates but decided against it: aliens in their escape pods would surely land in the area. They might have weapons; they might already be on their way to the giant, smoking crater.

He rummaged through the surrounding debris. Perhaps something useful could be found. Perhaps he could salvage his salvation from this chilled and somehow burnt wilderness. He worked to amass a pile of raw materials that would build another life, a bridge to carry him back to the world of men. Then his ears picked up a soft rumbling, and he lifted his head to scour the horizon.

Black utility vehicles roused a line of white from the frozen ground as they descended from a hill in the distance. They headed for the crater in a swift and certain path. Men were coming to investigate the crash, and to scavenge for what they could find. Orion raised one half-metallic arm above his head, waving as he walked to meet them.

Afterword

I have many friends and loved ones to thank for playing a part in making this dream of mine come true.

First and foremost, to my wonderful wife London: You encourage me to reach for my goals, and give me something to work for, which is the best thing anyone can do for a writer. You've taught me to simultaneously appreciate every little thing and yet never be quite satisfied. Because of you, each victory seems greater and each failure seems insignificant. We are simply meant to be, and you are the true reason why I write.

I owe a debt of gratitude to Matt Mucci and the developers, playtesters, and fans of *Xenoplicity*. Collaborating on this sci-fi/fantasy game with you was always a wild ride, and always inspirational. Role-playing is about inventing great characters with compelling motivations, and putting them in a rich world with powerful conflicts—it's the perfect spark for a writer.

Thank you to my beta readers, Joe Arbuckle and Monica Sharp, for your valuable feedback on my work-in-progress. Thank you for crawling through hundreds of pages of what might have seemed like sheer nonsense while helping me get my thoughts in order!

A very special thanks goes to my dear friend Kelly Creagh. Because of your priceless advice and direction, *Scavenged* is a better book, and I am a better writer. I can look at you and see what a real writer should be: dedicated to bettering their craft, and endlessly supportive of others. Writing and releasing a debut novel is not an easy thing to do, and your guidance made all the difference to me. Thank you so very much.

To my cover artist, Anthony Foti: you're a wellspring of talent. Thank you for distilling and sharpening my ideas and delivering a fantastic piece of art! Many blessings on you and your career. Thanks to Angela Fristoe for an excellent job with my typography.

And many thanks to my brilliant editor, Michelle Hope. You've been a pleasure to work with, and your skills with my manuscript will be appreciated for years to come.

Lastly, thank you to the magnificent #writerscommunity spread across all real and imagined worlds. Keep pouring your beautiful souls out.

About the Author

Scott Arbuckle was born in Louisville, Kentucky in 1981. In elementary school, he wrote many stories and poems, and won a Young Authors award for a fantasy short story. Scott's favorite subject was English, and he planned to become a writer. In high school and college, Scott studied Theatre Arts and Language Arts, and also developed an interest in fantasy and science-fiction role-playing games, a hobby that stayed with him into his adult years.

Scott now lives in central Kentucky with his wife, London. Together, they enjoy supporting zoos and aquariums while traveling around the eastern United States.

Are you interested in having your own adventures in the world of *Scavenged*? Check out *Xenoplicity*, the role-playing game! Follow *Xenoplicity* on Twitter and Facebook for details.

And be sure to keep an eye on www.twitter.com/starbuckle81 and http://www.ScottArbuckle.com for updates on *Augmented*, the sequel to *Scavenged*!

CPSIA information can be obtained
at www.ICGtesting.com
Printed in the USA
LVHW040044260719
625432LV00001B/32/P